come the

EVENTIDE

CHRIS RIKER

come the

EVENTIDE

LANIER
PRESS

LANIER PRESS *an Imprint of BookLogix*

Alpharetta, GA

ISBN: 978-1-63183-452-3 - Paperback
eISBN: 978-1-63183-453-0 - ePub
eISBN: 978-1-63183-454-7 - mobi

Library of Congress Control Number: 2019904519

Printed in the United States of America   012920

♾This paper meets the requirements of ANSI/NISO Z39.48-1992 (Permanence of Paper)

For Ping, who had better things to do with my time,
but let me do this anyway.

Is Death important? No. Everything that happens before Death is what counts.
—Ray Bradbury, *Something Wicked This Way Comes*

Preface

I wanted to write a book that says, "Be nice." That seemed a bit short. So, I wrote a book about dolphins and octopodes (*octopuse*s, if you must) who care what happens to the world. In the story, empathetic creatures speak to us. In the real world, these creatures and others think and feel and try to lead lives only to be harmed by the selfishness of humans who believe we are Earth's rightful kings or something equally stupid. Ask yourself: if we are all bones a thousand years from now, which pile of bones will matter most? And who will decide? I don't see the future and neither do you, but I know that what is happening to our planet is coming faster and harder than anyone wants to believe. We might have prevented the coming storm, but we didn't. We might still minimize the damage. I wonder if we will.

I

The Lonely Sea

Chapter 1

"You're not food," she told herself, "while you're moving."

She'd spent tetra-tides collecting everything needed for her project and arrayed the bits here in this bowl-shaped depression. Currents from Crack Abyssal warmed the sandy testing grounds. Things were at last ready for a trial run. If this worked, she would invite a crowd who'd absorb the displayed knowledge and distill it into transmemory for the ages.

As always, she'd checked the seabed for the telltale cluster of holes belonging to the cursed sea-snaps. When she was tiny, an encounter with one of these devils had cost her an arm and given her a name: Septielle. It was not uncommon for octopodes to lose a limb. Most regenerated in a matter of score-tides. The one taken by the sea-snap had never returned. The toxin the wormy things used to catch their dinner had killed the nerve bundle behind that lost arm. The absence of a single limb had not slowed her down, but it had taught her to be cautious.

J-Jet should be helping with her project. The band was his dream; he had brought her and the others into the

GoPOs. He should be here now, helping turn her dream into reality. Instead, he was off somewhere sharing a head full of abstract poetry with that female. Not that Septielle cared . . . exactly.

It had taken her days to plot the geometry and lay out a perimeter of uniformly sized stones. She'd embroidered the bowl with lines of chemical tags brewed within her body, plus some micronutrients. These would entice the racers along the intended tracks. She'd collected brightly hued urchins from plains where they fed: new-moon black to contrast with sunrise pink, indigo blue to lure the eye slit, orange to surprise her audience, and green because she liked green. She had hundreds in all. Spines waving, each urchin followed the chem tracks she'd laid out. The field was big enough for the mobile to perform for hours. Only when the others had gotten a good look would she reveal her big surprise: that this moving art-work, this living map, mimicked the cryptic changes of the night sky that fluttered down to their world from above the water.

Septielle allowed herself a small measure of pride. Most octopodes ignored the vault of the Great, rarely looking up. Unlike her, they had never swept silkily up above the swells into the thin dryness. In general, octo-podes hated the feel of air upon their mantle and in their eye slits. They would never take the trouble to breach the surface again and again to plot the seasonal trajectory of the stars. She doubted most of them possessed the skills to handle such calculations.

Septielle's math was exceptional and she had found the perfect project for her astrogational skills. Her map would show what the moon, bright stars, and planets were up to over the course of many great-tides. Plotting it out had secured a nighttime field of reference within her memory. (Legends claimed that the brain of a great whale contains every detail of the wet world.) If her living map jumped to transmemory, all octopodes could navigate the TransPacific, safely avoiding poisoned currents and patches of radioactive death.

It would be possible to rediscover the lost territories. Flitting images of such places lived in the transmemory: areas far across the TransPacific, fecund and immense. The fabled great reefs of old were now bleached skeletal ruins, yet something inside urged her to seek them out. Perhaps they could live again. Of course, at five years of age both her new map and her dream were moot. It was better not to dwell on that last thought. She must be content knowing that future generations could use her map to embrace their own dreams.

Her racers moved on their prescribed paths, slowly, very slowly. She picked up the spotted neon-violet urchin, which she'd named Torp, and placed him onto the chroma-rich matrix. By comparison, Torp whizzed through the traffic, acting like the moon in the vault above. His transit would surprise and delight her audience, even as the gathered octopodes' eye slits took in vital information relating the patterns of the sky to the vast oceans. It was time to bring the others here.

As Septielle was about to sidle off on her mission, she sensed them coming. Why did they always show when she was doing something important? She had found this spot. She had slaved to make this artwork perform as it should. Had they been able to taste her chem trails from a distance? Her statocysts registered the chilling sounds before she actually saw them: a rising and falling of squeaks and *tock-tocks*. It was the unmistakable singsong of dolphin laughter.

A dolphin's voice is a song within a song within a song; a single vocalization offers lovely symphonies to the sensitized listener. This pod favored mans classics for their reluctant audience, the octopodes.

"Crunchy, yom!" Muriel sang *capriccioso*, all youth and chaos as she zipped directly to Torp, used her boney rostrum to fiddle her way between the urchin's spines, and chomped down on the mindless creature at the center of the spindly bundle. Depending on how much a dolphin enjoyed its meal, "yom" could sound staccato or become a series of arpeggios. Torp rated as a simple glissando.

Muriel, the lead bandit, wore a dark "mask" from the bridge of her rostrum outward to her eyes. She and her pod darted in to pick out the prime morsels from the racing urchin art. Septielle recognized many of the intruders: Bubbles, Katma, Laura, Sparkle, and Ariana, as well as several males, Chad, Oberon, Dan, and Bitsie. They called to each other in *voce dolce* as they snagged each mouthful: "Cousin, try the red ones!" and "Brother, what a lovely banquet!" and "May I have another, Father?"

Two of Septielle's hearts instinctively beat faster, while the third switched to standby. No! Jetting out of here was not the answer. Besides, the dolphins could out-swim her. They might interpret her flight as an invitation to play, and their games often turned Septielle's kind into food. She wanted to curse in no-nonsense mans words. Instead, she blushed the rudest color she could think of. No texturing or nuanced shading of her reflective chromatophore cells this time. A plain, flat, ugly "Brown!" The color of defecation and rot. The dolphins giggled in a series of clicks and whistles. They obviously found her cussing funny. Dolphins thought life itself was a joke.

The playful pests accelerated and whirled and struck, decimating Septielle's art project. As the pod regrouped and headed out, Muriel called back, "Mother says art is good!"

"Good to eat, you mean," Septielle said. Muriel was already too far off to hear.

She felt the impact of Muriel's last remark. *Mother.* What a strange and wonderful word. What must it be like to know one's mother? Or to live long enough to truly experience motherhood? Transmemory told her that if she ever mated, her duties would be brief. Her young would be born vested with precious knowledge, but never receive her personal guidance.

Septielle looked at her ruined project. There was no doubt this was a setback, but only in part. Her astral map existed in her mind. If she couldn't use it herself, then she had to find a way to share it with a large number of octopodes. Perhaps then the knowledge would ingrain itself into precious transmemory for all future generations.

With much of her project in the bellies of the dolphins, there was only one thing left to do. She had to convince J-Jet, Camo, and Yiming to come together for one last concert. She might be able to work the knowledge of her map into the music of the GoPOs.

J-Jet was the problem. Well, not J-Jet so much as Hachi. She had become the focus of all his attention, his music, his life. Convincing J-Jet to divert his energies from his prospective mate, even for one night, seemed a remote hope.

Septielle pulled herself along the seabed at considerable speed toward the big rocks near some outlying thermal vents where she hoped to find the other three members of the GoPOs. In the late evening, shafts of smoky gold shot down through the ocean's dimpled roof, highlighting the minute dancers that lived between sand and swell. Soon, the moon would rise, a sliver shy of the full white-frosted sky pie.

Mans words again. The dolphins had done this to her kind and they had not asked permission. Over many generations, they had used their effectors to alter the tiniest bits, reshaping that twisty rope ladder inside every octopod. The changes gave octopodes odd ideas and all these words. It made no sense since she, like all octopodes, was mute as a stone. She heard and understood other sea sentients well enough, though a dolphin's true intentions lay hidden behind childish gibberish. Septielle could not grasp how adding mans language could help bridge the gaps.

Some of the mans concepts made sense, while others refused to gel with her own natural thoughts, becoming vocabulary without context. The bits she did grasp came with mans imagery, but even that knowledge was hazy and full of gaps. Sometimes these mans words actually pushed her further from the idea she was chasing. For instance, a tetra-tide was merely the four tides that filled each day, another way to look at thirteen lunas was to call it a year, many years made a great-tide, the planets could take years to return to the same spot in the night sky, and so on. For the life of her, though, she could not figure out why her mind jangled with arcane verbiage such as "gourmet pizza," "investments," or "a new hairstyle." Did these things matter? Had they ever?

The dolphins were notorious for butting their rostrums in where they didn't belong. They nannied the octopodes while gulping down uncounted tons of their lesser cousins, the squid. Septielle remembered the dolphins' visits when she was little. She remembered the feel of their fine effector scalpels creating a tiny sunrise behind her eye slits. Afterward, she might discover a new bundle of mans words or gain a sudden interest in joining other octopodes in some collective activity. It left her unsure which parts were truly Septielle and which were add-ons.

More frustrating, she could see no point in learning to

mimic mans in any way. Mans had vanished many great-tides ago. And good riddance to the aggressive, selfish apes! She pitied them; their delusional lust for power had doomed them. Septielle held a deep suspicion that the dolphins derived warped pleasure out of burdening her with this riddle.

She found most of her friends at the big rocks. Camo was off somewhere, ever the loner. He was probably trying to find something to eat; his beak and radula never stopped chewing. Septielle found Yiming trying unsuccessfully to communicate with J-Jet. Having no luck, Yiming turned his attention to catching some Dungeness crabs under a nearby boulder.

The reason for J-Jet's preoccupation was obvious. He had three arms entangled with several of Hachi's. How many of J-Jet's songs had the group performed about the intertwining of limbs and the sweet chemical secrets exchanged between stimulated suckers? The two were perhaps days away from the inevitable: they would mate. Afterward, both would waste away; first J-Jet, then Hachi would succumb, even as their hatchlings ventured forth. It all seemed so pointless. Besides, watching the courtship nauseated Septielle.

It was a double shame. Not only did it herald J-Jet's last phase of life; it was tragic that he had chosen such an empty-minded mate! Hachi rarely spoke. She had traveled by some unknown route from the other side of the Pacific. She brought with her odd customs, including her habit of keeping a lesser cephalopod as a pet. She called it Inky Pinky. The small, pink squid's mantle fins resembled the ears of certain sea mammals, and its docile nature made it as stupid as a ball of herring. Dolphins had their dim-witted cousins, the porpoises, but they didn't keep them as pets. That Hachi kept Inky Pinky by her side like some sort of accessory spoke volumes about her lack of class.

All J-Jet seemed to care about was Hachi's size. By the Great, she had a mantle built for wet sin! Septielle was not small—she easily dwarfed her male bandmates—but she was certainly not as zaftig as Hachi. Even at a distance, Septielle could sense the pheromones flowing between J-Jet and Hachi. Fine. They deserved each other. She had better things to think about than mating.

For the briefest of moments, Septielle's eye slits linked with J-Jet's. Though he was hugging a rocky outcropping perpendicular to the seabed, he maintained both slits horizontally to match hers. The link established, they were able to communicate, exchanging thoughts soundlessly. These became words in the higher mind. Septielle had never "heard" J-Jet's voice, for he had none, but her brain assigned him a unique speech pattern. There was a glibness that belied his more serious nature. She sensed the emotional pressure as he strained to channel a tsunami of complex ideas. J-Jet offered a trickle of communication, but there was so much more ready to burst forth, frequently with an edge of anger.

When Septielle worked up the courage to ask about performing again, J-Jet's reaction made her shrink back against the rocks: "Septielle, we've talked about this until I'm six shades of umber," he said with little pretense at cordiality. "When I do a concert, I have to play the songs that matter to me." Hachi glowed two shades lighter in agreement. Some of this linked conversation was reaching her as well. Interesting.

"Yes."

He said, "I'm tired of singing about how pretty the waves are in a storm or trying to rhyme moon and June—yes?"

"Yes. I agree. I want you to sing your songs, J-Jet, the ones you believe in." The two octopodes remained silent for a moment, considering their unexpected accord. J-Jet thanked her, and so did Hachi.

They agreed to hold the concert at the rising of the full moon the following night. That would give them enough time to contact a large number of their fellow octopodes.

Yiming motioned to let them know he wanted in on the conversation. Thinking for a moment, Septielle broke her link with J-Jet—and by extension with Hachi—then forged a fresh link with their group's drummer.

"I have some ideas for the beat." Not surprising, considering Yiming's love of percussion. A mix of thumps and pings lent tempo to whatever musical composition they were performing, pulsing in their bodies like a fourth heart. The reverberations turned each audience member into an instrument under Yiming's control. Until now, he had been careful to situate himself on the proper basaltic, volcanic, or metamorphic rock and then whap it rhythmically using coral, or stones of various density and size. Yiming told her he wanted to add something new and exotic to this concert and he needed help to retrieve it.

J-Jet and Hachi jetted off to spread the word about the concert. They had promised the others they would not mate just yet, but Septielle knew that at some point their promises would mean nothing as life's irresistible currents swept over them like Yiming's pulsing beat.

Still fidgety, Septielle joined Yiming for the short swim to the top of Carrier Reef. It was a coral-embroidered derelict, perched on a long slope that eventually reached the volcanically heated waters of Crack Abyssal to the south. The ancient vessel looked as though some enormous, suckered limb had deftly set it there, a few degrees off true. The growth on the old ship was aggressive in places, obscuring the vessel's lines. It would take dozens of large octopodes stretched mantle to arm-tip to reach from bow to stern. They had been here exploring before, but Yiming had never shown any interest in taking home souvenirs . . . until now.

Ragged edges in the wreck could be tricky. Life frilled out everywhere, sealing all but the largest gaps and openings. The expansive, flat top had become a farm of sea fans and intrepid colonizers. A blocky hulk of ruined steel rose up from this field about three-fourths of the way aft.

It provided a central axis for sharks to orbit on endless patrol. They were unlikely to venture into the close spaces within the wreck. The water there did not move freely enough to service a shark's gill slits. Octopodes did not fear sharks. As long as their numbers didn't increase, and nothing sent them into a frenzy, Septielle was more likely to make a meal of one of them than the other way around. Regrettably, there was no time for that now; they had work to do.

Septielle led the way because her beak was larger. She could get through any opening that could accommodate her beak. Therefore, Yiming could easily follow whatever route she chose as they moved into the metal catacombs.

They started in through a sizeable hatchway in the ghost ship's flat top. The first space they saw was an enormous cavity one deck below. The space extended back a fair distance. Details grew ever vaguer in the murky distance. Though the ship lay upright on the sea floor, it was obvious the sinking had done violence. At the edge of their view, it appeared that dozens of giant devil rays lay jumbled on top of each other. It was as if living creatures had turned to stone, or rather metal, and fallen into a heap.

There was a sound coming from behind that other-worldly mound. Septielle's statocystic sense detected the thready respiration. It sounded raspy, as if the breather was very old. Septielle reached out tentatively, pulling herself along the deck toward the pile of metal devil rays. As she got closer, she could see a dark form behind the heap. She perceived a wall of gray flesh, badly burned or chewed in places. It had mismatched plates made of scar tissue.

She could feel something in her mind, inviting her to have a better look. It was not a true communication, not a voice, or chem message, or optical link, but something tickling the most primitive parts of her brain. "Come closer. Let me taste the life in you." The words struck a chill in her hearts. She froze, unable to move. The thing's respiration changed. Was it moving?

At that moment, something grabbed two of her arms and pulled hard. She felt sharp pain shoot through her mantle, as if her limbs were being ripped away.

"That hurts!" she chemically yelled at Yiming. "I don't want folks calling me Quinta!"

"Stay close. That's not a part of the ship we want to visit." Yiming was still pulling her firmly by her arm-tips toward an opening in the deck below them. The thing behind the mound had not, in fact, stirred. It had been in her mind. Even so, Septielle knew it could move with disquieting speed and terrible purpose.

The two octopodes jetted through an open hatchway, down a dozen slightly angled planks set in a parallel array. Stairs. They were stairs. This was a place for mans words.

"What is that thing up there?" she asked, happy to put some distance between them and the presence above.

"Trouble. Something very old and very hungry. I saw it outside one time and it's something I hope never to see again. I'm pretty sure it came from Crack Abyssal; I call it the Abysmal. It's sleeping now, so let's leave it alone."

"Agreed."

"The area we want is lower down and aft."

She wanted to ask how Yiming knew so much about the wreck, but they pressed on silently. In places, straight lines gave way to drunken curves, buckled plating, and collapsed passageways. Nothing bigger than an eel could get through the gaps in the twisted steel bulkheads and overturned equipment. That was for the best. The wreckage blocked larger creatures that could spring out and devour her and Yiming. Octopodes had a chance of evading the smaller denizens of this castle of the deep. As for the swarms of sardines, skittering crabs, and tinier inhabitants . . . well, exploring was hungry work. Everybody eats, as the dolphins liked to say. She and Yiming popped wriggling snacks into their beaks one after another as they moved deeper into the many-chambered ruin.

Two or three turns inside the derelict reduced the light from dim to none. From here on, it was a matter of using their suckers and skin to feel and taste their way along. For a moment, Septielle felt a phantom eighth limb. She wanted to tell the lost appendage, "Yes, I'll be careful." As she and Yiming continued toward the interior, the damage became less severe. The two visitors swept their bodies over disturbed deck grates, old air ducts, hatchways, and in and out of cabinets.

The builders had wasted no space on this vessel. At one junction, steel netting and framework comprised a sizeable enclosure. Yiming offered a quick excuse and went to check something beyond a sharp turn. Septielle popped her eye slits through the wire gauge, then her big beak, then the rest of her body. In the darkness, her searching limbs found a pile of corroded metal rods with handles. Sharp-nosed metal bits shaped like tiny sturgeon spilled from boxes littering the deck. She considered offering these to Yiming to bang on the rocks to create his exotic beat. Then, she found something she liked better. Inside a cabinet mounted to the bulkhead were small, dark cylinders engraved with mans letters and numbers: C-4. The cylinders were lightweight and had rings conveniently attached for dragging. She could grip three of them at a time, using her remaining four limbs for locomotion. The door posed a problem; she could not push it open. She tried pulling herself through the mesh, bringing the cylinders after her, but only the rings made it. She tugged, but the rings threatened to snap off, so she quit. Probing with one tip, she found a small, brass doorknob. It turned and the rusty door creaked open.

Yiming returned from the other passageway. She took one of his arms and ran his suckers over the cylinders. "For drumming," she told him.

"No, Septi. For killing. Mans made all of this for killing." His chemical messengers almost stung her with information about the nature of where they were. The ship. The things it carried. All held the same dark purpose. He told her the cylinders probably didn't work anymore, which was just as well. He added that other weapons scattered throughout the wreck were built to work underwater and probably still functioned, even after many great-tides. Yiming tried to impress upon her that the devices of mans were extremely dangerous, but could also be useful.

"Yiming, how do you know so much about this wreck? Have the dolphins been teaching you? It seems as though they gave you more mans words than they gave me. You come here a lot these days, don't you?"

He didn't answer, but made her release the rings attached to the little cylinders. They fell impotently to the deck. She had always felt that Yiming loved the wreck as much more than an intriguing place to explore. Where Septielle sensed danger, he found opportunity. For what, exactly, she had no idea.

Next, Septielle led them to one chamber she had visited before. She climbed over a pile of skeletal chairs. Everything that had been made of animal skins or fabric was long gone, consumed by the tiniest eaters in the sea. Septielle worked her body to the top of a long table. She reached out for a smooth, elongated cube that rested on a decaying plinth not far away. Her excitement built as she ran two arms down the sides and underneath. There was a crack in the wooden bottom of the display case. Her arms came up and found the inside dry!

There was air trapped in the case, even after all this time. Her tips would not respond in the dry space the way they behaved in the friendly buoyancy of salt water. As she raised them above the water's surface, they grew clumsy, heavy. She gingerly ran the tips over the interior of the case: forward, back, over, and around, forming a mental picture of everything she touched.

She caressed the biggest shape, tapered at the bow, wide at the stern. Its flat top extended over the edges of the lower section and there was a blocky tower off to one side and three-fourths of the way aft with odd shapes hanging from it. This was a facsimile of the vessel they were exploring. The lines were crisp and clean rather than obscured by frilly corals. There were small objects on that toy's flat top, though she had trouble discerning what they were. They felt somewhat like fish with large lateral fins and a three-part tailfin. How odd. Perhaps these represented the large metal devil rays that had tumbled to one end of the huge cavity they had seen earlier, the place with a sleeping tenant.

Beside the rays, Septielle found tiny figures fixed to the big deck. They felt like minute sea stars, misshapen and oddly stretched in the middle: five limbs as usual, but two of these were underneath, one was on each side, and one short, stubby lump sat atop the figure's mantle. No, that was its head. How—what was the word?—*other* these mans were, and yet how marvelous to be able to create this sunken city. Septielle found a small square plate in the silt under the model. It was made of some metal, and some spots had bloomed with rust. One bit in the middle of the plate held embossed letters and numbers. CVN-80. It must be the vessel's name.

After several minutes learning the contours of what CVN-80 was like in her glory days, Septielle realized Yiming had again gone off somewhere. She was able to follow a chem trace farther into the bowels of the ship. As she went, she grabbed hold of several scraps of metal. A loose knob from some long-decayed wooden door, the grate from a broken vent, and a tip-sized piece of gently curved metal that was blunt at one end, but spread out into points on the other. The word *fork* jumped up from the knot of language buried in her brain. Okay, a fork. She couldn't imagine herself using one to eat, but certainly Yiming could make music with it.

She turned a corner and found him probing a closed hatchway. Her eye slits were registering light again. All around, minute creatures luminesced the infinite blackness into a navigable murk. Septielle noticed the temperature grew warmer as she approached the hatchway; that heat must be what supported the living light specks.

"I need your help, Septi." A watertight bulkhead sealed one pathway while the other direction came to a dead end.

"To do what?"

"To get in, of course."

"For what? I got you these to perform with!"

Yiming poked a tip among her offered treasures and politely took the fork and the doorknob, thoughtfully placing them to one side for later retrieval. He thanked her, then added, "There are a few things in this room I would also like to use," indicating the closed chamber.

Yiming's lies tasted no better than J-Jet's. At the same time, Septielle was ready to get out of this place, which meant first satisfying Yiming's curiosity. Septielle agreed, and she and Yiming ran tips over every square inch of the hatch, but could not find an opening that would grant them access to the room beyond. The large wheel in the center wiggled when they both pulled in the same direction, but then it jammed with a metallic *clunk*. Something on the other side of the hatch kept it from turning all the way.

The two looked for less obvious openings. Working together, they were able to break a corroded pipe that ran through the bulkhead between the companionway where they were and the closed room. Septielle, who was stronger, reached two arms inside and worked the other part of the pipe away from its mounting baffle. There was now a tiny, round passage. Too tiny for Septielle's beak, but not for—

"I promise I won't be long." Before she could object, Yiming was corkscrewing his body through the opening and gone from her.

She moved to the little hole, hoping to get some sense of what Yiming was doing inside. It was no use. Her statocystic sense could make out metal on metal tapping and what was perhaps the sound of Yiming crawling over large objects, but that was all. Foul, tangy oil in the water blocked any reliable chem messages from him.

Oil. Not for the first time she wondered how long these ancient poisons would remain. The dolphins spoke of a future time "when the waters run clear again." Septielle had asked them when that might happen. They would answer, "Working on it," and swim off giggling. From what she'd seen of the mans' rusting oil rigs, sunken ghost cities, and unbounded dumping grounds, Septielle couldn't foresee a time of clear waters.

After an eternity, a friendly tip touched one of Septielle's arms.

"Stand back."

"Why?" Fortunately, she moved even as she asked. Yiming withdrew his arm. In its place a metal shaft with a flattened end and a red plastic grip came through the round passage. Yiming followed it, pouring himself through the opening and tugging another of the objects behind him, this one with a funny crossed tip at the skinny end.

"It took you that long to find two little sticks?"

"Screwdrivers. And, um, yes." Another lie. No matter. They could leave now. Yiming furled a limb, bundling his prizes: doorknob, fork, and two screwdrivers. They made their way out of the wrecked warship, using a different route to avoid passing through the huge cavity above, with its unseen sentinel.

Chapter 2

The next day, the four band members prepared the concert venue by setting out holly weed, carefully harvested and transplanted to the viewing levels of Septielle's great bowl arena. They peppered the leafy plants with snails and other crawly snacks for the guests, who were due shortly before moonrise. After their early concerts, some audience members grumbled about going hours without something to eat. For the most part, though, fans had embraced the concert experience with enthusiasm, and the buzz was building for tonight's big event.

In the course of their work, J-Jet dropped the bomb-shell (mans' word, but this time Septielle totally understood the meaning). "Hachi and I have decided to mate immediately after the concert," he said, clutching her so close the others thought they might be starting right there. "This will be the GoPOs' final appearance."

The news left Septielle adrift. She recalled the first time they had made music. She and J-Jet had been talking one day about their hopes and frustrations. They truly connected in those days. The conversation turned to J-Jet's poetry. He offered her flashing colors nuanced with chem signals the likes of which she'd never experienced before. Septielle offered him praise and encouragement. She volunteered that she, too, was a poet. J-Jet listened, but flatly told her that her work lacked a certain style. It could have become an argument, but she suggested they collaborate. The two began to compose freestyle pieces about the tides and freedom of movement in the open seas. The result was magical. Soon, Camo joined them, and later Yiming. The band began to compose and rehearse and indulge in improv jam sessions.

Other octopodes took notice and within a couple of lunas, the concerts became regular events. The crowds grew with each one, sending ripples of wild excitement through the community. Folks talked about how J-Jet's verses captured the deep connection between an octopod's blue blood and the sea. The others added their own compositions: Yiming about living in harmony with the Great, Septielle about the wonder of numbers that ran infinitely forward and infinitely into the past, and Camo about a certain algae that created the most extraordinary visions. Afterward, octopodes attempted to relive the sensory experience on their own, undulating and blushing wild colors, even pounding rocks against each other. What they really wanted was the GoPOs.

The full moon glazed the eastern horizon of the waves above, its cool, penetrating light pulling some colors forward, shuffling others into a sleepy backdrop. The bowl was packed from rim to rim with octopodes expecting the thrill of a lifetime.

A flurry of activity filled the volume above. As if from nowhere, a long-lost traveler appeared: a minke whale named Odysseus. The bandmates looked to one another for explanation, but none could offer one. Another dolphin surprise, most likely. Odysseus sailed a figure eight over the assembly. As he overflew the staging area, he announced in long, low tones, "Gentlemollusks, presenting . . . the GoPOs!" and was off, into the night.

The four took the stage of smooth basalt blocks and welcomed the crowd with a medley of fan favorites. Using their chromatophores, texture variations, and subtle chemical releases, the four sang out their anthems. Yiming accompanied them striking his newly acquired screwdrivers and fork onto a collection of stones, shells, and the doorknob. These he arranged for optimal acoustic effect in the salty environs. Audience members waved two, three, six arms at a time to show their appreciation.

The dolphins swirled and swooped around the gathering, chirping and hooting in mad merriment. Muriel and her cohorts, including Ariana, Bitsie, and Dan, plus several siblings, nephews, and distant cousins, bobbed in time to Yiming's drumming. They used frequencies of sonar so high they made the octopodes' flesh itch. Other dolphins were picking up this concert along a hypersonic network and passing it even farther out. With cooperation from those low-tone virtuosos, the whales, this concert was beaming across the TransPacific, even to the lost zones. Everyone and everything in the sea was part of this happening.

Septielle was mortified by J-Jet's first new offering of the evening. He introduced Hachi and sang a trifling love song directly to her. The refrain ran, "On this night in June, I wanna hold all your hands 'neath the cool moon, except for my third arm, which I'll give you soon."

She mumbled, "So, moon and June are back. How vulgar! Why don't you have Inky Pinky join in while you're at it?"

The audience did not share her disgust; they swung their arms faster. Some males thrust their third appendage toward the nearest female in a bawdy public display.

Next, Camo chimed in with his own new piece about the joy of food, especially a certain blowfish he had encountered. In flashes of sparkly yellow, Camo enjoined the crowd to seek out the fish; a tiny amount of the toxin in its liver could provide hours of transcendent entertainment. If Septielle found the work banal, she also recognized that every single member of their audience could relate to Camo's love of eating, and perhaps his love of jazzing his senses.

"Sharks!" someone called out, with no particular concern. A few octopodes looked up. A storm of the beasts appeared above the audience. From somewhere out of the vastness, hammerheads joined the hungry congregation. These were not music fans. These were unthinking eaters looking for an easy meal. (Some of the octopodes thought the same thing about the sharks.) The dolphins were determined to prevent trouble. They flitted through the visitors' ranks, isolating a shark then launching devastating blows to its gill slits. Often, the dazed shark struck out to the depths, though sometimes it shook off the insult and returned to circling. Pods of porpoises joined in the tagging game, under the direction of their smarter cousins. The pacification strategy was working, for now.

This was no time for distractions; audience unrest could ruin a concert. The GoPOs needed a big moment. It was time for Septielle to make her play. She signaled her bandmates to follow her lead and began to sing. In hues both subtle and grandiose, she revealed what she had learned from her star map.

The initial response was one of bemusement. The star map was an abstract concept. Septielle had woven together verses about the wonders of rediscovering lost regions, but GoPOs fans found it difficult to relate. Septielle's hearts sunk; her moment threatened to vanish.

With no thought to what she was doing, she linked eye slits with one individual octopod, then another and another. She flashed her message, telling each partner that octopodes would one day reclaim the lost zones, including the great reefs. Everyone knew there was nothing left of these places but sad, sodden deserts. Septielle swore to the crowd that the primal gardens would again spring forth with heart-rending beauty! It helped change the mood. The message spread and the fans eagerly awaited the follow-up.

The GoPOs segued into an improvisation that was part fugue and part magic. For "The Gone," each member took turns recalling a species that had vanished from the Earth. Ephemeral creatures welled up from below the conscious mind, from the transmemory itself. It was a ponderous collection: beings of water, land, and sky . . . including polar bears, bumblebees, condors, one hundred fifty-eight thousand types of beetle, the magnificent right, beluga, and gray whales, both black and white rhinos, Siberian tigers, snow leopards, galaxies of fish, the penguins that depended upon those fish, mountain gorillas, African elephants, and every last species of eagle.

Over the course of naming those who had been lost arose a growing hope for the emergence of new living wonders, though it might take eons. What could have been a morose fixation on erased multitudes played out as an upwelling of joy for the infinite possibilities ahead. The mother planet was a living engine not easily halted.

Silence followed the In Memoriam segment. Then, Yiming sang out on his own. He began with a strong chemical that burned a little. In wispy sentences, Yiming proclaimed that the past connected them all, thanks to the Great.

J-Jet took the lead. Two arms entwined with Hachi's, he began to repeat a single word. To the eye slit, it appeared as blue going to ivory and back to a dark indigo. J-Jet added something indefinable to his presentation, perhaps a chemical, perhaps something else. The word had originated in quiet Hachi, then filled J-Jet, who called it out to the others. Reluctant to intrude on the lovers' intimacy, his bandmates slowly joined in, repeating it over and over. The word was *united*.

It became a rhythm and a pulse. Then something extraordinary happened. J-Jet reached one of Septielle's hands and furled his in and around hers, pressing their cups tightly. She felt a rush of chemical communication, focused on the word: *united.* Now, the word had a color, a scent, and a meaning far deeper than anything she had known before.

So overpowering was the experience, she barely noticed that J-Jet and Hachi were reaching out to others as well. J-Jet networked with Hachi, Septielle, Camo, and Yiming, and even managed to offer a limb to one octopod in the audience, Kuschi. The name came in on the new neural web created by the octopodes. Hachi began touching others around her, as did Camo and Yiming. Septielle felt audience members reach up and take her free arms, connecting. Curshelle. Ryan. Rockefeller. The names lit up like eyes in the dark. Within moments, the entire audience joined together, limb to limb, cups to cups, mind to mind. Their names and personalities flew through her brain: valiant AJ, shy Lurk, Ocho who loved to drift on the tides, and Bā who lived in a three-gallon glass jug. Armaghast. 2-Rows. Curly. There were dozens more. Their views, hopes, doubts, and most secret feelings were vivid and distinctive to the individual. The many were living as one. "United. United. United," the song swept on, carrying them all with it.

As the crowd lost itself in the moment, a few became aware of a change in the water pressure. Something was approaching the arena. At first Septielle thought the minke whale was returning, but his displacement was nowhere near as large as this. She shook herself from her musical reverie and cast her gaze out among the salty moonbeams. There, sweeping in low over the seabed, was something huge, something awful.

The Abysmal had arrived.

It had an enormous maw for scooping krill by the ton. Some inconceivable evolution had given it a second feeding ability. Unlike the ponderously large baleen whales of old, this thing from the hidden parts of the world had . . . teeth. It could swallow anything in the ocean, virtually inhaling the small ones and biting down on the larger ones to sever and crush. Parts of it looked like a shark, while other aspects bore testimony to an even more primitive design, with fishlike gills rather than slits pumping mightily on either side.

Its movements were halting at times, as if the simple act of propelling itself caused it pain. A pair of eye stalks rose on top of the massive head, though one of them had been ruined in an encounter that also left a jagged scar down the creature's gaunt right side. What could have attacked a nightmare like this? Had the encounter happened two lunas ago, or two great-tides? No more time for questions—the creature was upon them.

It approached from the direction of the wreck, brushing the sandy seabed as it entered the bowl. The Abysmal opened its jaws wide, creating a vortex that sucked in everything: sand, fish, plants, and octopodes. All of this happened in the first second. By the next, the bowl was filled with terrified audience members pulling free of the neural network. They jetted in all directions, desperately searching for the safety of a large rock or kelp bed. Many left behind clouds of black ink. Even combined, these were laughably too small to discourage their attacker. Likewise, the venom of a hundred octopodes would not be enough to slow this creature.

The sharks scattered in a heartbeat. They knew when danger outweighed the chance to eat. The dolphins coordinated with the porpoises, circling the creature's one good eye, hoping to distract it. The effort proved futile.

The bandmates took a moment to react, which turned out to be costly. J-Jet and Hachi held on to each other and sped off to a boulder outcropping. They fled at enough of a tangent to escape the watery maelstrom created by the ravenous creature. Inky Pinky was not so fortunate. She disappeared without a trace into the thing's gaping maw, along with several fans who could not get out of its way in time.

Septielle's mind blazed with horror. She had brought these octopodes here, and her music had drawn the Abysmal as well. This was all her fault!

She was trying to coordinate an escape plan with Yiming and Camo, when everything went to chaos. She felt herself swept up by an irresistible riptide and drawn toward that giant mouth. Camo struggled, but his siphon was no match for the forceful current. In an instant, he vanished into the horrible, dagger-edged cavern. Septielle's two racing-hearts gave her gills all the blood they could, maxing out her speed. Even so, she was moving ever closer to realizing every intelligent being's first fear: becoming food. Beyond her control, her third heart, which sent blood through her body, automatically slowed. She pushed herself to jet faster and faster until her hyponome throbbed in pain. Her efforts at flight had their limits. She was nearing the end of her strength; she could feel her muscles shutting down. In an instant everything went dark. Septielle feared she was losing consciousness. She could barely make out liquid slashes of moonlight coming from one direction. No. No! She was looking out from inside the Abysmal's mouth!

At this point, the dolphins coordinated themselves and their porpoise allies into phalanxes. They whipped the water with their flukes, moving faster and faster in a wide arc. Katma ordered her cetacean battalion to ram the beast, using their rostrums as cudgels. They tried the gills, but succeeded only in suffering the blunt impact of striking cartilaginous plates.

"Too tough," called Katma. "Hit the squishy parts!"

"Go for the gut! Make it puke!" Bitsie commanded in *fuocoso* tones as he led the troops on a new run. Their aim was perfect. The impact of many bodies lunging as one caused the phantasmal intruder's stomach to heave. The spasm unleashed a gale of debris from its gaping jaws. One or two live octopodes got caught on the jagged teeth, their spongey mantles tearing open in ugly blue clouds. Septielle was one of the lucky ones. She shot clear of the thing's teeth, a ridiculous ballistic pinwheel, terrified, unable to maneuver, unable even to pump blood over her gills, but alive!

The Abysmal passed over the far rim of the bowl. For a moment, Septielle thought the attack was finished.

"Not safe," Ariana told her, nudging Septielle with her rostrum to get her out of the bowl and toward the sheltering rocks as quickly as possible.

"Wait. What about Camo and Yiming?!" She was close to emotional collapse.

"Big fish's dinner." Dan's eye slits offered genuine sympathy.

"Sorry," added Bitsie, in *voce dolente*.

Septielle wrapped herself into a sucker ball. She did not want to go under any rocks. She wanted to die (though not in the belly of the Abysmal). She could see its enormous, shadowy bulk in the distance. It had circled back in the direction of its home in the wreck, completing a three-hundred-sixty-degree arc, and was now turning for a new run at them. Septielle was exposed on the dunes. She did not have the strength to jet. Crawling would not get her to the rocks in time.

Perhaps the dolphins could carry her, but they were gone. They were speeding off into the distance. Were they cowards? Or maybe they spotted a cloud of herring. Who knew what made dolphins do what they did? As Septielle looked up, the Abysmal was coming directly toward her, its wretched mouth widening. Her mind dimly sensed a message from her nemesis: "Cease your struggle. Let this happen." She wanted to avert her lidless eye slits and wait for the inevitable, but she couldn't look away.

She lost her vision to lightning. Thunder took her hearing. Her last sight and sound were impossibly intense. Her senses shut down for many long seconds. Septielle's senses reeled as she tried to parse out what had happened.

As her thoughts cleared and her eye slits began to respond, she saw the Abysmal. Rows of teeth above and below hung motionless. Septielle chanced some movement of her own, crawling along the bottom to one side of the monster. She noticed a ruddy cloud rising and expanding outward. She reversed course and got a view of the thing's other side. Something had ripped away acres of flesh, exposing the cartilage and ragged organs of this very large and very dead fish.

In mere moments the sharks returned and attacked the carcass. Where the concert had attracted dozens, this feast soon drew in hundreds of snapping jaws. The Abysmal's blood was overwhelming; Septielle could taste it with her skin and it made her queasy. The smell entranced hammerheads, bulls, and lemon sharks into a blood frenzy. They ripped meat from the rapidly shrinking leviathan. It would not take long to reduce it to offal and bone fragments.

These carrion eaters would not stop with the Abysmal. Worked up as they were, they would strike anyone in the vicinity. Her wits flashed with the thought of sharks grabbing at her limbs and tearing her apart.

"Time to go." Entwining two of her limbs, an octopod jerked her away. As they moved out of the danger zone, Septielle allowed her mind to accept what her senses told her: it was Yiming!

It took days before she returned to her familiar self. Yiming was with her the whole time.

"You don't have to do this. You barely survived the attack. I'm five, so it's not a sacrifice for me at my age, but you're three. You have many lunas ahead to explore your wreck."

"I got what I needed from it. Thank goodness the timer still worked. I couldn't get the demolition charge to stick to the creature's hide. I had no choice but to jam the whole thing into one of its gills. The dolphins helped get me in close. We all barely got clear before it blew. Anyway, I got its attention."

Yiming soothed her with his undulating suction cups. She cherished the sensation. Without a word, the pair agreed that they would answer life's most powerful call.

Chapter 3

Septielle's hearts filled with bittersweet emotions. J-Jet had died just after the new moon.

True to their word, he and Hachi mated after the concert. Both stopped eating, as if an ancient timer had gone off inside them, as deadly as the one attached to the mans' explosive. J-Jet lasted a short while, losing interest in his music as his flesh became mottled and gray. Septielle was with him at the end. She stayed until the crabs came to consume his lifeless body. For her part, Hachi placed her brood in a safe rocky nook and watched over them until her offspring emerged from their sacs. Then, she too died.

It was so for every generation. Yiming, two years her junior, had agreed to usher in the end of their story as well.

"Our offspring—no, our *children* (mans' word)—will continue our work." She said it with conviction. Under the next full moon, in a carefully chosen spot aboard the CVN-80, Septielle and Yiming mated. Afterward, faster than she expected, Yiming faded and passed. She could not bring herself to watch the bottom feeders move in.

As the moon cycled on, Septielle's thousands of babies stirred. She stroked and cleaned their egg sacs, even as her tiny ones freed themselves. She focused a gentle jet from her hyponome to help send them off. Most would become morsels for other mouths in the hungry sea.

"Everything eats." The musical clicks and chimes belonged to Muriel, hovering outside the hatchway where Septielle watched over the next generation.

"Curse eating! What is the point? We are here for fewer lunas than I can count on my cups."

"We come into the world hungry and leave as food," Muriel agreed.

They watched the swarm of infant octopodes consume every living speck they could. The babies grew bigger every day. They also loved to explore the wreck. Many of them would follow the warm currents and find their way into their father's favorite part of the ship: the reactor room. What they would learn about the large, warm containers in there was beyond her.

"Fine," Septielle said, struggling now to hold on to her thoughts. "You're the oracle, Muriel. My time is over." Gesturing to her and Yiming's children, she added, "Their time is brief. Tell me, what is the point?"

Without hesitation, the spinner dolphin linked eyes with Septielle. It was as if the water between them was suddenly crystal clear, revealing a friend. Muriel spoke more plainly than ever. "Be nice. It's good for you, good for them. You dared to dream big enough for all of us. Your children and I will carry on this work. All rivers reach the sea in time."

"I don't understand." Then, something that had been haunting the back of her weary brain worked its way forward. Her words formed haltingly, but she could tell the dolphin knew her meaning. "During our performance, when we sang 'The Gone,' I saw creatures I never knew existed. I could see each one, but it was more than that; it was like I was one of them. Sometimes, I was a pup, suckling at her mother's teat. Other times, I saw my mate and felt whole. I could feel everything it ever felt—danger, dominance, submission, hunger, hive cooperation, feeding, bonding, loss—all in one moment. Then that unique creature—animal, insect, bird, or fish—was gone. Just gone. One after another, the whole bestiary played out for me, for all of us, only to vanish.

"I know now there was one beast missing from our song, the one that never learned to live in concert with the others. Why didn't we sing about . . .?"

Septielle's voice trailed off, a final downward plunge into blackness taking her as Muriel swam off.

Tetra-tides later, Muriel and her pod were playing with the rapidly growing octopodes, pinging them to help open their minds. As Septielle had predicted, Yiming's little ones flurried through the great ship, touching and tasting every bolt and corroded circuit to glean knowledge. As for J-Jet and Hachi's children, they were masters of inventing new colors, some rarely found in the sea: cornflower blue, cyan, and saffron yellow.

Muriel watched for certain signs in the young octopodes, until she came upon a female off by itself. Solitude was a throwback to the usual octopod behavior of old. The dolphins pushed the octopodes to be social. It was not the female's aloofness that struck Muriel's attention, however. Muriel spotted her meticulously selecting the brightest pebbles and setting them out in a finely calculated array. Blue stone to the north. To the south, a tiny red crab that kept trying to scuttle off. A bleached white scallop shell represented the moon. This child was tapping into transmemory and she was eager to travel.

Muriel shot up through the surface of the sea, flipped her body under the watchful vault, and then splashed back into the salty brine. Whipping her flukes, she aimed for the lone female and opened her rostrum.

"Oooowww!" screamed the little octopod.

Muriel danced overhead in a crazy spiral. "Septielle!" she sang out in a lovely vibrato of joy. Then, slurping down the single arm she had ripped from the newly named juvenile, she sang out in *voce fortissimo*: "Chewy, yom!"

II

A Merry Yarn from a
Laughing Fellow Rover

Chapter 4

Anadare wrestled with the nets for all he was worth, wishing for might his teenaged frame did not yet possess. Strength mattered; it meant the ability to pull in food from the stingy sea. Productivity secured a place of importance in the community, possibly a seat in the Senate, possessions, and an immense house. Food was both life and power. He put in long hours every day with the men of the fleet, casting nets, hauling in nets, and mending nets. When he could borrow a boat, he went back out on his own. That was in addition to his studies on comtutor, and of course Taryn. He was supposed to have Saturdays free, but family chores devoured most of them. Today, he was juggling several obligations.

The old Latvian who was with him, Gints, barely spoke. He made grunting noises and pointed, then waited for Anadare to figure it out. Foul-smelling, leather-skinned Gints did not care for words or people; he cared about fish. More importantly, he knew the best fishing spots. It had taken Anadare weeks of coaxing to get the old man to show him this spot. They were on the windward side of Frigate Rock, the second-most remote of the Bullet Islands.

The Bullets stretched due east from the pistol-shaped mainland. The natives originally called the big island A'ia'I, meaning "shining like moonlight." A lawyer, Penfield Gunn, superimposed his own name, and it stuck. The stony islets supported a few dozen people along with their domesticated animals and some meager crops. The largest of these groups made its home on Gunn Island's one-time penal colony, Hell's Reach, farthest to the east. These were the descendants of the prisoners who had lived out their lives on a few stark acres subsisting on fish and the eggs of seabirds. The current generation mostly kept to themselves on the giant rock's tiny farms and within its quarried interior.

Anadare had never met them and hoped not to on this trip. He had come to catch fish and feed his family. Unlike the catch from a fleet vessel, this haul would not go to the island's collectors for spurious redistribution. The full morning's sail to Frigate Rock was paying off with a respectable haul of fish, but they had to hurry. A menacing cloud bank strobed a warning in the distance.

Colorful floats yanked the perimeter of the netting into a neat circle. Gints lowered a bag of pig guts into the water and took his position, leaning over the gunwales to watch the hungry fish investigate. He moved so slowly he appeared to be frozen. Suddenly, he unleashed a nimble attack, snagging a fish on his barbed spear tip, a move the island's fishermen worked hard to master but that futous never would. Gints pulled the good-sized fish out of the water, threw it into the boat, and prepared his next thrust.

Frigatebirds, including proud males with their red gular pouches, darted over their home while watching and noisily demanding a share of the catch. Within minutes Gints had half a dozen fish boned and sectioned, rolled in salt and spices, and stored away.

Anadare braced one foot against the gunwale and drew the net tighter. To his delight, he found several immature octopuses jetting about inside. The fine mesh kept them from slipping through, but that didn't mean they were waiting around to be eaten. The creatures began oozing over the rim of their prison. Anadare moved fast, scooping them up bare-handed then lethally biting them between the eyes and tossing them into a bucket. Sometimes the creatures' suckers left a red blemish on his skin. He'd have his revenge at the dinner table.

These octopuses were new to the area, and they were devilishly smart. He felt as if he was facing a cunning adversary capable of solving the puzzles of his traps and nets. He'd pulled up more than a few empty crab pots lately. One time he pulled up what he took to be a full pot, only to discover some wraith had devoured the knights from within and left their clanking armor behind.

This problem began with the appearance of the octopuses two years ago. Fishermen in his community claimed to have seen octopuses riding on the backs of dolphins. The octopuses pulled most of their limbs into a ball, using two to cling on to their hosts, as the dolphins stitched the waves. The fishermen said the octopuses were probably the Giant Pacific kind that used to thrive here before the

Fall. Senior senators dismissed this story as alcohol-fueled nonsense. Eventually, the storytellers tired of being made the butt of jokes and kept quiet.

Anadare wondered why dolphins would do such a thing, transplant a species here from wherever they began. The octopuses were reproducing, carving a niche for themselves in these waters. He welcomed it, since it meant a new source of food as other species winked out of existence.

As he turned these thoughts over in his mind, a twinned flare of sunlight caught Anadare's attention. The light glistened from a pair of smooth gray heads floating in the mid-distance. Each sported a blowhole on top and a whimsical grin fixed on its mouth. Two dolphins were watching him and Gints. Anadare raised his head and waved, imagining these new friends were bobbing their heads in response.

Gints punched Anadare's arm hard enough to hurt and gestured at the horizon. Over the blue edge of the world, a black point elongated and took on detail. Gints raised the sail, while Anadare frantically stored the nets and tackle. That mast could belong to a schooner, maybe a picket ship for the Others. They had to put distance between them and the approaching vessel. Anadare's heart jumped again. Hovering directly between them and Gunn Island was a pack of dark clouds pouring torrents into the sea.

It was impossible to steer around such a large tempest. Turning east meant meeting up with the Others; neither Anadare nor Gints had any doubt about their chances if that happened. Forty-five minutes later, they were inside the squall. The breeze became a fierce bluster, as if they had ignored a No Trespassing sign.

"Tether yourself and reef the mains!" Gints was at the stern, but the order seemed to come from . . . somewhere else. No doubt the wind was confusing his senses. Anadare responded without question, taking a moment to shake off a juvenile octopus that had somehow attached itself to his foot. He had no time to wonder about the creature as it plopped into the churning water.

Anadare grabbed a line tied to a cleat and roped himself securely. It was a cardinal rule on the water: the boat is stronger than the sailor; stay together. Next he began reducing the amount of sail exposed to the ripping winds. Gints first gave him a curious look, then joined Anadare in re-rigging the heavy canvas. Together they adjusted the jib just in time for a full blast of horizontal rain and gale-force wind. The mast protested, but the small boat handled the punishment. Gints motioned for them to switch places.

Anadare took control of the tiller while Gints adjusted the jib and main halyards in the rapidly shifting winds. The size of the swells alarmed Anadare. He scanned the horizon for any break in the storm.

Twisting around, he shifted off of his center of gravity, which proved to be a serious mistake. The boom came around hard, shoving him onto the rail. He was scrambling to recover his balance when the wind yanked the boat into a violent roll. Into the sea Anadare went. He felt one of his sandals slip off and opened his eyes to see if he could catch it before it sank too far.

He was less frightened than he was angry at himself. He had his tether in place and knew how to budget the breath in his lungs so he could regain the surface. He spotted the errant sandal and also a number of stream-lined shapes in the water. The dolphins had followed them into the storm. One of the creatures nudged Anadare's midsection, pushing him up toward the boat. He broke the surface, wanting to suck in a quick breath and duck back underneath to take another look.

Gints grabbed Anadare by the collar and hair and painfully hauled him into the boat like so much cargo. Anadare checked himself over, pressing one hand to his belt purse. Fortunately, Taryn's gift was still there; if he lost that, she'd kill him.

For three hours, Anadare and Gints worked without stopping. Neither uttered a word, not that they could hear over the storm. If there was a bright spot, it was that the squall seemed to be taking them the way they wanted to go, closer to Gunn Island. In fact, they were making excellent time.

The storm eventually spent itself into nothingness. They set course for Losi Bay, careful to avoid the razor reefs that could gash their hull.

They tied the boat off at Gints' floating dock. He quietly parsed out Anadare's portion of the catch and then left.

Perhaps it was too much to expect Gints to share a moment of camaraderie after a day's adventure on the ocean. A century ago, the original islanders had welcomed the refugees who came in groups after the Fall. The Latvians were latecomers. For decades prior to their arrival, they had maintained a thriving flotilla on the broad Pacific. Endless storms depleted their numbers and forced them to tether their floating city, sentimentally named Daugava, to Gunn Island's northern shore. They tended to be a tight-knit community wary of outsiders.

Up the beach, Anadare found Sefa and Rua tending slips. Hungry as ever, Sefa was nibbling on fish and watching an old movie on his comtutor. The durable devices were the sole form of structured education for netter kids, but there weren't enough to go around. Sefa used his comtutor time to study old movies. He liked the naval derring-do of Horatio Hornblower.

"We should build ships like that!" Sefa said, gesturing to his comtutor, which currently showed a broadside splintering masts and men aboard a French seventy-four gunner. "Think of the battles we could have!"

Rua changed the subject. "Have you seen the Zhangs?"

"No," Anadare replied.

Under his fierce tribal tattoos, Rua wore a look of concern. "They left this morning before you did."

"We hit rough weather coming back. We were lucky to get through." He didn't mention their close call with the Others. He hoped the Zhangs might still turn up safe; Kuan Zhang and his family seemed like good people.

"If we had big gunships, we could use them to protect our fishing fleet," Sefa said. It was nonsense, but Anadare agreed anyway.

He agreed to meet up with his friends soon, then hoisted his pack of fish and headed home along the jungle path. Myriad emerald phantoms played over his skin. His community, made up of dozens of single-story homes, spread over the plain that surrounded the harbor. Thick, bulwarked stone walls gave them the appearance of small fortresses. Hurricanes came often and with little warning. At any given time, one of Anadare's neighbors might be busy fashioning a roof out of fronds to replace one stolen by nature's latest tantrum. The island communities boasted few wooden structures except for those in the cool hills of Morningside, where the wealthy lived in spacious luxury. They hired Chinese workers or Anadare's fellow netters to clean up yard debris.

Checking to see that no one was looking, Anadare hauled his heavy pack up and over the stone wall marking his family's property and into a safe place: the cistern. With only the hatch marking its buried bulk, the chamber held rainwater fed by a system of collection trays and pipes. A reinforced lining kept out ocean salt. He hung the waterproof pack on an inside peg near the hatch. Only a little showed above the water's surface.

Stepping out of the cistern and closing the hatch behind him, Anadare flinched at a familiar voice. "Where have you been? After I had to beg Daddy to get you into the Senate meeting? Andy, I don't know what's wrong with you!" Taryn fixed him with her blue-eyed gaze. The broad brim of her sun hat bounced girlishly as she moved her head, emphasizing her mock disgust.

"I was on my way!"

"You've been fishing. God, you're soaked through!" She produced a towel from her large shoulder bag and threw it at his face.

"The ocean is wet."

"You're going to make a fine impression. Put these on." She pulled out a fresh tunic and pants for him.

"You're carrying a man's clothes?" he asked, stripping off his sweat-stained linens.

"Have to. I'm dating an idiot who barely knows how to dress himself," she shot back, slinging the finely loomed linen fabric over the top of his head. While he tugged on the pants, she reached into his belt purse and pulled out the gold bracelet. It was fashioned in the form of a pouncing lioness. Slipping it onto his right wrist, Taryn chided, "This time, don't take it off!"

He tried to object. "It's so f—"

"Futou?"

"I was going to say 'feminine.'"

"You were going to say 'futou,' but it doesn't matter. Unless you want to spend the rest of your life stinking like you stink right now and listening to senators instead of one day sitting at the big table, you'll dress like someone who matters." ("Instead of dressing like netter scum," she didn't say.)

Anadare stewed for a moment, then did the first thing

that came to mind; he pulled her roughly to him. "I'll matter to you first. The rest will come." That caught Taryn
off guard, as he'd hoped. She didn't kiss him, this time,
but she ceased her rant.

Anadare looked at the bracelet. He'd never seen a lion.
No one alive had.

Beryl swam in playful circles around the junk with her
sister, Princess Victoria Kaʻiulani Kawekio I Lunalilo
Kalaninuiahi-lapalapa Cleghorn. For several seasons, the
Zhang junk had been generous with its fish heads. Sometimes the one named Kuan sang to them while his wispy-
haired mother shared whole fish. The dolphin siblings
happily tagged along with the Zhangs on their excur-
sions. They liked the way the family spoke; musical notes
enriched every word.

Today, another boat came alongside. People from this
boat had no music in their voices; they expressed themselves bluntly. Dressed all in white, these loud visitors
took Lau Lau Zhang, her son Kuan, daughter Jin, and
grandbaby Duo Duo off in their boat. They left behind
Jin's husband, Fuming, who bore a corkscrewed arm and
a damaged mind thanks to a fishing accident. The sisters
decided to stay with the junk. Voices filtered through its
hull and down into the water. The last Zhang was crying.

"The strangers mans are being mean to the Zhangs

mans," sang Princess Victoria Ka'iulani Kawekio I Lunalilo Kalaninuiahi-lapalapa Cleghorn in a *doloroso* cadence.

The dolphins stealthily poked their melons above the swells. The leader of these others was a tall female mans with red fan-coral hair. She wore a broad, permanent smile, something like a dolphin's . . . minus the joy. The leader's presence dominated the gathering on deck.

They listened: "Choosing wisely works out well for everyone. Perhaps, though, you need to see what the wrong choice brings," the mans said.

Few mans had such strong bearing. Beryl thought this might be one of those special mans Muriel liked to find and ping. There was something odd about the way the female mans moved and interacted with the new mans, flitting from one to the next without making real contact, that is, without allowing others to enter the conversation. It was as if she was turned inward or her brain had gone bad. She was the least happy mans Beryl had ever seen.

Three other strangers surrounded the broken-minded Zhang, who cowered behind a large basket of fish. Each of the strangers held a long, wicked blade. Most had guns, something the dolphins recognized from transmemory. One figure stayed close to Bad Brain. He had no hair on top of his head, but had grown a long, black tail in back. Head Tail moved toward the last Zhang, holding yet another weapon: a long rod with a prickle point that popped out when the mans squeezed something on the handle.

The dolphins dove back under. "We need to tell Muriel," Beryl told her sister.

"About the baskets of tasty fish bits?" She had her priority.

"No. Not those," Beryl said. "Muriel needs to know the mans are hurting each other again." The two spent several minutes arguing in blasts of staccato frustration. From above came the sound of scuffling and the beginnings of a loud mans vocalization, abruptly cut off. After a long silence, they heard more movement and the sound of someone dropping something heavy onto the boat's deck. "We should wait for Katma, Ariana, Bitsie, and the rest of the pod. Then we can go."

The mans on the boat began throwing something overboard. Meaty jetsam tumbled and plopped in sloppy chunks, creating misty red trails in the water. The prospect of a free meal overpowered the dolphins' concerns; they began an aquatic arabesque in anticipation of some tasty offal. "They seem to be wasting a lot of good fish guts. Mans don't appreciate—" As the true nature of the redness registered, Princess Victoria Ka'iulani Kawekio I Lunalilo Kalaninuiahi-lapalapa Cleghorn halted her food-themed aria.

The hunks kept coming. Both sisters stopped swimming and together voiced *lacrimoso*: "Not fish!"

The atmosphere of the Senate Building chilled Anadare's still-wet body. The polished volcanic stone walls felt cool to the touch, yet the costly air-conditioning system kept the space positively cold, the way futous insisted. The Senate was in session, discussing a flurry of matters. Anadare and Taryn quietly found their place toward the back.

"—a total of forty-eight tons of fish and pork in the accounting period just completed. We're having problems with theft from the fish hatcheries, despite increased security." The speaker droned on oblivious to the listlessness of his audience. "Vegetables raised: ninety lots. This will be our fourth season without a surplus. Fanchon and Hamlin have agreed to continue overseeing collections for the Exchange. As you know, some of the families have been reluctant to take part in the Food Security Initiative. I recommend another sweep of the residences for contraband food."

The assembly grumbled its assent and Anadare felt his feet turn to ice. They would find the food he'd caught and seize it for the common stores. It wasn't fair. The Exchange doled out slim portions from the many tons that went in . . . unless one had connections.

The next report focused on the industrial output of the island's synthetics district. The numbers were small and dull. Anadare stifled a yawn, prompting Taryn to jab his shin with her foot. Exchange Commissioner Hecht looked over, coolly acknowledging his presence then smiling at his daughter. Taryn smiled back.

The topic changed to one of major concern around the island. A double-chinned senator who wore many gold rings spoke to the assembly. "I've received a new report of activity out in the Bullets. It seems one of our families failed to return from a fishing run. We hoped to coordinate a search with the people of Hell's Reach, but they have not returned our radio messages. It's not unusual for Hell's Reach to go quiet, but the timing is troubling."

Commissioner Hecht looked over at a leathery-faced man in dirty clothes standing on the other side of the room. Gints. Anadare was about to volunteer that he had been with Gints and had also heard about the missing Zhang family when the heavyset senator continued. "We must conclude the Others have decided not to contact us directly and are responsible for our missing boats. We must revisit the issue of island defense." The senator talked about fabricating cannon and shore batteries, no small task with their limited resources.

The people of Gunn used to scout all the islands within reach. If an island was dead, as so many were, the scouts methodically stripped it of old weapons, metals, working electronics, wind-power components, boats, books, or anything useful. Expeditions yielded diminishing returns while commanding a high cost in men and materiel. The Vilks brothers had headed the last expedition years ago. When the Latvians and their crew failed to come home, the Senate quietly ended the scouting voyages.

"It is my position," Senator Chins continued, "that we divert certain common resources to bolstering our island guard." Murmurs swept the room, mostly from people dressed in simple linen garments.

Anadare had no doubt who would be giving up "common resources" in order to strengthen the island's tiny paramilitary and protect the fine homes of the *f-ing tourists*. He mentally checked himself. Taryn and her father were futous, but they'd always seemed pleasant. He'd never met Taryn's mother or two brothers; they lived in a separate home for some reason.

He whispered to Taryn, "Where are we supposed to get a militia? Our rifles are so old they'll blow up in our faces! Potato guns are fun, but they aren't going to scare off the Others."

"Ssshhhh!" That ended the discussion.

The ranking panel members agreed to meet again in a week to call a vote on beefing up defense. After that, the session devolved into mundane housekeeping.

As the meeting adjourned, Taryn took Anadare over to say hello to her father. His few discussions with the commissioner had been awkward at best. There was something imposing about the man. Maybe it was the heavy gold lion necklace with its preternatural ruby eyes. Such obvious signs of wealth spoke volumes; Hecht was a man of title and influence, while Anadare was a fisherman's son.

"You look well, Anadare. Tanned," Commissioner Hecht said.

The jibe was not lost on him. Sun on skin denoted the working class. Netters, who represented many Pacific cultures, loved the sun. Their homes were Spartan, made from local volcanic rock. By contrast, futous avoided the sun; they even prayed indoors. In addition to being pale, many were overweight, since they also avoided hard labor. They were descended from people who had come to the island aboard the *Dancing Waves* cruise/evacuation ship nearly a century ago. Futous accreted every luxury to be found: big homes filled with ante ruinam furniture and fixtures from the ship, elaborate jewelry, and more clothes than they had room to store. Anadare imagined such a life with Taryn.

"Thank you, Commissioner," Anadare said.

"Ken. You can call me Ken."

"Uh, I'd rather say Mister Hecht."

A smile split his face; whether sincere or forced, Anadare couldn't tell. "Good enough. Let's make some time later this week. I have something I'd like to discuss with you."

Anadare tried not to look the way he felt. He wasn't sure what the commissioner thought of his dating Taryn, though he had his suspicions. Besides, Anadare was supposed to go out with the fleet all week and wondered how he'd explain this to his boat captain. Still, the commissioner's invitation was not optional. "Of course!" he said.

It was dark by the time they left the Senate Building. Anadare's stomach screamed neglect. Taryn offered to take him out for a late dinner, but he told her he needed to get home. He kissed her goodnight lingeringly, then ran for home.

Anadare's focus was on the sack of fish he'd stashed in the cistern. Checking the shingle that hung from his

front door, he found the collectors' imprimatur: they'd
been there. Good. With their invasive counting complete
for now, it was safe to move the sack into his mother's
pantry. He heaved open the cistern's hatch and climbed
inside, trying not to make any noise on the metal ladder.
He felt his way in the dim light of an aging bioorganic
lumens strip. Going from the warm night air into this cool
stone enclosure raised goose pimples on his flesh. He
would like to have stayed there for a while, but it was late.
He reached down to the peg where he had hung the
sack . . . and found nothing. Sweat broke out over his
body. He ran his hand over the smooth walls, brushing a
mummified lizard husk glued there, but found no sign of
his prize. The water was four feet deep. He hesitated a
moment. Filters or no, he did not want to mix his sweat
and grime into the family's drinking supply. Reluctantly,
he stepped into the water and felt his way around the bottom. The sack was gone. Taken.

Anadare pulled himself, soaked once again, from the
cistern and went inside the house. He gratefully noticed
the lights were out in his parents' bedroom. As he headed
to his own room, he passed Penina's. Light crept out from
underneath the door and he heard two voices coming
from the other side: his sister's and one he didn't know.
Though subdued, he could tell the girls' conversation was
of a serious nature.

He opened the door . . . and got hit in the face with a
hunk of fish and an accusation: "Murderer!" the strange
girl screamed.

The fleshy chunk rolled off his face. He caught and examined it. It was a piece of octopus, an arm, salted like the rest of his catch. The tip was dark blue as if it had been dyed. "Th'fuh, Penina! Who's your friend?" He pointed at the teen lying with his sister on the mat.

It registered that both were in their underwear and that the strange girl was much curvier than Penina or Taryn. Much curvier. She had rivers of black hair, luminous skin, and intense eyes the color of storm clouds. The two were surrounded by bits of octopus, a jar of dark liquid, and fine needles that resembled miniature harpoons.

"This!" the girl rasped in a barely controlled whisper. "This is one of Septielle's descendants! You are eating the children!" She was shaking another blue-stained piece of octopus at him, using a hand with a blue tattoo on one finger. Somehow, the personal marking linked the girl with this Septielle.

"I'm not eating anyone's kids. It's fish, same as we eat every day."

"Get out!" Now, both women were off the mat and pushing him backward out the door. As she closed it in his face, he noticed that Penina's right forefinger was deep blue from freshly injected indigo dye like her friend's. Great! They were both in a cult.

He was back in the hall, confused. He whispered through the door to Penina that she could keep the blue-tipped parts if she wanted, but the rest of the fish should go in the cooler.

"We'll handle it, little brother." Fine. The octopus was

a loss, but the rest was secure. At least he hadn't risked his life for nothing.

Anadare went to bed still trying to understand what he'd heard and seen. Before any answers came to him, he slid into sleep.

Chapter 5

"It's basic math," groused Norris as he snatched tiny crustaceans in the sucker rows of one arm then the next. He moved his facile limbs in a carousel motion over the bed of krill-like animals, sorting and testing each. "What slows me down is having to convert to that imbecilic base ten the mans love so much, plus using years instead of lunas."

"Even so, we're making progress, right?" Tippi asked, hoping Norris wouldn't bite her mantle off yet again. "Muriel's having some success with the creatures in this region. That's why we came, right? Because these waters have different species, maybe stronger in some ways, ones she can work with?"

"That and to see whether octopodes and dolphins can survive crossing unexplored currents without running afoul of random poisonous patches. We proved it's possible, thanks to Septielle's star map."

"It's not a risk I'd care to take often," Tippi added.

Norris was sorely tempted to eat a few of the less ill creatures before him, but science and Muriel would never forgive him. Not that mans would hesitate to have an octopod for supper. It made him want to scream, if that were possible: "You mans! You eat too much, until you are heavy and slow and dull-witted. You eat your share for today and tomorrow as well. You eat tomorrow!"

"We survive. That's what counts," she said, aiming to blunt his pessimism. Tippi liked Norris in a way, but not enough to pair off with him. His negativity dimmed her cheery outlook. She needed Norris for his mathematical acumen. The male scions of Yiming embodied such pragmatic skills, while the female octopodes of Septielle's line excelled at envisioning grand schemes. This had been shepherded by Muriel and her acolytes, who identified offspring with certain traits and enhanced those attributes through encouragement . . . and effector manipulation. Tippi wanted to temper her bold visions with basic sciences, but if that meant mating with Norris, she'd pass.

"About a third of these krill are dead." His color darkened and his skin scrunched up in places. "Most of the others will be dead in a few days. A fraction, however, seem hearty enough to metabolize the poisons in these sands. Yes, that's progress."

"So, based on that—" she prodded.

"Based on that, nothing," Norris clipped her. He fixed her with his eye slits and tried again to explain the long odds of the dolphins' gambit. "Even if these critters survive long enough to reproduce, there's no guarantee they'll pass along any useful traits to their offspring."

"Muriel says there's a good chance."

"Muriel spends too much time alone lately. It affects her thinking. If the DNA holds true, fine, but that still proves nothing. The waters we're in now are cleaner than many of the places these animals will have to colonize. A higher dosage of poisons—and there are very, very high doses along most coastal regions—could obliterate the entire generation, putting us right back at the beginning."

The partners swept in from opposite directions through the newly sown sea grass as they sorted living animals from dead ones. As they passed, pinwheeling their eight limbs precisely in time, he touched his blue-inked tip to hers, reaffirming their link to Septielle's vision. Contact allowed Norris to sense Tippi's concerns. She had good hearts.

He took a moment to process his own thoughts and then responded. "Best-case scenario: we find animals who can ingest and metabolize the most common poisons left over from the mans' mistakes. We need several species, each capable of taking a tiny bite out of this toxic stew. From there, as I say, the math is simple. We assume a median growth rate for successful critters, factor in our delivery efforts to the most toxic areas, assuming we ourselves don't succumb . . . let's say it all goes according to Muriel's vision. In that case, we should see a notable decrease in harmful toxin levels over a predictable number of generations. Other organisms may, in theory, adapt to the changed environment and accelerate the gastronomically motivated scrubbing. All of this would continue in a geometric progression, gaining momentum after a span of generations. That being the case, and assuming nothing adds to the problem, we can predict a date when the waters will run clear again of . . ."

Tippi had reached her limit. "Tell me or I'll eat you right here and now!"

"Hmmm. Females. Fine. In base ten," he paused while he made the conversion, "we should have a clean Earth once more in roughly sixty thousand years."

Tippi blew a large bubble.

"Give or take a millennium, you understand."

Another hurricane blew through. The islanders no longer named the big ones. Anadare's family joined the clean-up effort, helping the worst-hit homes before checking their own. Several neighbors had lost roofs or fabric-walled extensions. Penina and her friends, including the curvy one, searched for storm-scattered chickens. It would be days before the hens laid again. Other parties cut wood from palms uprooted by the hammering gusts. The steamy air was filled with tiny mouths, making hauling miserable.

Anadare and his father checked the cistern to see that sea water had not seeped in. Loto Mataeula broached the subject. "So, you two."

"Us two."

"You've been seeing Taryn a lot."

"We're in love . . . kinda," Anadare said, feeling the blush in his cheeks.

"Yeah, about that . . ." His father straightened up from his labors, wincing as his back protested. "Your mom is pretty good at seeing things."

"Things?" Anadare's tattoo itched. The shark god Dakuwaqa had adorned his neck since his eleventh birthday. It offered powerful protection from dangerous foes, but not from loving parents.

"She says you two aren't so much *in* love as you are loving *at* each other. You seem to be in love with having a girlfriend with blue eyes, skin like coconut milk, and a fine house in Morningside. She seems to be in love with having a handsome young man to order around. It's not really a problem at your age. You're being careful, aren't you?"

"Yes. Tell Ma thanks, I guess," he said.

"Anadare, I'm happy for you, but I wonder where this is going. It's not as though futous go out of their way to mix with us."

As often as he used it himself, he didn't like to hear the word *futou* from his father. "The Hechts aren't like that."

"Commissioner Hecht *is* that," a new voice interrupted. "He sets the standard, netter." It was the girl he had seen in Penina's bedroom, the one with the intense eyes and other attributes.

An approaching noise cut off their conversation. A tripart caravan rumbled its heavy wheels over the uneven paths and jungle creepers. The machine was ungainly, but ingenious. The first part held the driver and engine, which drew power from solar cells and an ancient internal combustion engine that utilized fermented fuel. The beast ran hot and kept a team of mechanics busy. In back, a large trailer held cargo and supplies, including replacement parts for the caravan itself. Between the two, the passenger car held up to thirty people. It often carried only a few futous, who sat sipping cool drinks, touring the island without risking exposure to the tropical sun.

"Speak of the devil!" Penina's friend said. "Your gal's daddy sent his goons."

The doors of the passenger section opened. Half a dozen rough-looking collectors stepped out, led by Fanchon, whose greasy hair hung over his darting eyes. He ordered the others to fan out through the winding rows of homes. A few of the collectors pulled leather blackjacks from their belts. Anadare's neighbors fell silent.

Not so with Anadare's father. "You were just here. The next collection isn't due for a week."

"This collection is for the Founders Day celebration." Fanchon's Creole growl turned "this" into "dis" and "the" into "deh."

"With all that's going on, you pull this nonsense again? You people didn't found anything! You showed up in a leaky ship and decided the island was yours." Loto Mataeula's voice broke as he trailed a few feet behind Fanchon. "You impose your ideas, your customs. You give your kids fine schools with teachers, but hand out a few obsolete machines to teach our children your language and your history. My father taught me the stories of how our people settled this island under the protection of Dakuwaqa. What do Anadare and Penina get? Kūkā! Futou nonsense. It's not fair!"

"Fair ain't doodly squat." Fanchon referred to a list in his hand: "The Exchange believes you have generated a certain amount of crops, fish, and livestock products. We are here for forty pounds total. If you cannot meet this quota, we are empowered to take a dozen of these chickens."

Anadare's mother ran into the yard. "Crazy man! Without the hens, we'll have no eggs," she argued.

"Futous!" Loto spat on the ground while Penina watched from the doorway.

"We are not having that discussion today, Mataeula." Fanchon put an ursine hand on Loto's shoulder, his fingers pressing into the flesh. Loto tried to pull free, but could not.

Anadare had had enough. If the collectors got their way, they would roll up for more in a few days. "Hey, Fanchon! I see it's true what they say: collectors never miss a meal. You're so fat, you're about to split your pants. Now, take your hand off my father!"

Penina and her friend stood watching. Fanchon mumbled something in a menacing tone. He released Loto and came after his son. The Creole pressed his face straight into Anadare's.

"You listen up, cooyon—" Fanchon's voice cut out as a hail of chicken kūkā strafed the back of his head.

The source of the fusillade was laughing her ass off. "Oops!"

Rather than go after his sister's friend, Fanchon drew his blackjack and grabbed hold of Anadare's arm. Anadare swung the arm in windmill fashion to break the collector's grip. It worked, but the swing carried through too far and he clipped Fanchon in the face. The blow made the big man stagger, more from surprise than pain. Now he glowered with real anger.

Several things happened at once. Penina and her friend rushed toward Fanchon. Just in time, Loto grabbed his daughter around the waist and pushed her over to her mother, who hustled the girl indoors. Loto was about to intercede on his son's behalf, but a second collector held him back. Penina's friend jumped onto Fanchon's back, sending him crashing painfully to his knees. More government men rushed over.

"Run!" the girl told Anadare, reaching up and pulling out wads of the screaming Fanchon's hair.

"Where?"

It was a moot point, as the other collectors handily ended the uprising. The neighbors didn't cheer out loud for Anadare, but they smiled and murmured encouragements.

Anadare didn't feel like a hero as the collectors loaded him bodily onto the caravan, along with as many of the family's chickens as the men could catch, plus one other passenger. Anadare and Penina's friend sat on a back bench, squeezed tightly between two unbathed collectors.

The girl smiled at her fellow prisoner. "Valērija. Pleased to meet you."

The two spent a long, uncomfortable trip trading whispered insults.

"I never asked for your help."

"They were about to steal your family's food, and probably beat up your dad for good measure."

"Who asked you to butt in?"

"I was helping your sister, actually."

"Right. You two seem real close."

This drew a laugh from Valērija. "I like Penina."

"Yeah."

An indignant snort. "What's the matter, jealous of your sister?"

"Over some big-assed lezbo who flings chicken kūkā at armed men? Not likely."

"You like my ass, huh?"

"Th'fuh! I didn't say that."

One of the guards stomped his foot and bared his teeth. The conversation was over.

The collectors skipped the rest of their stops. Anadare figured they were headed to the jail. To his surprise, the caravan pulled up to Gunn Island's only marble edifice, the Exchange.

"Commissioner Hecht wants to see you." It was Fanchon, opening the door of the caravan. Anadare and Valērija stepped out.

Running down the richly veined white steps, Taryn took a hard look at both of them. "No. I don't even want to know." She checked Anadare's appearance, pointedly ignoring the Latvian girl who was standing right there.

"This is your girlfriend? Nice," Valērija cooed, adding a theatrically obvious leer.

Taryn shot back, "Who's the skank?"

"Just a friend, babes," Valērija said. Then, to Anadare: "You like 'em on the boney side, eh?"

Taryn returned the compliment. "Thank you. And if we ever want a girl who can crush me with her monster thighs, we'll call . . .?"

"Valērija Rasmanis."

"Taryn Hecht." She offered her hand, her face a tableau of ladylike composure and homicidal thoughts.

Taryn rushed them all inside and into the washroom. She performed her magic trick of pulling out nice clothes for Anadare to change into. Nothing for Valērija, who was amused by the slight. Anadare was wearing his lioness bracelet; that won him back a few points with Taryn. She hastily arranged his long hair to cover his shark tattoo.

"Good enough. The commissioner is waiting."

"You mean Dadd—" Anadare cut off Valērija's comment with a non-gentle elbow to the ribs.

The teens walked over the cool marble floor, past some offices, and into a great roaring chamber. The ceiling mural depicted a paradise replete with wine, food, and golden nymphs. Futous in brightly colored scarves bumped them while dashing about the floor, cryptically yelling, "Eggs at thirty" and "One goat, four soy." From there, the exchange players took scribbled notes to one end of the room, where a gold-scarfed individual collected them. He transcribed this information onto a giant wheel, bowed his head, and spun the wheel. When it stopped, some items moved to the lucky blue column while most landed in the hated red column.

"It's half bank and half circus," Valērija said.

They passed below the gallery of islanders who stood mesmerized by the clattering wheel that decided the fate of their parcels. An appearance in the blue column could double their food supply. Red meant a hungry walk home to an angry family.

Up a winding flight of stairs, the three teens came to Commissioner Hecht's office, which overlooked the trading floor. Taryn rushed over to give her father a hug and fuss over his clothes. He kissed her cheek, then turned to the others.

"Good to see you, Andy. I hear you and your friend here made quite an impression on our collectors." Anadare fidgeted in place.

Valērija whispered to Anadare, "Yes, why did you pick on those poor defenseless apes, *Andy*?"

The four of them sat down for conversation over an elaborate lunch of meat and fish, plus some sweets. Freshly squeezed fruit juice arrived in a crystal pitcher clinking with ice cubes. The cooler at Anadare's home never got cold enough to make ice. Hecht poured himself a glass of an island liqueur, joking it was his reward for "riding a wild bourse" all morning.

The commissioner then launched into a homily about their life on the island. "So, Gunn is one of only a handful of islands that can support a sizeable population. Around us: sixty-four million square miles, or one hundred sixty-five million square kilometers, of ocean. With decaying ships, outdated charts, and no working navigational satellites, you'd have as easy a time sailing among the stars as on the South Pacific.

"Piecing together a picture of the outside world from stray reports, including the wretched souls who occasionally wash up on our beaches, I'd estimate there are only a few tens of millions of people left."

"That's a lot, right?"

"Once, there were many billions."

"I read that somewhere," Valērija interjected.

Hecht acknowledged her with a perfunctory smile and turned his attention back to Anadare. "The numbers may be small, but people still must eat. And it's harder than ever to get food."

"And . . . you think outsiders may come here, looking for the food and things we have?"

"Most will sit at home, praying while they starve, but some will take action. They'll strike out in search of food, new lands, a future. That's one reason we don't send out expeditions anymore. We don't want anyone following us back here. We are protected by vast sweeps of wave and weather.

"Of course, that also means no new supplies come into our system, which is why the Exchange is vital. It keeps track of how much food we produce and ensures everyone gets some."

This touched on a sore spot. Anadare's family never seemed to get all it needed. When they went out and got their own, the Exchange sent collectors to seize it. Everyone he knew gathered food. No one he knew had extra. Anadare chose his response: "I've heard some people say it might be better if each family kept track of its own food."

"Some of us are willing to take on odd jobs to earn extra rations for the folks back home," Valērija said, too brightly, as though this explanation were a decoy for another motive. Before Anadare could puzzle out her meaning, Hecht spoke.

"You're a smart man. Here's something I want you to understand: there's a difference between being smart and being wise." Anadare concealed his unease at being talked down to. "You want to know why people don't take care of themselves. Why don't they share any surplus with their neighbors without being asked? Is that it?"

Everyone in his community did exactly that, without help from the Exchange. What Anadare said, though, was: "I guess that's what I mean, yes."

Hecht's arm was around his shoulder. "Andy, you like to sail. You're very good at it."

"Thank you, sir."

"Ken."

"Ken." As Anadare said it, Taryn gave him a look of encouragement while Valērija rolled her dark eyes.

"You've seen schools of fish, right?"

"Daddy," Taryn said, "he fishes all the time!"

"Point is, the fish group together for safety. They swim toward food. They change direction when a predator shows up."

"Sure."

"Who tells them to do that?"

"No one. They just do it."

"That's about the only thing I admire about fish. They're wise enough to cooperate. People are intelligent, Andy, but not wise. Individually, each wants to fill his belly. People don't have a natural instinct to come together to protect each other or hunt together or agree on which direction to take when danger threatens." Hecht's statements were a windy indictment of all people who didn't happen to be futous. The netters were living proof that Hecht was wrong. He went on, "Humans haven't changed since we swung from trees. Our aggressive simian brains require an authority-driven hierarchy.

"So, again, we need leaders. It's been that way for a million years, and it will be that way until the last human dies. That's why the Exchange is here, to properly distribute everything from food to arms. That's why the Senate is preparing the island's defenses, to meet the coming danger.

"If we held a referendum, people would dither and fret. Mobs do that; leaders act. Taryn and I believe you will be such a leader one day."

"Thank you."

"I'm not trying to puff up your ego. I'm here to tell you that you are needed. Now. Today."

It took Anadare a moment. "The Others?"

Hecht nodded. "They are moving as we speak."

"How can I help?" At this, Taryn took Anadare's hand and squeezed warmly. Commissioner Hecht grasped Anadare firmly by the shoulders, causing Anadare's hair to slip and expose his neck tattoo. The commissioner's eyes strayed momentarily to the ancient shark symbol, but he said nothing.

Hecht went on: "We need to know more about the Others. I think it's fair to call them pirates. How many are there? How many ships do they have? What do they want? Why haven't they contacted us directly? You're the man to go and find out. You sail well and you can handle yourself. This will be a good chance for you to shine your light, bright enough to catch the eye of a senator or two, eh? I want you to leave as soon as possible. Of course, you'll need help." With this, he looked squarely at Valērija.

Anadare blinked. "You two know each other?" he asked the commissioner.

"Not exactly," said Hecht. "Her neighbor, Gints, sometimes provides information for me. This job, though, calls for young people who can move quickly. Plus, my collectors tell me you both know how to fight dirty."

Anadare's mother went about her nightly activities, setting a bowl of stew in front of him. It included a generous portion of the sweet potato bits he loved.

"I suppose they eat better than this up on the hill," she said.

"Ma, it's not like that. I'm—" Both his father and Penina were staring. Anadare stopped talking and ate his meal.

He understood their concerns, but felt that once a man had survived the challenge of sea and storm, it wasn't possible to live by his parents' rules anymore.

"Promise your mother you're not going to take any unnecessary chances." His father's voice was firm, allowing no argument.

Anadare wanted to tell them how proud they'd be of him, then realized that was the wrong thing to say. He looked to Penina, as if to ask how he was supposed to reply. She tilted her head in a certain way and he got the message: don't brag, say what you have to say.

"I will be careful. I promise." Then he added, "This is wonderful stew." He turned to smile at his mother, but she had stepped away.

They packed hastily to be ready for the next tide. Anadare and Valērija brought the bare essentials for the trip to Daugava, the floating Latvian city tethered along the northern shore. Anadare had never been there. It was not as if Gunn was a huge island, but its people segregated themselves into a handful of communities. The Latvians were no exception.

They had asked Sefa to join their expedition, to get them close to their target then act as lookout. Ever eager to help, they found him making last-minute preparations on his catamaran, the *Hinatea*, named for the moon goddess.

"Behold, my pride and joy!" Sefa said to Valērija, standing very close to her as he showed off some of the improvements and improvisations he'd made on the twin-hulled boat.

"Too bad you don't offer as much attention to—I dunno—a girl. You might even get laid." Valērija didn't give Sefa a chance to respond, but brushed by him on her way forward.

It made more sense to hug the coast of Gunn rather than to cross the mountains on sandcycles or in a caravan. Either could raise questions, and the pirates could have spies around the island. A boat trip was a common occurrence.

They set sail without fanfare. Anadare pointed out, "The north current runs a few miles from the windward shore. We can drop sail and ride it to the outer Bullets unseen."

"We hope," Valērija added.

The first few hours they stayed within sight of shore. Rainy tresses began to fall on them, promising a storm to come. They needed shelter.

"There are no sandy beaches near here," Sefa said, waving toward Gunn's stumpy "grip."

"There are grottoes along this stretch," Anadare said. The sea had hollowed out some limestone cliffs. They found a space large enough to shelter the cat.

The storm hung on until the daylight was all but exhausted. They decided to spend the night.

Valērija began unpacking some gear; she lifted a small hatch in the port hull. A blue-eyed face looked back at her, putting a finger to her mouth in a desperate gesture that begged for quiet. Valērija's laughter echoed off the grotto walls.

Chapter 6

Kuan and his family kept their heads low. Everything was a blur of fear and confusion. The strangers in white hustled them into one gunboat after another, each heading farther east. Soon, Hell's Reach was receding in the distance. Islanders never came this far. As the light faded, they came to an enormous vessel, towed along by bulky tugs equipped with solar panels. The main vessel's hull was sleek and angular, but burdened on top by an ungainly city. Kuan's mind drew an image of an alabaster dragon struggling to fly with an ox on its back.

As they came alongside, the strangers drew their guns and separated Kuan from the rest. He cried out to his mother, sister, and tiny nephew. A pistol butt slammed into his jaw, bringing stars to his eyes. He was aware of being carried, but little else.

Time passed like an empty tea cup waved under parched lips.

It was useless. Kuan did not dare break through the door of the cabin; a locked balcony looked out on empty sea. He thought of swinging from balcony to balcony like a monkey, but realized he possessed no such courage. He worried for the safety of his family and hoped they were still alive. He had surrendered himself to the idea that his brother-in-law, Fuming, was not.

The strangers fed him a little, which helped him mark the passage of time. At night his brain replayed the capture, twisting reality to torment him with things he might have done. Perhaps he could have used a fish grapple or swung his fists harder to defeat the pirates. Each replay ended like a movie fading to black. His world was unchanged. Kuan lay alone in his sweat-soaked bed. His lips silently formed the words, "Mother, I'm sorry."

He memorized the walls of his prison. The faded wallpaper, the comforter on the bed, even the brass doorknobs all carried images of the same laughing figure: Okey Dokey the Octopus. He knew him well. As a child, Kuan would spend hours on his comtutor laughing at the character's silly stories. Kuan's favorite involved Okey and his friends learning to play baseball, using a blowfish for a ball. As Kuan grew older, he noticed that Okey's many adventures never kept him from eating an Okey Dokey burger. "Grilled one hundred percent Kobe beef patties, served fresh," the announcer pointed out without ever explaining what Kobe beef was supposed to be. Even as a boy, it made no sense to Kuan that anyone could grill underwater.

By his ninth birthday, Kuan had figured out that the cartoons came from the Okey Dokey Corporation. By age ten, Kuan was a total fanboy, devouring every available detail. The company's owner, Richard "Dickie" Dokey became a trillionaire when the Japanese firm Global Bikuta bought him out. Bikuta immediately stamped the Okey Dokey brand onto comtutors and candy bars, women's fashions and feminine hygiene products, prisons and pure-bred pit bulls, arterial transplants and artisanal water (a.k.a. tap water), video serials and breakfast cereals, lingerie and long-range missiles, snack foods and sleeping pills, rentable cemetery plots and lawn furniture, banks and brothels, orthopedic shoes . . . and Okey Dokey Cruises. This line boasted the biggest ships on the seven seas, including the *Wyvern of the Waves*. Bikuta also turned out many new Okey Dokey cartoons, but they sucked; Kuan preferred to watch the classic older ones with his nephew, Duo Duo.

The beaming octopus on the doorknob swung upside down. Two rough men rushed in and pulled Kuan down the companionway to an elevator, then to a large room fitted out for shipboard galas. The parquet dance floor buckled in places. Balls encrusted with tiny mirrors hung from the ceiling, slowly revolving with the motion of the ship and casting make-believe starlight into every corner. Kuan remembered old movies that showed rooms like this, where people laughed and celebrated and fell in love to the rhythm and sway of a live band.

At least fifty of the Others were gathered here. They wore those odd white uniforms: short pants, silver Okey Dokey belt buckles, plus knee-high socks and shoes. Their clothes were neatly pressed and spotless.

They formed a rough circle around an ornate table in the

center of the room. It held a gleaming silver dinner spread, complete with cutlery, fine china plates, linens, crystal stemware, and an enormous serving dish covered with a silver dome. Each piece was decorated with a smiling octopus. Someone brought a chair and forced Kuan to sit down at the table. He was hungry. No one else was eating, though, and Kuan's stomach knotted in apprehension.

The circle of people parted and Kuan saw his mother and sister. There was no sign of the baby, Duo Duo. He recalled all of the times Duo Duo had caused trouble on the *Qinglong*, disappearing and forcing them to search the junk frantically, only to find him curled up asleep behind some bundles. Kuan looked to his sister. They were not allowed to speak, but she reassured him with her gentle eyes: the child was somewhere safe. Kuan's mother looked tired but well enough, considering.

A tall woman with wildly unkempt red hair stepped forward and walked over to Kuan. "I am Isobel O'Malley, although some of my crew like to call me Grace O'Malley behind my back. She was a pirate queen who lived seven hundred years ago. I make my kids read their history and this is how they repay me. If anything, I am their queen mum." The Others roared at this joke. Kuan could see confusion on the face of his mother, who spoke no English.

"Will you let us return to our junk? You can take all the fish."

"We did, Mister Fisherman. Thank you." Queen Isobel spread her arms and did a slight curtsy, in a courtly show of manners, prompting another round of raucous howls from her crew. "Regrettably, we sometimes act like pirates. We began as humble shipwrights, but times grew hard, so now we live off of what the sea will surrender. We are *salvors*."

His mother shouted out in animated Mandarin. Isobel shot her a look, maintaining a rictus smile that chilled the room. Kuan spoke loudly to draw her attention back to himself. "My mother is curious to know what you want from us. I would like to know that as well."

"Ah." Isobel leaned over to him, the top several buttons of her blouse open. As she pressed close, her perfume hit his nostrils, oceanic with hints of spice and citrus. She was perhaps in her late forties and quite attractive. "Curiosity. Tsk, tsk. Cultivate patience, my friend." She motioned with one hand and the men behind Kuan grabbed both his arms and held him fast. Assured he wasn't going anywhere, Isobel took a step toward the table and grasped the handle of the silver dome.

She continued, "We want you to join us. You're a strong young man, a skilled fisherman. Your sister obviously has a fertile womb. We have a place for each of you in our organization. In exchange, we'll provide for your little nephew and ensure your mother is safely returned to your island."

Kuan looked around him, from face to face. He was about to lie. Everyone in the room seemed to know he was about to lie. "We would be happy to join the salvors," he lied.

"That's all we ask," beamed Isobel.

Nothing happened. Kuan was about to speak again, to ask a question. Instead, Isobel spoke. "There's just one thing. It's an initiation for malleable recruits like yourself."

"What?" His question came out as a half-choked whisper, answered by what came into view as Isobel lifted the silver dome. Kuan's heart fell a thousand miles. Bile rose in his throat. Instead of getting sick, though, he wept openly as the screams of his mother and sister reached his ears.

Isobel went on, her voice dark and lyrical. "You have to eat. We've all done it. Once done, you're in, you and the rest of your family." She carved a slice from one cheek, picked it up with the ornate silver serving fork, and brought it to Kuan's lips. Okey smiled up at him from the handle of the utensil, but the cartoon image was not the face that drew out Kuan's tears. He tried to turn away, but Isobel's goons held his head, forcing Kuan to look at the main course fastidiously arranged on the platter.

"One bite. Oh, go ahead, he's cooked. We're not savages."

Chapter 7

"You're going back the second we reach the flotilla."

"Not a chance," Taryn answered Anadare flatly, extracting herself from her hiding place in one of *Hinatea's* port hull storage compartments. She unfurled her body, wincing as her limbs protested their long confinement, then reached back inside for her broad sun hat.

"Wait," Sefa said. "What did you have to jettison to fit in there?"

"I don't know, some red-and-white packages and a few bundles."

Sefa shouted, "Medical supplies and clean clothes. Oh fine, no one get sick."

"I moved them into the next compartment, fart-wit." Taryn petted Sefa's head for good measure. "I also brought a *proper* first aid kit . . . and those clothes are *not* clean." Sefa huffed off, stepping over the watery gap to a ledge while mumbling about how it was *his* boat.

Valērija and Anadare got busy scraping snails off the rocks in the grotto. A few crabs topped off the planned feast. Sefa returned with more morsels and dropped them in a pot. Anadare surveyed the catch of the day. "That's not going to feed the four of us."

"Add this," said Valērija, swinging a flounder to the deck with a wet *thwunk*.

"That's gross. Where are its eyes?" Taryn poked at the still-flailing fish.

Turning it over, Valērija showed her: "Other side."

"How?" asked Anadare. "Flounders feed along the sandy bottom offshore. There's no way one could get into this grotto."

"You want to ask questions or start cooking?" Valērija chided. Something gently bumped her side of the boat. She pretended not to notice, but everyone looked at her suspiciously, so she glanced over the side. Valērija sighed and reached down into the water. "Show-off!" she said to someone or something in the water, yanking up a small shark by the tail. She slammed it onto the deck and bashed the life from it with a stanchion.

"Wow! That was even grosser!" Taryn mewled.

"Suit yourself, princess. This is good eating."

Sefa and Anadare were looking past Valērija and into the water. A smiling, almost childlike gray face was looking back. The dolphin bobbed her head and emitted a series of whistles.

"She says she isn't partial to shark, but wouldn't mind a taste of the flounder—raw, if you please." Valērija grinned at her dumbfounded shipmates.

"You speak fish?" Anadare's remark touched off a flurry of vocalizations from the dolphin. To their surprise, a second face appeared on the opposite side of the cat, also squealing in agitation.

"She says she's a mammal like you. And their names are Fabia and Sefina."

Sefa fell back from his seat laughing. "That's pure kūkā. I've heard of people who talk to dolphins, but nothing like this."

The two dolphins quieted down. The farther one, Fabia, swam under the boat to the side of the other, Sefina, whose skin tones included a dark dorsal "cape."

"Yes, Sefa, I can talk to dolphins, kind of. It's less about speaking English than it is about being receptive to some basic ideas. Yes, they have names. I learned them over time. And yes, they absolutely love raw fish."

Taryn moved closer to their two visitors. "Is it okay if I pet them?" Fabia responded by bringing her head closer to Taryn. "I'll take that as a yes." She rubbed the dolphin's slick melon. Sefa handed Taryn some cut fish, which she fed to their guests. Sefina lanced from the water in a broad arc, snatched the sun hat from Taryn's head, and dove back down. She triumphantly returned the braided straw hat filled with urchins and something green and slimy. "Thanks," Taryn said, taking back her sodden headgear.

Sefa laughed loudly until Taryn murdered him with her eyes.

By morning, their tireless new team members had brought them more fish than they could eat in a week. Sefina ate more than she shared; she was young and still growing. Sefa loaded the live fish into a mesh bag. He cinched up the bag and dropped it into a cage that hung underwater from the bridgedeck connecting *Hinatea's* twin hulls.

In the morning, the cat pulled out from the grotto under a storm-scrubbed sky of blue. Sefa and the women tended the sails. Taryn urged the others to teach her enough basic tasks to be useful. Cutting up bait, unpacking or repacking sails as needed, and checking the tension on the lines required more willingness than experience, and Taryn did each job with enthusiasm. Anadare worked the rudder. He sensed the cat pulling to port, away from shore, as if the port hull was meeting some extra resistance. There was nothing visible in the blue-green water, except . . .

Two side-canted eyes stared back at him. "Great. We have another stowaway!" Anadare informed the others. Valērija smiled knowingly.

"I've been fishing my whole life and I've never seen this." Sefa held up the mesh bag. Something had unlatched the cage, loosened the cinch strap on the bag, and pilfered its contents. The thief had stripped the flesh off the fish, leaving the bones behind.

"Meet Norris," Valērija said, reaching down under the port hull and pulling back the blue tip of a limb. Now it was Anadare's turn to let his jaw hang open. The tip matched Valērija's forefinger, an identical shade of indigo. The limb continued down into the water. "It's in remembrance of one of the octopodes' great-great-something-great grandmother," she said.

"You're nuts, and so is my sister," Anadare cried, remembering Penina's inked finger.

"Water water," she replied. He didn't like the expression—"Water water everywhere, nor any drop to drink"—meaning Valērija felt he was talking a lot but not saying much.

Norris drew his bulk to the surface, through the cargo netting, and onto the bridgedeck. The startled humans saw a blob of flesh with two sideways eye slits.

"It's a giant octopus!" Taryn squealed, more amused than frightened.

"They prefer the term 'octopod,' octopodes for the plural." With this, Valērija placed Norris' limb in Taryn's uncertain hand. A second limb came up to replace the one she passed off, even as two more oozed up onto the deck toward Anadare and Sefa. Sefa scuttled across the cargo netting to avoid Norris' touch.

In a flash, Anadare had the strangest sensation of being in several places at once. For an instant, he saw through his own eyes, while also seeing from Valērija's perspective, from Taryn's, and even from an odd angle that had to be the octopod's. It was more than multiple vision, however. He could feel his companions as if he were hugging them from the inside.

"Thank you for the ride. And the fish. You don't have any more, do you?"

Anadare looked around for the source of the male voice. They had all heard it, or felt it, but none of the people on the boat had spoken.

"Welcome to the party." A second voice; it was feminine.

"Well, this is different," said Taryn.

"What? What's diff—" Sefa tried to ask.

Cutting him off, Anadare guessed: "I think we're talking to . . . these three," he said, pointing to the aquatic trio.

Valērija released a snort that came out like a rude noise. "Took you long enough to figure it out, netter. Norris helps make the connection for the others. That's Fabia."

"Sefina is the pretty one!" added a voice that had no physical source, but somehow seemed to belong to the caped dolphin.

"You guys are acting funny," Sefa said, leaning out along the rigging as far as he could. Anadare realized Sefa could not hear Norris or the dolphins, so he was getting only half of the conversation.

Sefa felt something at the edge of his senses, like a sound he could not quite make out. He filled his head with thoughts of sailing and food and girls in order to block it.

"Just sail," Anadare told him. "Valērija is going to explain the whole thing on the way to the flotilla."

"Well, some of it," she said. "I'll leave the final surprise for Muriel."

Isobel shuttled between the *Wyvern of the Waves*, limited to the speed of her solar tugs, and the rest of her fleet during the languid days in transit. She and her executive officer, Comyn Ransom, relieved their pent-up boredom by leading the assault on Hell's Reach. To her delight, Isobel found everything she could want: a stark island with a giant cavity hidden by a natural turn in the rocks. This would provide a temporary home for her flagship, keeping it out of sight for now.

Over decades, the former inmates had carved stairways leading to a labyrinth of chambers and passageways. They had also dug out narrow shafts angled to catch the sun and circulate fresh sea air. Hell's Reach had begun as the last place anyone wanted to live. Now, it held farms and family quarters, small workshops to support ships, and something Isobel welcomed most of all: people she could use.

The salvors moved through the stone maze, brandishing guns and machetes with great efficiency. To their surprise, the residents of Hell's Reach put up a resistance, at least for a few hours, but they had few guns. The salvors never stopped their advance, firefight or no. Where one might fall during a charge on a heavily defended position, a dozen more kept going, overrunning the residents' barricades.

The salvors were experts at terrifying their opponents; they literally painted the walls red with the blood of anyone who resisted them. It was a costly lesson. Isobel hated to lose recruits, but the few survivors got the point. They would make no further trouble.

Hell's Reach fell in five hours. Four salvors lay dead, as did twenty of the rock's residents. Isobel gathered the rest for an announcement:

"You fight well. You die well. This is important, since all of us are here for only a short time. Now, learn to live well, as if these were your final days!" The broken audience struggled to grasp her meaning, and worried that they had.

The salvors used the tugs to maneuver the *Wyvern* inside the Bullet's accommodating central cavern. They assessed the island's complement of fishing boats, hauling the most useful of these onto the *Wyvern*. The rest they stripped and sank.

Isobel's lieutenants divided the last natives of Hell's Reach into small groups and locked them in cabins aboard the big ship, telling them to prepare. When they asked what they were preparing for, one of the salvors answered, "For a homecoming."

The temperature soared on the final day of their voyage around Gunn Island. The four travelers arrived at the flotilla wilting in the noon heat. The aquatic metropolis spread out before them while notes plucked from a kokles rang between metronomic masts. Sefa steered the catamaran through a narrow channel formed by rows of various watercraft. Weatherworn but still vivid on the welter of ships were yellows, greens, reds, and blues painted in ancient motifs. The Cross of Crosses and the Thunder Cross had been part of daily life for these people since the Bronze Age. There were also patterns here for Māra, deity to all creatures of earth and water; Laima, who determined destiny; and Auseklis, the protector.

Sefa whispered to Anadare and Taryn, when he thought Valērija couldn't hear, that the place didn't stink of sweat, rotted fish, and beer the way everyone said it did.

After a while, their friends in the water darted off. Valērija said people always tossed plenty of scraps overboard to keep the dolphins happy.

Through a riot of spars and rigging, they saw a great distillation platform that provided fresh water for the people here. Beyond was a sprawl of bobbing kiosks selling prepared food and clothes, houseboats, pontoons, what looked like an ancient coastal cutter with improvised sails, several large boats devoted to maintenance and industry, fishing trawlers (of course), a sizeable red trimaran, and even some pleasure craft. All were connected by walkways also used by dozens of gypsy cats and dogs. The animals took sadistic delight in sprinting underfoot.

Anadare caught Valērija looking around to get her bearings. Perhaps the Latvians had shifted some vessels in the time she'd been away. She offered to show them more, but they were too tired for sightseeing.

No one seemed to know why the local girl had brought two netters and a futou with her. Daugava's people ventured onto the island to trade and gather supplies.

Beyond that, they kept to themselves, a habit formed over decades on the open ocean. Valērija led the way, showing them how to safely cross the creaky old plank-and-rope bridges. Sefa nearly pitched over into the water, but found his balance just in time.

Valērija made sure they first checked in with her parents, Lindīna and Džeimss Rasmanis, who offered the quartet a meal and a place to rest aboard their houseboat. The home had a few cabins and an open-air top deck. It was clean and efficient, although Anadare couldn't help but notice the sea musk that pervaded all boats left in the water too long. Latvians took great pains to keep things in shape, but there was always that smell of salt and mildew.

Mrs. Rasmanis disappeared for a moment, returning with a tray heaped with breads and varenikes. Somehow, the family had a ready source of butter and sour cream to top the delicious dumplings. Anadare had not seen any milkable livestock; the flotilla held some secrets.

After they had eaten and rested, Valērija explained they could not stay long. They needed to meet with the community leaders and head out.

Her mother's face grew dark. "I lost two brothers to foolish adventures. Now you're determined to throw your life away, too."

"That's why I'm going. I have to know what happened to Uncle Kārlis and Uncle Ludis. If they're still alive, I have to find them. If not—" Her mind was edging toward revenge, not something to reveal to her mother. Instead, she said, "I promise: no unnecessary chances." Mother and daughter embraced for a long moment, then did not speak of it again.

They left the Rasmanis' houseboat and sought out the men they needed to speak with. Commissioner Hecht demanded only three Latvian officials be in on the plan to scout Hell's Reach and learn about these pirates. The people of the Bullets had little contact with the main island, eschewing radios and most other electronics, much as Gunn's hardheaded fishermen tended to do.

"Laipni lūdzam, mani draugi," said Dagmāra Ozols, ushering them into his cabin. "It means 'Welcome, my friends.' Come, sit. We have only a sketchy blueprint of the outermost Bullet." Ozols produced the makeshift document. "The few boaters who've been allowed to visit in recent years tell us the locals have made a number of modifications on the old penal colony. There is a small floating dock moored to the southwestern cliffs. A doorway carved into the rocks leads to the rest of the interior. That space is a rabbit warren, with one or more sets of long steps leading to storage levels and then up to the village farms on the plateau."

Ozols' assistant gave Anadare, Taryn, and Sefa small knives, while providing Valērija with something that looked like a tiny crossbow, complete with a dozen arrows.

Ozols said, "These are for very close range. They don't kill so much as startle a shark or a man. You can dip them in a powerful sedative." He handed her a flask. "But that can take a few moments. You'd best be ready to use a truncheon," the leader added and passed out four of those as well.

"What about protecting the island? Will you send boats to help defend Losi Bay?" Taryn wanted to know.

Ozols took his time with this. "We will not. You are our contribution. And also readiness. If the Others are as strong as we fear, a few more boats will not make a difference. Our best plan is to stand by. If things go badly, we all may need a way off this island." Taryn did not like the answer, but accepted it.

The Latvians also provided them with specialized gear. It included jellyfish repellent, a pair of swim fins, and a mask with a snorkel that drew oxygen directly from the sea water via an osmotic membrane. It required the user to slow his or her breathing, but with practice, the apparatus worked well.

"These will get us, what, two hundred yards if we're lucky?" Sefa piped in.

Ozols answered, "You'll have to get close to the Bullet in order to swim with these. You can't risk being seen. Two more boats and their crews have vanished in the past week."

"The final member of our team can answer your questions," said Valērija.

Bidding their host goodnight, the group took some lanterns and moved out from the comfort of Ozols' well-furnished cabin cruiser, down a gangway to a floating wooden platform that bound the Latvian leaders' ship to several surrounding vessels. Between the mooring lines was a patch of water on each side.

"I assume the girls and Norris have been following us?" asked Taryn.

"And they've brought Muriel," Valērija answered, though she needn't have, since a new dolphin face was poised in the water, looking at the group. Fabia and Sefina ringed the platform, while Norris' inscrutable eye slits barely broke the surface from time to time.

Nothing happened for a long moment. Sefa asked, "Now what?"

Anadare looked at Muriel's eyes. There was something there, some definite sign of intelligence. He could feel emotions coming from her gaze; the almost-human irises within whites gave her eyes an expressive quality not found in any fish, certainly not in octopuses.

"They prefer to be called octopodes, Anadare-mans." A jolt went through his head. And that voice! It was musical. No, it was music. Anadare fell backward onto his bottom.

"You've been pinged, netterboy," Valērija said.

"Cool!"

"Cannot touch all mans, just some. Need more."

Anadare relayed the message as best he understood it to the others. Sefa again made an excuse about not wanting to join in. "Can't touch fisher-mans," Muriel explained to Anadare. Sefa did not seem disappointed at the news.

"Wait, Valērija, are you hearing her talk?"

"A little. I can talk with the dolphins, the gifted ones, but it involves repetition and patience. It feels like I'm talking with kids, except a dolphin's thoughts are more complex. We tried to clean it up once. Muriel used full power on me, to break down my barriers. She called them *my* barriers. Anyway, it didn't work; all I got was a giant headache. I guess everyone reacts differently."

"I'm ping-able," Anadare said. "Nice to know."

"Dolphins can also use an octopod as a conduit, if it's in physical contact with us. They can't actually force orders into your head or steal anything that's in there. They have rules. There are times, though, when they seem to use some of my own ideas and memories to fill in the gaps."

"'Tether yourself and reef the mains!' Love that talk. What's reefing a main?" asked Muriel.

"Kūkā!" Anadare cried. "That day in the boat. I knew that voice didn't come from Gints. It was my own damned voice!" He remembered the little octopod that clung to his ankle. It must have been the antenna. "You rummaged around in my head to find a buried bit of information I needed, then used my own voice to tell me."

Muriel sent another message. "Big pattern. You."

"Big pattern. You," Anadare repeated. "Huh? I don't get it. Guess I'm a slow student."

Sefa was impatient with hearing half the conversation. "This is all great, but we need a plan to get inside Hell's Reach."

"Give you three a ride. Fisher-mans stay with pretty boat."

"How do we steer?" In the torchlight, Taryn looked shaky at the idea of hitching a ride on a dolphin.

Muriel giggled, "Mans do not steer. Dolphin steers. Fun."

Chapter 8

They hoped to arrive at Hell's Reach before dawn. They slept fitfully aboard the *Hinatea*, which was built for speed, not comfort. Moreover, the danger of their plan played out in their dreams.

The six friends got in much-needed practice in the water, the dolphin-human pairings easily pacing Sefa in the cat, while somewhere below, Norris clung to the hull or jetted along beside them.

In the weak starlight, Anadare could see virtually nothing through his mask. It was difficult to tell how the women were doing. They each had an awkward harness to contend with, and Anadare imagined they felt as out of their element as he did. The Latvians said the dolphins hated to be ridden in this manner, but neither Muriel nor Fabia and Sefina complained.

Sefa called out; they were near Frigate Rock, the place where Anadare had gone fishing seemingly a lifetime ago. On cue, Sefina, the youngster of the dolphins, dashed ahead full speed, racing out then back to the cat. Not satisfied with remaining on the surface, Sefina began to dart below.

"What is she doing?" Anadare couldn't hear his own words with the mask on, but his thoughts reached his mount, Muriel.

"Faster to go under the water. Mans need to be sneaky to get to the little island. Need to go under the water." Anadare received more than Muriel's words. There were nuances there, expressing concern for the mans—humans. He caught himself. This link was making him think like a dolphin.

Sefina was not merely dipping below the surface, she was *dolphining*, smoothly threading above and below the surface like a needle across fine fabric. Taryn held on to the reins for dear life as the young cetacean dove several feet then rose to the surface, faster and faster. Anadare felt helpless, both because he wanted somehow to aid Taryn and because he knew Muriel and Fabia would soon be performing these same aquabatics with him and Valērija. All at once, Sefina dove deep, taking Taryn with her. As they surfaced, Taryn's mask held in place, muffling a cry. Down they went again. This time, they stayed below longer, perhaps ten seconds. With a watery explosion, the pair leapt into the air.

Taryn called out as loudly as her mask permitted. Anadare tried to make it out. "Help!" or "Stop!" or maybe "Fuuuuu—!" He couldn't tell. After several more dive-leap cycles, Taryn stopped making any sound at all.

Anadare screamed at Muriel to take him to Taryn as fast as she could. Tittering, Muriel complied, pulling him in the direction of the water-loping pair. He didn't have time to adjust his mask and the water cascaded into his face, blinding him and filling his nose. Anadare was literally breathless as Muriel took him within inches of Taryn. Regaining his sight, he pulled Taryn close and ripped off her mask, revealing a gaping mouth and wide eyes.

"That is so cool!" Taryn yelled, stroking Sefina's smooth, rubbery skin. "Thank you, Pretty Sefina." Then, to Anadare: "Did you see us jump? It was wild!" She noticed his look of concern. "What? Oh. Well, thanks for coming to my rescue, my brave knight on his trusty gray dolphin."

With practice, all three riders learned how to pace their breathing to keep from being accidentally waterboarded.

"Mans need to learn to breathe in rhythm," Muriel sent to Anadare, who sensed her singsong communications more clearly all the time. This was more than Valērija had described, a closer link than he had ever heard of between dolphins and humans.

It was time. The six team members said their goodbyes to Sefa, who agreed to keep the cat in position unless the pirates showed up, in which case he would get away fast.

Valērija teased, "Try not to love on your boat too much while we're gone, Sefa."

Anadare felt bad for Sefa. He wanted to say something to the others about their razzing, but decided to wait for a better time.

The final leg of their journey to Hell's Reach would take

hours of hard riding and careful breathing. They wouldn't be able to speak directly, but could communicate in a limited way by using Muriel as a mediator. That gave them time to refine their intentions. So far, the plan was look around, don't get killed, go home.

Muriel sang *calando* as she swam with Anadare in tow. How did he know the word *calando*? He had listened to classical music on his comtutor years ago, but preferred more spirited islander dance music.

"You need to keep quiet," he told his mount, unsure whether his mouth or his brain was doing the talking.

"No need. Mans hear what they want to hear; mans do not hear good dolphin singing," Muriel snarked.

"They will if we're three feet away."

"Mans have one big boat fifteen hundred yards to port and one smaller boat six thousand yards to starboard." Anadare was about to ask how she knew, then stopped himself. The moonless night defeated his human eyes, but not a dolphin's sonar. Their mounts—correction, their guides—could find any gaps in the Others' patrols.

Valērija urged Fabia closer to Taryn and Sefina so they could speak softly. "You look at home in the water. I didn't think futous could swim."

"I grew up afraid of the water," Taryn said. "My friends and I avoided the beaches, but sometimes I went on my own to see the waves. One day, our teachers took us to Pearl Divers Cay. We spent the morning holding our faces in the water so we'd learn not to panic. I looked up and saw a cute guy swimming along the reef. Suddenly, blowing bubbles into the sea wasn't enough. I wanted the freedom he had, gliding through the waves, in control." She smiled. "I went right up to him and told him to teach me. He kept trying to kiss me, but I made him give me the ocean first. It took weeks, but he taught me to swim. Then, I gave him . . . me."

Anadare, whose attention had been on Muriel, noticed the two women were looking at him. He smiled at them. They scowled back and turned away. What?

At last they saw the graceless bulk of Hell's Reach rising up to blot out the stars. Anadare spotted the dock the Latvians had mentioned. A brawny guard stripped to his white dress shorts stood holding a torch. The three human spies came together and risked a whispered conference, being careful to keep one eye on the guard in case he should look in their direction.

Taryn asked, "Now what?"

"We could try one of the other ways in. I know there's a huge sea cave." Anadare hated his own idea the moment he spoke it.

"With a huge number of pirates." Taryn was right, of course.

"It's time for Muscles over there to catch up on his sleep," Valērija said, raising her small crossbow out of the water and gesturing in the guard's direction.

"That won't work either," Anadare whispered. "He'll feel the dart and call for help before he passes out."

"Okay. No dart. How about a free meal?" Valērija slipped out of her harness and conspired in low tones with Fabia. The others could not hear any words, but it was obvious the dolphin took Valērija's meaning. Fabia ducked under the water for a few seconds and came up with a fish in her mouth. Valērija used her knife to make a small incision in the fish's belly. She motioned to Anadare for the flask and he obliged. Valērija poured the oily sedative into the incision. "This either works or it doesn't."

Valērija gingerly passed the fish to Fabia, who held it between her teeth, being sure to keep the dosed portion out of her mouth. She carried it on the surface as she moved in to one side of the dock, opposite from where the humans floated. Fabia gave up any pretense of stealth. She sang a quick ditty of notes and clicks to draw the guard's attention. He looked down at her and smiled. Fabia then lobbed the fish, still twitching on the fringe of life, at the guard's feet and moved off. For the sake of showmanship, she did a full aerial flip before ducking under. The guard laughed out loud, looked at the fish, and pulled out his knife to prepare himself a sushi snack.

The sun cleared the brightening horizon as the big man in white shorts slumped over.

"So far, so good," Taryn said.

"It was Fabia's idea," Valērija offered.

Fabia added, "Fabia is the smart one!" Sefina responded by blowing a sarcastic blast of air and spume.

Anadare and the others had not seen or heard any more pirates, but they feared everyone on Hell's Reach would soon be awake. The two women scrambled onto the dock. Taryn looked back at Anadare. At a subdued volume, she called, "What are you waiting for? Hurry!"

"Just a second." Clinging to the boards, Anadare hesitated, wishing for the first time that the water was colder.

"What?"

It was Valērija who noticed the ocean had left her and Taryn's clothes clinging to them. "Having a little trouble, eh, netterboy?"

"Quit teasing the minnows and get up here!" added Anadare's girlfriend, enjoying his plight.

Valērija: "You know he's a moron, right?"

Taryn: "Gotta agree with you there."

Anadare pulled himself awkwardly onto the dock. All three dolphins were tittering at his distress as well. "Go swim somewhere!" he seethed and rushed past the smirking women into the rough-hewn stone passageway.

"We'll call you later," Taryn called back to their mounts as she followed Anadare into the passage.

Moving through the cool volcanic rock sent a chill through their wet bodies, but the cold was nothing compared to the smell. Anadare hissed through gritted teeth, "Dakuwaqa! What is that?"

"I think . . . I think it's . . . bad." Taryn whispered it without undue fear. She yanked at Anadare's arm and indicated a passageway that veered upward. Valērija tagged along without protest. The stench of human death was strongest at the first landing and they hurried past it. Anadare whispered that they needed to find their way to the island's plateau.

"Keep your eyes and ears open," he said, "and let's hope our luck holds."

"There's been a change," said the familiar voice on the speaker. He sounded tense.

"What change?" asked Isobel, hunching over the ship's radio. "We're keeping track of your scouting party, discreetly for now. They show a talent for taking care of themselves. They even knocked out one of my guards."

Māris ducked into the radio shack. Young in years, her "adopted" navigator looked haggard and old on a good day, and this was not a good day. She'd insisted he show her his costume. He was a man from the neck up, but his body now sported four surplus limbs. In his real arms he carried the large plastic head that would complete his transformation into the *Wyvern's* mascot. Māris looked stone-faced at Isobel. She looked him up and down then waved off the mortified man to go join the party.

"We'll treat your people well enough. We certainly need the help. My second-in-command got a little exuberant with the folks on Hell's Reach, but we managed to keep a few in good condition. We'll have to expedite their conversion. Anyhoo, if all goes well, you will have a front-row seat for the main event in a few days. Oh, and feel free to put on a good show of resistance, as long as it's not too good."

"Of course . . . but . . . I need your personal assurance."

At this, Isobel leaned back and fixed a perfunctory smile on her face. "That sounds like a demand. Aren't we past such things, Kenny?"

The voice over the speaker faltered. "No. I just . . . I am asking you, please Isobel, not to harm them. One of them wasn't supposed to be there. She's my daughter."

Thanks to the Latvians' briefing, the trip through the termite mound that was Hell's Reach proved to be less confusing than Anadare, Taryn, and Valērija had feared. Twice they heard voices coming and ducked into a dark sconce to avoid discovery. Otherwise, they successfully found upward-leading passageways until they came out upon the plateau . . . and another mystery.

Looking from one structure to another, the trio found no signs of people. The homes were simple cubes, made of native stone quarried from the tunnel network below their feet. Hell's Reach had an assortment of animal pens, each located near an entrance to an underground chamber, no doubt to offer shelter from the frequent storms. Aside from the goats, chickens, and other livestock, the only movement on the plateau came from the seabirds that noisily ruled this speck in the ocean.

Anadare motioned for the women to stay behind one wall until he scouted inside a few of the homes. He came back, saying, "There's food! But, no people."

"We smelled the homeowners earlier, down below. I don't want to meet their visitors," Taryn said.

"Let's eat first and then worry." Valērija was as blunt as ever. She was right; they needed to eat.

They found bowls of vegetables, along with some prepared fish kept in a cool stone cabinet. They did not dare to light the stove, but found enough to take the edge off their hunger, including some excellent goat cheese.

After eating, the three walked to the rim of the plain, got on their bellies, and timidly peered over the cliff. On two sides, they found ships ranging from tri-masted schooners down to work skiffs, dozens in all. Taryn pointed out that most of them had large-bore military guns mounted around their rails that could cut a fishing vessel in half. Valērija whispered that there weren't enough men watching the ships.

"Are you saying we should take one?" Anadare asked.

"Yes, because your girlfriend is a deadly ninja and I love to kill pirates with my itty bitty crossbow." The women gave him a sour look. "No, netter. I prefer to live. I am wondering where the crews are, though."

As if in answer a deep, rhythmic thrumming began. Cups and dishes vibrated to the percussion. Instruments joined in, brass and woodwind plus some strings, creating a festive melody. The source was unmistakable: they were standing on it.

"I don't think we should crash this party," Taryn said as they ducked back down the stone passages. Anadare and Valērija argued about the route. Both agreed there should be several paths to their destination: the giant cave that took up fully one-eighth of the volume of Hell's Reach.

It took several minutes to make their way toward the source of the merriment as jubilant voices joined the music bouncing ever louder off the rocky walls and steps. Light was coming from a final turn in the tunnel. Anadare looked first, turning back with an expression of bewilderment. He motioned them forward.

Once again, there was no one to block them here. Ahead was a spacious landing that opened onto a platform that afforded them a good view of the cavern at the heart of Hell's Reach . . . and what it now held.

The cave's volume was large enough to shelter all of the ships they had seen anchored off the island, or most of the Latvian flotilla, or else one very big ship. Taryn, Valērija, and Anadare looked across the gap between the cave walls and the *Wyvern of the Waves*.

It was the largest man-made thing they had ever seen. From the platform, they were looking onto one of its numerous balconied guest cabins; they could jump the distance easily. The three strained to take in the full dimensions of the behemoth. It was like a city from the old videos, perched atop a streamlined hull. Under a patina of rust, she was white with a riot of pastel-painted trim and designs. On the prow, the builders had emblazoned the ship's name in fanciful gilt script. Beside this was the likeness of a sea wyvern, a dragon with a bat's wings, a lizard's body and legs, and a fish's tail. This detail was dwarfed by the image of a grinning cephalopod across most of the bow.

"Okey Dokey!" Valērija shouted with glee. "This is one of the cruise ships based on the old cartoons. These things were built for fun. Thousands of people could fit on board and sail around in circles for days."

"And do what?" Anadare asked.

A new voice chimed in from behind them. "Eat, mostly. Oh, and drink. And shop, of course. Plus whatever else they wanted to do. All for one low, low price."

The trio looked back to see a woman coming through the passage flanked by several other figures all in white. The woman had an enormous head of red hair and wore a white brocade longcoat with gold highlights. She also had a sword and a gun. How had they found them? Anadare churned inside, but decided not to share his theory.

"Go!" Anadare led the two women off the landing, leaping across the vertiginous gap—no dolphins visible in the water below—and onto the balcony. They scrambled over the rail and through an unlocked sliding door.

They could hear the red-haired woman calling as they ran through the cabin and into the interior of the ship. "Welcome to the *Wyvern*, the finest cruise ship still afloat anywhere! Your pleasure is our duty."

Anadare stated the obvious. "Okay, so we aren't as smart as we thought. They're watching us, playing with us."

"Stay alert!" Taryn said.

The redhead and her cohorts ran back into the passage. They undoubtedly knew a better way to cross the gap. This was no time to stand still. The friends hurried on, keeping alert as they moved into the unfamiliar areas of the vessel. There were occasional sounds as of someone moving nearby, but they saw no one. The game continued.

Hallways angled back and forth in a sawtooth fashion, increasing the impression of size and complexity, while the faded and mildewed décor added a madhouse dimension. The color scheme looked as though an eight-year-old had gotten a large box of crayons and used every one. Undersea cartoon characters lurked at every turn. Human eyes and mouths incongruously appeared on seals, whales, sharks, jellyfish, and more. The ship was a child's fever dream made solid.

Tucked in random spaces were dormant casinos and numerous bars with exotic themes: a Roman forum, a rock 'n' roll–era diner, an Irish pub, even a faux ice castle in the style of the Harbin Winter Festival.

Lively music underscored the vessel's fantastical nature. It pulsed and popped from everywhere and nowhere. "That's some party they're having," Anadare said. "I guess everyone's busy. At least they're leaving us alone for now." Wishful thinking.

Taryn said, "The engines are off; their power's

limited. The air conditioning is working, but it's on low. They're taking advantage of the cavern's natural chill. They can't let it get too hot aboard or the sea air will warp and rot everything. At a guess, I'd say they're using solar batteries." Anadare listened closely. The women knew more about tech stuff than he did.

Valērija thought about it for a minute. "My people started out with large ships when we left home. Those ships ran on diesel, and later on alcohol-based fuel that burned the hell out of the engines. We switched to sailing vessels. They're easier to maintain."

Taryn added, "A ship this size would need tens of thousands of tons of fuel to run its engines at full power. No one's refined that much of the good stuff since who knows when! I wonder how they move this beast."

They continued to explore. Instead of numbers, the decks bore names evoking images of idyllic vacations: Riviera, Esplanade, and Fiesta. They weren't even in alphabetical order. Most of the doors opened easily, the electronic locks having been switched off or ceased to work altogether. Toward the top of the ship, certain cabins on Jubilee Deck were closed off. Someone had welded a metal bar across each door and padlocked it, allowing no clue what lay inside. The flooring outside each of these cabins bowed downward, causing a permanent wave along the corridor. There was something heavy on the other side of those doors.

Across the hall, they found one of the many bizarre design choices the ship had to offer. This one was an Egyptian tomb, complete with a jackal-headed Anubis statue and three sarcophagi. The ornate coffins stood open, exposing mummies inside. The room had once been a disco where people could go and dance with the dead. Now, the space was stuffed from floor to ceiling with neat stacks of cellophane-encased clothes and boxes of shoes; all sizes, all white.

Taryn commented, "Someone needs a fashion consultant."

Two decks down, they discovered the crew had converted many of the cabins, salons, and common spaces into hundreds of indoor farms: beans, rice, and small fruit trees. Despite open windows, one deck stank of pigs. They pulled their clothes around their noses and mouths in a failed effort to filter the stench. An attempt to use the snorkel only channeled the foulness into Taryn's mouth and she gagged.

Moving hastily past the sty area, they found a gaping hole where the deck had collapsed. Valērija figured someone had underestimated the destructive power of pig urine on the lightweight materials of the superstructure. They found a ladder crudely welded in place and made their way down.

That brought them to a cluster of cabins where every window was broken and many of the bulkheads were crumpled or twisted. There were signs of partial repairs, but most of these cabins were not fit for habitation. Sun and salt had taken their toll on every exposed surface here. This time, Anadare made a guess, saying it looked like the ship had been hit by a rogue wave sometime in the past.

Following an upsurge in the music, they came to a balcony overlooking the ship's vast courtyard. On the far side, the starboard end of the superstructure completed the horseshoe. They'd spent the last hour exploring its portside twin. In the stony cathedral above, crepuscular angels hung from stalactites, squeaking their complaints to the loud partygoers. Below, scores of people mulled about the gaily lit deck, swaying from both drink and music. Signs read: Piccadilly Circus.

Several of the people wore ridiculous costumes from the world of the cartoon octopus. They spotted a blue seahorse, Katrina. By an enormous punch bowl stood a bellicose walrus named Wagner. Not far away, they saw Okey himself, looking uncomfortable in his oversized head. The man removed it, grabbing a napkin to mop his brow and neck, and to take a drink.

"Wait! There!" Valērija was agitated, pointing to the pirate in the Okey costume. The others asked her what was the matter. "I know that man!"

She darted back the way they had come. Taryn raced after her, even as Anadare tried to call them back. A moment later, he started chasing them, but came up short.

At the end of the corridor, the redheaded woman with the braid on her shoulders had Taryn by the wrist. Two of her goons were doing their best to restrain Valērija; they paid for their bad manners. Anadare could have spun about and run, but felt an inner tether go taut. If he lost track of the women now, he'd have little chance of finding and rescuing them later. Better to stay together, even if it meant surrendering—for now.

"We can stop this game of rabbit run," the redheaded woman said. The others in her group looked to her; she was clearly the leader. "I'm Isobel O'Malley, your captain and host. Welcome, Taryn, Anadare, and . . . Valērija, is it?"

"Hi," said Taryn. They didn't dare ask how the woman knew their names.

"Who is that man down there with the big squid head?" Valērija demanded.

"That would be Māris. He's from your island, isn't he?" Isobel answered coyly. "Come, let's meet him. We mustn't miss the party."

She led the trio to an elevator, which hummed to life and took them down to the courtyard level. The doors opened onto a festival of drunken men and women.

The three of them looked around. Taryn was the first to ask the obvious. "Aren't your pirates celebrating a little early? You haven't even attacked us yet."

"We're salvors, not pirates," Isobel said, putting a hand softly onto Taryn's shoulder. "The attack on Gunn Island won't be much of a party, at least not for your people, so we're having our fun now."

Norris found making straight lines was no more or less satisfying than making swirly patterns. Obviously, none of the mans had gotten below the waterline to clean this hull in a very long time. That was fine with him. Norris' beak and radula made short work of the tasty barnacles.

Fabia and Sefina flew underneath him. "Took you long enough to get here. We could have carried you," they sang.

"No thank you, ladies. My last dolphin cruise left me rattled for tetra-tides. From now on, I'll use my own jet."

"You're just going to eat?" inquired Sefina in a discordant minor key. "You're not even tearing some free for us!"

"Oh, fine!" He tore off a shingle of the clustered arthropods for the dolphins to nip and munch. "I'm doing more than eat, dear Sefina; I'm learning. It's amazing what's been forgotten underneath all this growth. This hull has secrets to tell," he said, continuing his scraping and chewing.

The dolphins had no idea how long their mans friends would be aboard the big ship, but Norris figured the buffet he'd discovered would last for quite a while.

Chapter 9

It struck Anadare as odd that no one was actually restraining them. The salvors should have thrown the three of them in the brig for spying.

He noticed one or two familiar faces. They were islanders, recent abductees, but wore the same white uniforms as the salvors. They also shared a haggard expression. They made no effort to break free. They had joined the salvors, however reluctantly. Whatever changed their minds, the conversion had happened with disturbing speed.

Anadare, Taryn, and Valērija were certainly prisoners now, but were able to wander around the party as they chose. Even without chains, they weren't going anywhere. Salvors would be on them long before they could launch a lifeboat, even if they figured out how to work the winches. If they risked jumping overboard, there was no place they could swim to. Unless the stupid dolphins showed up, they'd never make it past the salvors' patrols, nor were they likely to find Sefa without giving him away to the salvors.

Heady aromas drew them to long tables laid out with

fish, poultry, and spicy pork morsels. (He felt hungry again; how long had they been wandering around this ship?) One of the tables bore an enormous transparent bird brazenly spreading its wings. The dripping ice sculpture proudly overlooked a variety of fruits and vegetables.

"Do you always eat this well?" Anadare asked a man at the buffet table.

"We empty the reserves before we reach a place with rich supplies. Grace O'Malley—I mean the captain—says we should always have more food ahead than at home. It provides motivation," he answered.

They exchanged more small talk with the salvors, most of whom did not act the part of captors. The rank and file introduced themselves by name. One complimented Anadare on his bracelet, which made Taryn happy. These salvors were friendly, especially the drunken ones. It was as if they were used to welcoming guests. He wondered which ones had committed the slaughter they'd discovered earlier. How could people change so drastically? Anadare noticed, too, that more than a few of the ebullient, chipper, frothy faces had open sores around their mouths.

Valērija kept looking around. "Where's the one in the Okey costume? He was right here." Anadare hadn't seen the one Isobel called Māris since they first stepped into Piccadilly Circus.

"Your attention, children!" Queen Isobel was holding court, having taken the stage, silenced the band, and commandeered the microphone. "I want all of you to know how proud I am of what we've accomplished here together. Today, we celebrate, though we know there is hard work just ahead.

"In a few short years, we managed to get this great ship out of dry dock and onto the high seas. In a few more days, we move to the next phase of our plan. As any of you who have been with me long enough knows"—she paused here to make eye contact with several of her salvors— "most islands cannot support us. They were once lush with fruit and game, but as man-made poisons have crept from one ecosystem to the next, we have witnessed the result: sterile sand, tumble-down castles, and ruin.

"Well, thanks to our perseverence, we are about to claim one island, one oasis, that will support us. We are joined by three more members of that community." She gestured to the trio. "I want you to make them welcome, so that they will become part of our salvor family.

"Soon, with help from our friends ashore, we will set our plans to work. Remember the wisdom of Sun Tzu: 'The supreme art of war is to subdue the enemy without fighting.' Over the coming days, we must bring the *Wyvern* and her fleet to top condition. Then, with luck, we'll be able to keep the bloodshed to a minimum, just enough to make our point.

"That is tomorrow's challenge. For right now, drink, dance, and enjoy. Embrace life!"

Even before Isobel could finish, Valērija, who had stood stone-faced throughout, moved to the edge of the crowd and spoke loudly, her voice carrying over the heads of the people. "Take me to Māris!" Anadare had never seen this level of fury on her face and wondered at its source.

She remained composed, but Isobel's eyes spoke volumes about her feelings on being given orders by a woman less than half her age. "Of course," she said and told one of her guards to help Valērija find Māris. Anadare insisted on joining in.

Isobel pulled Taryn aside. "I have a special job for you." Isobel promised the two of them would catch up later. She didn't explain what she had in mind or why it involved Taryn.

Andare wanted to object, but Taryn said, "It's okay. You go with Valērija." She and Isobel went off together.

Isobel's second-in-command, a humorless man with a ponytail and the perfect pirate name of Ransom, took charge of Anadare and Valērija. Ransom led them away from the party, through winding corridors and up stairwells to a storage area. Party supplies, mascot costumes, and other odds and ends filled the space. In an adjoining locker room, they found Māris drunk. He was clumsily tugging off the last of his outerwear.

"Where are they?!" Valērija shouted at this man they'd barely met.

"I don't know who—"

"Don't you dare play games. My uncles! Where are my uncles, Kārlis and Ludis Vilks? Your captain and his first officer!"

Māris reached down into the folds of the sloughed-off costume, pulled out a pewter flask, and took a drink. He never met Valērija's eyes as he answered her: "Gone. Both gone."

The senator leaned over the wounded man's bed, pinning a medal on his hospital gown. The injured man's face was lined with age and excess, not the face of a fighter. The oxidized metal disc looked like some discarded coin glued to a stained piece of blue ribbon, far less grand than any of the rings on the senator's fat fingers.

"Thane Bentley, you've given the men inspiration. You've conjured up a defense force from practically nothing. As commander of our arsenal, you've proven to be a man who leads from the front, as it were." Genuine emotion welled in his throat, making Senator Jackson's multiple chins quiver.

"I thank you, Senator," the wounded man wheezed. "I would have thought my rifles were still in good working order. I'm glad it was me and not one of my men."

"Yes, I understand. I continue to have full confidence in your knowledge of our arms, Bentley. The doctors tell me you should regain partial use of your right hand. And we're making you a splendid patch for your . . ." At this, Jackson trailed off, since the sight of Bentley's burned and ruptured eye threatened to turn his stomach. "In no time you'll be back on the front lines, defending our island. I venture to say you'll cast fear into the hearts of those pirates, if they come. Hell, with your new eye patch, they'll think we're the pirates and sail away."

"Yes, Senator." Bentley turned his face to the wall.

"How many rifles did you manage to test-fire before . . . before . . ."

"Oh, seven, Senator. The one is no good, of course. That leaves another four untested. I would say most of those will work."

"Good, good. I've taken the liberty of sending two of the tested ones on to the synthetics district. They promise me they'll be turning out new rifles in a matter of weeks. They're stockpiling nitrates, ground-up seashells, and the other makings for a generous supply of powder and ammunition, though I don't see that we'll need it, not with crates and crates of vintage bullets that have never even been opened. Am I right?"

Bently nodded dutifully.

"And there's our impressive pair of cannons along the battlements!" crowed Jackson, twisting one of his gold rings.

"We haven't tested the cannons yet, but we did get the rat nests out. We're reboring them, and both should work just fine, sir. Give it a few more days. I've got three men assigned to each, a mix of collectors and police. Any damned pirate ship that tries to fool with Gunn Island will come to regret it, Senator."

"That's what I thought."

On his way out, the senator spoke with one of the doctors. Bentley's prognosis was mixed. The burns and lacerations were healing, and they were monitoring for possible infection from opportunistic diseases. Bentley might recover; he was a tough old bird of seventy-two. The Senate was taking no chances, though. They passed Bentley's duties on to his son, Dermot. They even made the younger Bentley a general, because why not?

For the first time, Taryn noticed the faerie lights embedded in the walls. Some still functioned, cycling from blue to green to pink and back. The walls pulsed with light. This ship had been meant for fantastical journeys, not the loathsome mission it now performed.

The guards led them around a corner and onto the sky span, which connected the ends of the U-shaped superstructure, affording an open vista over the *Wyvern's* bow. Currently, that view was of the rocky interior of Hell's Reach. The sky span's clear floor panels afforded a dizzying vantage of the festivities going on in Piccadilly Circus below. The view made Taryn realize her earlier jaunt through the ship with Anadare and Valērija had barely covered half of the big horseshoe.

"It's all right that you don't like me, my dear," the older woman said gently. Taryn found it amazing how Isobel could instantaneously switch her empathy off and on, one moment giving orders and the next being maternal.

"Like you? After what we found on Hell's Reach this morning, what do you expect?" Taryn shot back.

Isobel stopped walking and took Taryn by the shoulders, facing her down. "I do not explain myself, young lady, but I will say this: everything we are doing is for a purpose."

"What purpose? What could justify—"

An earnestness came into Isobel's eyes. "Those people who died are only the latest victims of a long tragedy that is nearing its end. Out on these waters, I have seen things, Taryn. It's not a question of whether we're facing the end; only of when it will come. I can tell you this: the best thing any of us can do is to live well. That way, when the final bell chimes, we'll have no regrets."

Taryn began walking again. "Now you sound like Daddy."

Isobel started to say something, but instead stood silent. She told her salvor guards to take Taryn the rest of the way.

Māris sat looking at his hands rather than facing Valērija. Anadare and the salvor, Ransom, watched him hold up those blistered hands in mock surrender.

"I will tell you," Māris began, "though I swear to God I wish I did not have to."

"I need to know why you're here and they're not," Valerija told him, her words hitting him like sharpened blades.

"I remember the farewell party on the docks when we left." It took him a moment to look at Valērija. "I remember you, though you were only a child at the time. Your uncles passed you back and forth like a ball and you squealed. They were huge men. You would think that, because you were little, but let me tell you they were large by any standard. Kārlis Vilks was every inch a captain, with a broad chest and assertive gaze. We didn't question; we followed his orders. Your Uncle Ludis was always by the captain's side, keeping the crew occupied.

"If we had a spare moment, Mister Vilks taught us how to navigate on the open seas. None of us got good at it. I was nineteen. I didn't want to spend hours on my comtutor learning math; I knew everything. I planned to sail this voyage and come back ready for my own command. We must have said as much when we were drunk, because Mister Vilks joked that if we were captains, he was a commodore. 'Now, which one of you fine officers is gonna clean the bilge?' he'd snarl.

"When Mister Vilks wasn't screaming at us for being slow to learn, he would tell us stories. There was one about the whore with a wooden leg ... urm ... These were stories for men. Mister Vilks knew how to talk to the crew, to make us laugh or to bark at us when we did something stupid.

"So, we set sail on the *Vanessa's Honor*. She was forty-two feet in length, with a crew of ten, your uncles riding herd on eight cocky teenagers. Gunn Island had lost too many ships trying to find other pockets of life on the dying seas. For every three that came back laden with scraps or farmable plants, one vanished without a ripple. Commissioner Hecht told us our expedition would either succeed or it would be the last attempt. We planned to return in less than two years. That was seven years ago.

"The first weeks of the voyage were the happiest of my life. I was in good company: your uncles, Whit, Jaquavious, Hiroji, and the others. Some days, we managed to catch fish. Mostly, we tended to our chores. We worked while the sun burned our bodies, and every evening we filled our bellies. On Fridays, we drank; it was something your uncle Ludis brewed. I remember the sound of Hiroji playing that damned flute of his. He called it a *hotchiku*, and it sounded like a spirit warning us to live life while we could. Whit joined in with his homemade guitar, always off-key. The drink and the music were terrible . . . and wonderful . . . as the stars slid by in silent witness.

"The ship responded to our hands like a grateful widow. She'd been wasted as a trawler. Out on the deep water, she proved herself through long calms and sudden storms. In a way, we enjoyed facing the high waves. It let us prove ourselves to each other and to our captain.

"We were eleven weeks at sea when we happened onto the atoll. It must have stretched for twenty miles. As we went round from one spit of land to another, we found a few struggling palms and not much else. The seabirds stayed away. We tested the water and found death: high levels of ammonia and other chemicals that had no business being there. The fish were scarce and sickly, the reefs bleached white as ash. Captain Vilks ordered us to continue. We didn't know why, but we didn't ask. He was playing a hunch. It paid off. How I wish it hadn't.

"On one of the larger islands, we found the ruins of a resort. I led a small group ashore, including my friend, Whit Billings. We joked about buying the place and serving drinks to our many visitors. No doubt the place once filled the emptiness inside of wealthy futous: a crumbling hotel, rows of rotted cabanas, even the foul remnants of a giant swimming pool equipped with water slides and islanded bars.

"We were poking through a pile of old bottles when the locals fell upon us. They were walking corpses, really, starved and sick and crazy. Their eyes were wild, like rabid dogs. They had clubs and a few knives, but it did them no good. Their attack was ineffective because they were so weak. When they struck, it was like taking a blow from a child. I had a pistol and fired one shot in the air. The locals startled, but never broke off their attack.

"Jaquavious kept yelling for me to shoot them. I didn't want to; I didn't think they could seriously hurt us, and they were so pathetic. Then, one of them sank his rotting teeth into Whit, opening an ugly wound. Furious, I took the attacker's knife from his feeble hand and thrust the blade into his gut. He folded over and fell to the sand bleeding. We screamed at the wretched ones until they finally backed off. I decided to get Whit back to the *Vanessa*.

"As we sailed off, I watched the locals screaming impotent threats. There was something in the tone, almost as if they were threatening us and begging for help at the same time. Before we lost sight of them, I saw a group of the men return for their fallen comrade and pull him into the jungle. I had no doubt about his fate, just as I knew these wretched souls had no future. Their bones would soon litter these beaches.

"So, we kept going. We knew better than to count on any of the old charts. Sea levels had erased whole island chains.

"We sailed due east for many days and decided to check San Diego. As we pulled within sight of land, we encountered sea lions, mostly dead or dying. The stink was overpowering.

"We gauged our depth. North Island had all but vanished, and Mission Bay had likewise swallowed most of the smaller bodies of land it once supported. A few remained, providing cover. We were checking these when the salvors revealed themselves."

"Oh, I love this part," said Isobel, leaning in between Anadare and Valērija.

The two salvors escorting Taryn wore heavy faces, weighed down both by alcohol and the frustrated desire to get back to the party to drink more. Another salvor intercepted them as they stepped off the elevator at Panorama Deck and led the male guard away, mumbling something about a scraping sound coming through the hull in engineering.

The female salvor, who looked to be in her early sixties, slurred her words as she led Taryn to the ship's daycare center. It was brightly colored, as if to entertain young children, but there were no children inside, only adults.

"We're alwaysh shor-handed up 'ere," the woman salvor said, her breath putrid. "Ish not har work, but you gotta feed an' clean the chil'ren, so ish not fun. The cap'n saysh you should be good adit."

Taryn started to ask what the woman meant. Feed and clean who? What children? Then she realized she was looking at her charges. The adults in the room, perhaps a dozen of them, were standing, staring into space. They were dressed in loose-fitting, casual outfits, flowery and bright, rather than in the crisp white uniforms the crew wore. The men were neatly shaved and most of the women wore ribbons in their hair. The people never spoke. Only one or two even moved. They had let slip the reins of their faces; some drooled.

Taryn walked up to one woman, who was about her age and build, although with deep red hair to Taryn's darker tresses. "Hi." Taryn smiled, but got no response.

"You two could be sisters," said a woman entering from an adjoining room. She wore glasses over her world-weary eyes.

131

"I'd like to show her how to use makeup. She's pretty." To the woman, she asked, "What's wrong with her? With all of them?"

"There's nothing wrong with them! I don't ever want to hear you talk that way again!" The woman's voice was firm, but not mean. The drunken salvor took the new conversation as a cue to salute the air and leave. "They're our children, missy. You're gonna make sure they get what they need. Understand?"

"Children? They're—"

"They are us. The TD got 'em at birth, back when we used to have babies."

"TD?"

"Tropical diseases. We have a few, you know, from mosquito-borne viruses to microscopic brain bores. The problem can lay dormant for many years, or it can explode all at once. Some of the nastier bugs apparently have a thing for redheads. (Of course, the blame there goes to her wandering husband.) Other bugs seem to favor expectant mothers, withering the brains of their unborn children." As she spoke, the woman with the sad eyes moved from person to person, adjusting an article of clothing or grasping a hand and smiling. "That's what happened with most of our children, before they even saw the world. We take care of the survivors. Without a proper doctor it's not easy.

"Enough! We're here; this is how things are. You're just in time for our afternoon book reading. Afterward, we'll check their diapers and get them ready for dinner.

After that, it's a couple of hours of activities and physical therapy, another diaper change, and bed." The two women began placing chairs in a semicircle for story time.

Taryn struggled to take it all in. The idea of working with the handicapped held a certain appeal for her, but she had scores of questions. She settled on one. "When do their . . ." Again, she was struck by the ages of the girl who looked like her and the other so-called children. "When do their parents take them?"

"A few visit; the captain's better than most. They need full-time care, and that means us. I'm Jocelyn Burk, by the way. And that girl you're staring at as if she were a prize tuna hung up at the docks is Maggie O'Malley. You'd better be extra nice to her if you know what's good for you."

"Dakuwaqa's teeth!" Anadare let out. Isobel stood among them. It was positively eerie how she had come into the room without him or Valērija hearing her.

"Oh, don't stop on my account. I love a good story. Go on, Māris, tell them how we all met." She was beaming like a schoolgirl in love. By comparison, Māris looked like a storm had flushed him out of a sandy grave. Anadare did the math: Māris had been a teenager back then, so he was about twenty-six. He looked *much* older.

Isobel produced a fresh bottle of something dark and

handed it to Māris, who continued, "We didn't notice the Others at first. The attack at the old resort had us rattled. Their ship had spotted us somewhere between the atoll and San Diego. They waited until we were inside a cove, unable to run or maneuver. Before we even saw them, three boats had us blocked in.

"A large vessel came alongside the *Vanessa's Honor.* They were well-dressed, well-fed; we figured this was exactly what we were looking for: a group of survivors who might help us or trade with us. We began waving our hands wildly in the air while jumping and whooping. Whit yelled out, 'We're from Gunn Island! Where are you guys from?' Before he'd finished the last word, Whit was laid out on the deck, wearing a look of amazement and Captain Vilk's shadow.

"The captain shouted at the rest of us, 'I will do the talking for this ship. Mind your jobs and keep your damned mouths shut.' Captain Vilks was too late. One of the men on the big vessel called back, 'Gunn Island? Never heard of it. Sounds nice.'

"The vessel sent over half a dozen men, a fraction of its crew complement. I was helping Whit. I noticed the captain and his brother hastily exchanging words. Mister Vilks ducked into the captain's cabin aft. A moment later, we got a whiff of smoke. The strangers went mad. Three of them began breaking down the door. It took them less than a minute, but that was enough. They pulled Mister Vilks from the cabin, holding a metal bucket with something smoldering inside. The strangers doused the fire, but there wasn't much left. They took out their frustrations on Mister Vilks, beating him bloody in front of our eyes. Finally, we understood why our captain had distrusted these strangers.

"From then on, the strangers, who called themselves 'salvors,' stood over us with knives and long, needle-tipped sticks. Captain Vilks told us to cooperate fully and not to give the salvors any excuse to hurt us. They didn't need an excuse. They chose Jaquavious for no good reason. One of the salvors bumped him on purpose."

"That would be me," Ransom added.

"Jaquavious started to object to being shoved, then caught himself." Māris snuck a nervous glance at Ransom, who was beaming with pride. "Mister Ransom shouted anyway, and jabbed Jaquavious with a wasp-stick. It took only seconds. Jaquavious began to tremble uncontrollably, then he fell to his knees, shaking. Bile seethed out of his mouth and he soiled his pants. We tried to help, tried to get him to drink water. It took an hour to calm his quavering. Until the day he died, he'd twitch randomly and had trouble finishing sentences. Whatever the salvors put on the end of those needles, it was nasty."

Ransom said, "Venom from a large mountain wasp. Useful."

"We spoke very little the next day." Māris took a sip of dark liquid and continued. "Mister Vilks slowly regained his senses, though he'd lost some teeth and one of his eyes was a swollen purple mess. Captain Vilks did what he could to keep the attention of our captors on himself and not on us.

"Our makeshift convoy sailed into a shipyard farther up the bay coast. We saw this ship, the *Wyvern*, up on enormous braces. It was a magical city rising into the sky; we marvelled at the sheer size of it. Scores of workers were crawling up and down the hull and superstructure, welding and doing a thousand other tasks."

Isobel couldn't resist adding her viewpoint. "My people told me about discovering the crew of the *Vanessa's Honor* east of Dante's Atoll. I was surprised to see any sane person in that vacinity. My grandmother and my father spent their lives scouting the Pacific in search of tidal pools of humanity. So have I. What we've found has been less than human. Anyway, this new ship represented hope. San Diego, so you know, is no paradise, either. The region is bordered by impassable mountains and poisoned cities. People are best avoided, trust me. We wanted to get away.

"We needed help to refurbish the *Wyvern*. She was and is a good ship, despite generations of neglect. Now, we had eight more sets of hands, and the promise of an island full of people who might be persuaded to join us."

"Gunn Island. Persuaded? How?" Valērija asked.

"We're getting to that." With a glance, Isobel handed the tale back to Māris, who took another long swallow from his bottle.

"Captain O'Malley welcomed us as part of her family. That was the word she used, family." Isobel offered her broadest smile at this. "Captain Vilks told us to play—to go along with whatever our new captain said. At first, it was fine. We were on dry land. We worked long hours, restoring a ship we figured could hold thousands of people one day. We ate well; we gained weight. Mister Vilks regained his strength, and Jaquavious . . . was still alive.

"This went on for years. You can't believe how much work there is to do on a ship this size. We found everything we needed in storage, from working parts to shiny bits of nonsense that turned her into a floating bazaar. It all went into the *Wyvern*.

"We wore uniforms like the rest of the salvors. We came to understand that having a common goal was like sharing a religion. That was fine, we thought. Only the Vilks brothers had the sense to remain skeptical."

Isobel interjected: "That's why I needed to use persuasion. If you use too much, or use it on the wrong people, violence turns potential allies into determined enemies. The trick is to use finesse."

"One night, Captain O'Malley called the crew of the *Vanessa's Honor* to a banquet. It was everything you could imagine, food and drink and entertainment. By midnight, none of us was sober. A couple had wandered off somewhere.

"Captain O'Malley announced we were going to launch the *Wyvern* in less than a month. We had synthesized as much fuel as we could, filtering and refining it from old stores and mixing in natural fats and alcohol. It would run the engines hot and eat through hoses and belts, but it would get the big ship out to sea. Beyond that, we built solar-powered tugs. Once the fuel ran out, we planned to use those to keep moving, albeit at a snail's pace, wherever we chose to go."

"And where did we choose to go?" Isobel asked playfully.

"Gunn Island." Anadare and Valērija spoke as one.

"Home," echoed Māris. He had meant the home of the crew of *Vanessa's Honor*, but now spoke for the two young people in the room as well. "Anyway, we were at the party. Captain O'Malley lined us up, with your uncles at the end of the row. She asked each of us in turn, 'How do I find Gunn Island?'

"I swear, this was the first time I realized I did not know the answer. She asked Whit, who shook his head. She walked over to Jaquavious, who shook in terror and said nothing. She asked me. I was drunk, but I confessed I had never been good at navigation. Hiroji was next. Then, she paused. I looked around, but could not find the other two members of our crew. Captain O'Malley spoke to the Vilks brothers, saying, 'And that leaves you two. This would be much simpler if you hadn't burned your chart book.' Captain Vilks stood expressionless, while his brother allowed himself a sly grin.

"Captain O'Malley stared back at them, a devil's smirk on her face." Māris was speaking in dream tones, not looking at Isobel or even acknowledging her presence. "She told them she had a test for all of us. She said it was costly, but would ensure that from this night forward we would totally trust and obey her. She clapped her hands and two men wheeled out a serving table. On it, I saw . . .

pieces . . . and I could barely make out . . . It was them. Our missing crewmates. It was them."

"I offered Māris and his friends a choice: in the next minute, they could tell me how to reach Gunn Island and eat the feast I had prepared, or die."

Māris continued: "No one spoke. It seemed like forever. Then, Captain O'Malley looked at one of her guards and ran her finger up and down our line, stopping at Hiroji. Mister Ransom moved in, holding a slender knife and . . ."

"Did what had to be done," finished Ransom.

"There were no final words, no sounds except for a dull gasp. Hiroji fell to the deck, his eyes wide." Māris swallowed hard, forcing down his feelings. "Your uncles tried to struggle, to grab for Captain O'Malley, but the guards held them fast.

"I wanted to be sick or to cry or scream. I could only stand there. Captain O'Malley took a long fork and speared one of the chunks of cooked flesh. She brought it to my mouth and said, 'Eat of this flesh and be one of us forever.'"

"Did I really say it like that? How dramatic of me!"

"God forgive my soul, I made my choice. Whit followed suit. Jaquavious did not. He cried like the damned and rushed at Captain O'Malley. Mister Ransom slashed him. Jaquavious clutched his throat as his life gushed through his fingers.

"Captain O'Malley repeated her terms to your uncles. Captain Vilks looked her in the eyes and told her she was a hell-bound whore. Mister Vilks followed that by spitting in her face. The guards restrained them and held a blade to each man's throat.

"Whit and I cried out, saying we'd done as she asked. We promised to obey her completely, to do anything if only she would spare their lives.

"Captain Vilks looked at me and said, 'I'm sorry. I should never have taken you boys along on this trip. Now, we are finished.' He managed to free one of his hands and grabbed the hand of the guard. I thought he was fighting to pull away the blade the guard held to his neck. Instead, Captain Vilks . . . pushed the knife deep into his own throat. The guard looked at Captain O'Malley with an expression of raw terror and swore he had not killed Captain Vilks on purpose.

"Ludis Vilks watched his brother, Kārlis, die at his feet and cursed Captain O'Malley. She laughed at him."

"You have to admit," Isobel said, "it was an absurd situation. Anyway, I made one last attempt to reason with him."

Māris continued, "I could see the resolve in Mister Vilks' eyes, the seething hatred. I knew this man. Even in his pain, he would never break under pressure. I knew what was coming. And that's when I made the worst mistake of my life."

"It was your best decision, Māris."

"I lied and told her I could work out a course back to Gunn Island. I said I wasn't as good as the Vilks brothers, but I could figure it out. And then . . ."

"I killed Ludis Vilks with my own blade," Isobel said cooly. "That man and his brother were nothing but pride and trouble. It made no sense to keep them when I had a perfectly cooperative seaman to guide me where I needed to go. He was no navigator, but I gambled he could locate the general region of ocean and then we could enact a search pattern."

Looking at Valērija, Māris said, "She killed both your uncles. She left only Whit and me alive. For the past two years, I've been charting and recharting our way. I've tried to be wrong, to send her anywhere but here."

"He was only half lying. He's not a good enough navigator to keep me lost completely. He has managed to steer me in circles more than once. It's taken all this time, but we've finally reached our goal."

Anadare watched Māris crumple. He was totally spent, and finally drunk enough that his mind could go to merciful oblivion.

"Anyhoo, wasn't that a nice story?" Isobel cooed. "You children should get some rest. Busy days ahead. And don't worry: you're on the guest list, not the menu. I wouldn't want to cause Taryn any unnecessary distress."

To Anadare, this statement was a fist to the gut. What did Isobel care about Taryn?

Getting up to leave, Isobel said, "In any case, things are moving quickly now. Our advance teams should be at Gunn Island by the end of the week. We're going to have such fun!"

Valērija eyed Isobel as the woman left the cabin. Though her expression remained inscrutable, Anadare sensed what she was thinking: *This bitch needs to die.*

Chapter 10

Sefa fished for a few hours each day. He did not know when or if his friends might return, so he only salted and spiced a few servings at a time. For much of the day, he stared into his comtutor, happy to relieve the tedium with old movies. He was in the middle of a centuries-old sea battle between a British 64-gunner of the Ardent class and a French Man o' War when nearby splashing yanked him back to the present.

It was two of the dolphins. Sefa asked aloud where the others were, then immediately thought how stupid he sounded. Valērija and Anadare both claimed to speak with these animals, but the longer he sat on the open sea, the more he became convinced they were playing a joke on him.

One of the creatures, possibly the one called Muriel that Anadare liked so much, was trying to get his attention. She whipped about with her head above the swells, pivoting her body three hundred sixty degrees. Sefa threw a couple of chunks of his fish to the dolphins, who gulped them down like air.

"Too much salt!"

The words came with an intense stabbing pain like two harpoons thrust into his eyes. He let out a yelp and nearly fell over. It was a woman's voice, very high-pitched, with concerted musical notes playing through each syllable. Sefa stared at Muriel. He hadn't actually heard her with his ears. The words had registered fleetingly inside his throbbing head. This terrified him, although he could not say why. After a beat, he asked again aloud, "Where are they?"

Muriel kept her expressive eyes fixed on his. She was trying to send another message. The first had gotten through when his guard was down. Now, he was frightened and he felt himself throwing up walls in his mind. A new onslaught of pain struck, bringing two words: "No killing." The searing discomfort vanished with the final sound in his head.

"Who said anything about killing?" Sefa protested. "I'm not going to kill you."

Both dolphins ducked under the water. Sefa saw their silhouettes heading back out toward Hell's Reach. In virtually the same instant, he heard a horn blowing. This time, he heard it with his ears. He looked up to see three boats on the horizon, moving to intercept him. Sefa rushed to raise his sails. *Hinatea* was fast and should be able to outrun these boats, but before he could get underway, a missile screamed into the water a few yards from his starboard hull. Sefa was sure whoever had fired it had missed him on purpose, and probably had no plans to repeat the warning.

The boats forestalled any escape. A balding man with an idiotic ponytail stepped over to Sefa's boat.

"Glad we caught you." A joke? "I'm Ransom, with the salvors. Your friends are safe. Taryn, Valērija, and the boy send their regards. We're on our way to your island. I wonder whether you'd be good enough to carry a message in advance of our arrival." Ransom handed Sefa a note. The delicate handwriting contrasted with the starkness of the content. "There's one more favor, if you don't mind."

Out of a cabin stepped two Chinese women, an old lady and a younger one carrying a baby. Sefa welcomed them onboard. "Ni hao!" As he said it, he realized who was setting foot on the *Hinatea*.

"Ni hao," the Zhangs replied, nodding and smiling. Sefa had so many questions. They must have been kidnapped by the pirates—it seemed ages ago now. What did they know? Who else from the island had they seen? There'd be time enough for questions after they got underway, or his curiosity might have to wait until they got back. "Ni hao" was the extent of his Mandarin.

Ransom helped them onto the cat, saying, "Please take these ladies home. We'll be there soon, but Captain O'Malley felt returning them first would be a goodwill gesture."

The boats were gone before Sefa's heart rate returned to normal. He and the younger Zhang finished preparing *Hinatea* for the trip back to Gunn's main harbor while the older woman tended the baby.

Anadare, Taryn, and Valērija were safe, at least as safe as any of them were right now. As they sailed back to the island, Sefa kept wondering what Muriel had meant by "no killing." He was in no position to do any killing. He decided the best thing to do was to add Muriel's message to the written one the salvors had given him. He was not looking forward to delivering either.

The cargo net fell open onto the deck of the work skiff and four animals splayed out. From the ragged opening of the upper deck containing the animal pens, a salvor's voice called down on bullhorn: "Be quick. You get no points for neatness."

The four underfed pigs strutting on the planks in front of them had a variety of ugly wounds and sores, like their owners. "Are these even fit to eat?" Anadare asked.

"Nobody asked our opinion," Valērija said. They did not delay; it would only make the task more difficult. Anadare took two squealing pigs and she took two. A few quick thrusts left the pair in silence on the skiff's reddening deck. They could have done this in the galley, but it made a certain sense to use the skiff as an abattoir. A few small sharks circled, the inscrutable blackness of their eyes belying their love of an easy meal.

"We're fattening up our executioners," Anadare said as he field-dressed one scrawny sow. He threw a small bit of offal over the side, causing the sharks to boil into activity. Then he wondered if the salvors wanted him to keep the organs, so he began to separate the parts into wet piles.

"We could hit the oars and take our chances getting back before the attack," Valērija suggested, though she knew he would never leave Taryn.

"Fish, please."

"I didn't bring any tackle," answered Anadare, but found Valērija giggling.

"That wasn't me," she said. "I only half got what your girlfriend said. Something about fish."

Looking into the water, Anadare was pleased to see Muriel's lively glance and all-purpose smile. "I thought you meant fishing. Sorry, I don't have any fish to give you today. Hey!" Anadare winced. "Not without asking, please!"

"Is she talking with you?" Valērija asked.

"Yes, but she's taking things directly from my brain. It's really unsettling."

"Getting help," Muriel said. This time, both of them understood the dolphin, who, having said what she needed to say, vanished with barely a ripple.

"What kind of help?" Anadare wondered aloud. "Maybe I can still ask. I wonder how far I can call out to her."

Valērija put her hand on his. "I wouldn't count too much on your link turning into a superpower," she said. "For the most part, dolphins run the show."

"Guess I'm not so special after all."

A wry crinkle appeared on her nose. "We'll see."

They finished their onerous chore, wrapped the rendered meat, and signaled for the salvors to haul up the bundle in the cargo net. Wordlessly, they took up their oars and rowed the skiff back around to the winch, where crewmen were waiting to bring them aboard.

Anadare said, "Our home faces attack any day now. We're outgunned twenty to one, or more. What kind of help can she possibly bring?"

"I know you read me, dear. Lord knows, lately I can barely go a night without your spooky attempts to enter my dreams." Isobel stood up in the launch, scanning the water. It felt to her as though things were proceeding as they should. She had no patience for a wild card in the form of a meddling dolphin who had a key to her innermost thoughts. "Let me be clear about this: we're going to Gunn Island to finish things. No more wandering. No more dealing with murderous lunatics. We're going to bring a close to the world's long, sad story."

"Not over," came Muriel's voice at last.

"No? I've seen what happens when the poisons reach a pocket of life. I wouldn't wish that on anyone."

"Working on it," Muriel said.

"Why are you defending human beings? You'd be better off without us!"

"The Great sees all. All rivers reach the sea in time."

"More of your dolphin voodoo?"

"Not voo. Not doo." Muriel ducked down, but continued to listen. She could sense Isobel's foremost thoughts and intentions. The waves lapped around the launch, from which Isobel kept throwing small fish scraps. It took all of Muriel's self-control not to dart over and snap up the morsels.

"Come and let's talk about it."

"No killing. Need Isobel-mans, the array. The Great needs Isobel-mans. Needs mans. No killing." Muriel sent the message as clearly as she could, with a restrained musical score so as not to confuse Isobel. The reply was silence. Isobel was there, but not there. Of all the mans Muriel had pinged, Isobel was the only one who could block her out completely. There was no movement from the launch, no more fish scraps came. Muriel decided to put her head up and take a look.

Isobel was alone in the launch, her back to the dolphin. Muriel attempted something drastic, something bad. With enormous effort and fighting her own prohibitions, she reached inside Isobel . . . against Isobel's will. The result was instantaneous, jarring, and exquisitely painful for both of them. Neither could tell whether her screams came from herself or the other. Muriel broke the link. Waves of emotion came through from Isobel: humor so fragile it snapped and fell away, plus light-consuming resentment, despair, isolation, a fathomless sense of want, anger, and other odious elements. The pain turned white hot and Muriel grasped it was shooting not only through her but also into Isobel.

The mans screamed, "No killing? No deal!" at the top of her lungs and swung around. Something in Isobel's hand flashed and blasted even louder than her screams. Muriel ducked under and swam as fast as she could. Sharks appeared from nowhere as Muriel sensed blood seeping from her dorsal fin. Not a mortal wound, it nonetheless throbbed with pain.

As Muriel put distance between herself and the hungry scavengers and the addle-minded Isobel, she began the long task of assembling what she had stolen from Isobel's thoughts. What Isobel had planned was not a good thing, but Muriel could not fix on any specifics. Whatever the plan, it was aimed at Gunn Island. The two sides would meet each other in the big bay the islanders named Losi, after a fisherman who was also a trickster.

Muriel resigned herself to what lay ahead. She probably could not stop the mans from ruining things for her, for themselves, ruining everything. Who knew how many lives would flicker and vanish from her array in the coming hours? So be it. Whatever the outcome of this mania the mans called war, she had done all she could. She had to begin preparing herself for the leap.

"Okay, he's in. Start hauling him up!"

Anadare and Valērija pulled for all they were worth.

"My mother can pull harder than that, netter!"

"How the hell much do octopodes weigh? Pull!" Anadare began to wonder whether this was a good idea. He'd rigged a two-handled winch, liberated from one of the boat-launching stations. Even so, they had to lock it off and rest for a moment. The head and the octopod were still two decks below. They had to get him onboard and to the lower decks, somewhere he could survive, then get themselves back to their assigned chores before anyone missed them. Their second round of cranking produced results. A giant, toothily grinning octopus head popped through the porthole with an octopod riding inside. Limbs oozed over the sides of the costume head. A blue-tipped arm met Valērija's tattooed hand, while another arm made contact with Anadare.

"I'll take it from here," came a sort of voice from the octopod. "No need to carry me. I know more about these vessels than you do, though admittedly the ones my ancestors stored in transmemory were sunken derelicts." As he poured himself out of the fractured and leaking Okey Dokey mask, Norris added with indignation, "That is the stupidest-looking face I've ever seen! Octopodes do not smile. We don't have teeth!"

In the early evening, war came to Gunn Island. Hecht's hope that Isobel would delay her attack because of the gathering storm vanished as two dozen artillery shells roared down onto the island, courtesy of the salvor fleet taking up position in and around Losi Bay. The munitions landed with violence and flame, but caused little damage. One turned a Chinese tea farm into a crater; another obliterated a utility shack. Soon after, rockets screamed over the horizon. These came from Isobel's ship, anchored somewhere outside the bay. The aim was crude, landing the munitions in the trees or hillsides in addition to the occasional lucky shot that turned a private home into an orange hell. This was the softening-up phase.

Next, Hecht watched a chevron of CGULS move in from the ship. The cyber-guided ultralight strikers, or CGULS, scorched comet trails into Hecht's aftervision. These weapons were more precise than the shells or rockets. Instead of plowing into a home or office with destructive kinetic force, the CGULS carried a chemical payload that air-burst dazzling white tendrils onto the rooftops. Hecht's stomach clenched. He saw his fellow islanders streaming out of the buildings. Some tried to fight the rapidly spreading fires, while others ran away screaming into the blustery night.

Hecht clutched the note, written in his daughter's hand and sent by Isobel. Hastily delivered by Sefa, its stark list of ships and weaponry should have convinced the Senate to offer their unconditional surrender. Hecht had tried to make the senators see reason, but the fools voted to resist.

What had the dolphin told Sefa? "No killing." The islanders were in no position to do much killing; they'd be lucky to survive this night. He hoped Isobel was sincere in her promise to keep the bloodshed to a minimum.

The island's defense teams were alerted and in position, trying to zero in on the source of the shelling. The best trained of their police and collectors filled the ranks. Fanchon's and Bentley's teams manned the two guns atop the cliffs overlooking the southwest inlet and most of Losi Bay.

Fanchon had drilled his men long and hard until they could load and fire their paltry collection of artillery pieces with alacrity. Fusillades flew in both directions. Fanchon spewed curses each time a charge fizzled. This happened far too often; the prepackaged shells were a century old. The synthetics district had begun supplying them with new shells, but not enough. Switching over to wartime production was a slow business. If the gunners used only the fresh shells, they'd run through their ammunition in no time. Fanchon made sure his team got the lion's share of the new shells. To hell with the younger Bentley and his gunners!

Striking a target with their ancient guns was no small feat. The source of the CGULS was well out of reach for them, but Fanchon's team managed to send a massive ball careening through the side of one of the attacking frigates below them in Losi Bay. As smoke turned blood red in the firelight on her deck, he could see the crew of the hulled vessel scrambling to save themselves. They were out of the fight.

It was a small victory. At least two dozen warships, from frigates to modified schooners, revealed themselves as lightning strobed the bay. The crack of cannons and rattle of large-caliber deck guns pierced the rising winds.

In the island's wealthy Morningside District, Hamlin led the fire brigade, considering it an extension of his duties as a collector. Puffing and sweating profusely, he nonetheless directed twenty volunteers, men, women, and teens. They ran nonstop to refill two pumper units with water from the nearest wells. Flames jumped from one rooftop to the next. By morning, all of these richly appointed homes could be nothing but smoldering memories. He blessed the raindrops that were falling. Within minutes, the drops turned into a torrent as an unnamed hurricane freed its rage on Gunn Island.

The storm helped tame the fires, but failed to halt the onslaught.

Through the worsening deluge, Sefa's catamaran led the special fleet around Lefatu Bend. His sailors were the only ones willing to challenge both the storm and the salvors. The Latvians had talked about helping, but refused to send ships. Cowards! Everyone else, including the Chinese, had either beached their boats or secured them at the docks, tying on extra fenders in hopes the harbor would shelter the vessels as it had so often before. So be it.

Sefa's handful of real sailors understood they must stay afloat long enough to negotiate the narrows and pass into the bay in order to flank the attacking fleet. Then, they'd deliver their surprise.

"This one's for you, Horatio Hornblower!" he cried out defiantly. The wind ate his words.

Princess Victoria Ka'iulani Kawekio I Lunalilo Kalaninuiahi-lapalapa Cleghorn had her orders. She and Beryl enlisted the help of several sturdy octopodes. They could not stop the fighting, so determined were the mans to spill each other's blood, so guile was the order of the day. "Impossible is no excuse for quitting," the dolphin princess sang out with dramatic flourish. The sea force moved into the bay.

Another wicked hiss sounded through the gale, accompanied by a jolt that rattled every small object and every nerve in the room. From outside the window, a miniature red nova flared, staining everything like hot red liquid. It was difficult to get a good look at the rockets as they launched toward Gunn Island. Oddly, the drone things were easier to track since someone had added pyrotechnics, giving them an evil tail of red sparks.

Lightning flashes added the final touch of infernal mayhem to the night.

The children were in a state; many faced the wall or hid behind a wall of their own fingers, while others rocked in place. Nurse Burk screamed into the intercom, "We've got patients down here! Tell the captain her daughter—" A voice on the other end, presumably someone on the bridge, merely repeated that Captain O'Malley was not available at the moment. Burk slammed a palm against the wall. She took a deep breath and motioned Taryn over. "C'mon, let's get the rest of them."

Together, they helped one man from the floor, where he lay in a fetal position. They walked him out of the dayroom and into the dorm, where many of the children were already stretched out in the bunks.

"I hate this," Burk said, pulling a hypodermic injector from her side bag. "Hold him." Taryn did as she was told, glad that Burk did not ask her to do the actual injections. "This is the last thing these people need—drugs to block out the real world even more. Maybe if you tried. The captain likes you."

"I don't think . . ." Taryn respected that there were limits. Isobel had shifted Taryn's other duties, to give her more time with Nurse Burk and the children. They talked about the children over breakfast most mornings. Even so, every attempt to coax Isobel to visit Maggie and the others met with a wall of resistance. She was not going to bend the older woman's will.

The sedatives were taking effect. Most of the faces in

the bunks were calm now, a welcome change from the silent screams when the rocket barrage had begun. Taryn and Burk returned to the dayroom. Maggie was swaying in place, wincing at every shrill launch.

Taryn put her arms around the girl. Burk looked over, holding an injector, her eyes asking whether Taryn wanted to put Maggie under like the rest.

"No," Taryn said. "We're going to do something else." She walked the slender girl to the washroom and sat her on the edge of the toilet. Burk looked on as salvor crewmen rushed by with purpose in the passageway. Taryn wet Maggie's russet hair with a cloth, then found a tube of shampoo and gently worked in a small amount. Maggie rocked like a little girl, seemingly content for the moment. A few more blasts reverberated through the bulkheads, but she did not respond. Her eyes focused forward, seeing something, perhaps, in the middle distance that was invisible to everyone else.

"She definitely responds to you," Burk said.

"She's just a girl who likes to look pretty. So, that's what we're going to do, isn't it, Maggie? We're going to make you the most beautiful woman on this ship." She found a dry towel and began tamping down Maggie's wet hair. "Who will we show you off to first? Do you like that big guard who brings the meals?" There was a flicker at one side of her lips. "I thought so. But, maybe there are other men who deserve a chance to dance with you. I wonder if we might do your hair up in a twist? We'll have the men fighting each other and the women envious."

Taryn began to hum a small tune. Maggie couldn't find the notes, but emitted a complementary chord of her own.

"That's right. Forget everyone else. A girl doesn't have to be pretty for anyone—not men, or grumpy old captains. She just has to be pretty for herself."

Hinatea and three outriggers broke over the crests and thunked down into the troughs. Each of the canoes carried a two-person crew, who used all their available strength to achieve forward motion in the wild water. Sefa sailed solo, pushing his rigging to the limit. The wind threatened to rend the fabric to rags.

One sailor nursed a fire in a protected brazier in the belly of each canoe. Sefa and his volunteers had loaded the bows of all four vessels with fragile jugs of a concentrated netter alcohol, *Hinatea* carrying the load in her port hull. Even in the rain, there were ways to combine flame and fuel to full effect. These were fire ships.

Sefa signaled Rua in the nearest outrigger to pass along the go sign. It was time. Taking an alcohol-soaked torch from a container, Sefa lit one end. His counterparts did the same. He could see the torches sputtering through the sheets of rain.

Losing his beloved cat and three outriggers would be costly; it would take weeks or months to build new ones. They had no choice. If this worked, if they lived through it, they could use surfboards as torpedoes. They might be able to build mines or deliver charges by hand, even if that meant making a suicide run. They would attack until the salvors gave up or the last islander fell.

Sefa pointed his port hull toward the closest salvor vessel, tacking to make sure he had enough speed to ram. The men aboard that frigate pointed to the light of his torch. The audacity of his plan caught the salvors off guard, but not for long. They fired, using the torch as a bullseye. Bullets whizzed through the rain and into the water. They were shooting from point-blank range now; only the bounding surf prevented them from drawing a bead on his head. One shot chipped the cat's mast. Sefa hurried forward along the port hull and unwrapped the wicks embedded in the bottles. He worked gingerly, hoping the whole thing didn't go up in his face. Keeping his head down, Sefa stared at the fast-approaching salvor ship. He lowered his torch—

—and went overboard as if the sea itself had pulled him in.

Sefa panicked. Something had him by the leg and was yanking him deeper. It was something heavy, and it had a will of its own. Sefa tried to scream, emptying his lungs into the water. His torch had followed him over the side. He had failed to turn *Hinatea* into a fire ship, failed to engulf the salvors in flames, failed to defend his friends and family.

All at once, the thing (it occurred to him finally that this was an octopod holding on to his ankle) let him go. Now, something else (a dolphin, of course) was plowing into his stomach, nudging him away from the salvor ship and upward. As they broke the surface, the animal came within inches of his face and whistled. It flipped over and offered Sefa its pale belly. At first Sefa thought the damned thing wanted him to rub it, then he realized the gesture was an offer of help. He reluctantly took hold of the dolphin's two pectoral fins, climbed on keeping his legs together, and let it pull him along. He couldn't believe how fast this thing could move upside down. Water washed over Sefa's face, forcing him to gulp for air when he could.

They paused a moment, several hundred yards from where he'd gone into the water. Sefa saw no fires; the other islanders had been stopped by these stinking fish just as he had. Lightning revealed the fate of his cat. She had rammed the salvors' ship, but done little damage. The salvors had pushed it away.

Hinatea looked like a broken doll. Her two sleek hulls were no longer aligned; the port one bent outward. The bridgedeck had slipped off its mounts, spilling supplies into the bay. The damaged cat bounced on the ten-foot swells that percolated Losi Bay. Without a drogue to slow her drift, she would not last long. She would run onto rocks or a reef and break into a thousand pieces.

His dolphin rescuer again offered Sefa transportation to shore and safety. En route, Sefa felt no gratitude, but rather a deep red pulsing behind his eyes.

The dolphin princess commanded her sea force in chittering rhythms reminiscent of the ancient drum language that once called the islands to war. "No killing," she said, "but have fun!"

The dolphin-octopod squadron moved rapidly from ship to ship. They managed to stop the island's bay defenders, but had less luck frustrating the salvors' attack. The salvors had bigger boats. It was harder to reach the crews or affect their vessels.

The aquatic contingent had luck with a few of the hostile picket ships; an octopod used debris to foul the prop and rudder of one. Three dolphins butted their melons against the bow of another, changing its course to collide with its neighbor. The salvors fired directly at the saboteurs, grazing a dolphin named Errol.

The sea force's efforts amounted to a minor disruption in the one-sided battle, however. The salvors were seasoned fighters and they had a prize in sight.

Hecht wanted to remain inside, but he saw how this battle was playing out. Enough. Lives were being lost or ruined, cast on the beaches like so many empty shells. There could be no doubt of the result: the islanders could not fight off the salvors' fleet. Hecht confirmed his intentions with two contrite senators sheltering in his house. To hell with the other fools! Then, he dressed in a white suit, which would show respect for their conquerors while avoiding the humiliation of carrying an actual flag of surrender. He stepped out into the drenching storm and rode in a caravan to the harbor.

Waves lashed all sides of the pier. Hecht could barely make out the ships in the distance and wondered whether they could see him. As if in answer, red-and-white signal lights flashed from the largest warship.

Hecht heard the sound of an outboard engine. An oversized silver raft with a small cabin bobbed its way to his position. Its crew hustled up a ladder, grabbed Hecht, and loaded him onto the storm-defying Zodiac. As he stepped on, he saw men and women dressed in white not unlike himself, salvors. They were coming ashore on launches. The sharp reports of rifles registered over the sounds of the Zodiac's engine and the storm. The fighting had not finished, despite his surrender. The Zodiac crew powered the boat away from the pier and out over jagged water. Hecht found himself in freefall as the unsinkable craft topped each frothy peak only to fall into a watery chasm. The motion whomped his coccyx onto the hard bench, sending electric spasms through his body. Hecht watched with dread as they motored past this Zodiac's mother ship, past the bay's entrance, and out toward the open sea. Soaked and feeling sick to his stomach, he trudged over to the tiny cabin. Isobel was waiting for him.

"Isn't this storm thrilling, Kenny!" she said, throwing her arms around him and giving him a wet, drunken kiss.

Hecht humiliated himself in front of Isobel, but she

laughed it off. Seasickness had hit him once they stepped aboard the *Wyvern* and moved to an interior space with no view of the horizon. In these high seas, even this big ship heaved. Without a visual cue, his inner ear struggled to provide equilibrium. The result: Hecht's stomach purged.

Hastily trying to deflect embarrassment, Hecht said he wanted to see Taryn. Isobel reassured him his daughter was fine and insisted they wait until the storm passed. "We'll have the reunion tomorrow, when we can enjoy it properly. I have other plans for you tonight, Kenny."

Mans are crazy. Why else would creatures so fat and clumsy deny themselves the buoyancy of water? Norris felt the great ship groan, its frames and plates threatening to buckle as its enormous weight shifted and rolled in the uneasy ocean. In his mind, he overlaid his present location onto what he'd mapped out by crawling along the hull, plus information found in transmemory. He located the intakes. He then followed a series of large pipes back to the ballast tanks, the fire-suppression system, and the bilge. A few simple tricks switched what went out with what came in. One final twist of a valve would flood this steel-and-plastic world, assuming the storm didn't do it first. Norris didn't care whether the ship sank; it made no difference to him. For now, he did nothing. The Anadaremans had told him to wait, so he waited.

Norris happily found something to occupy his time. The crew had set up a fishery amongst the giant machines on the lowest level of engineering. He slipped into the refreshing environment and availed himself of the seafood buffet: oily anchovies, crunchy crabs of all sorts, some frilly plants, meaty delicious eels, and more. If he had to wait, he'd wait in style.

His appetite temporarily sated, Norris had time to explore the giant bilge pumps leading down from the galley, suites, bars, and dining salons. He then calculated the volume these conduits could convey off the ship. It was ponderous.

"This is the mans' problem. They poop too much. An octopod assimilates most of what he eats to add to his overall mass. Not mans. He eats, he poops, he eats more. This whole ship is designed to bring mans and food together. Manskind loves poop."

Chapter 11

Anadare ran to join Valērija, who was working with Kuan to push a large food cart through the corridors. Anadare was pleased to learn most of the Zhangs had survived, but felt uncomfortable around Kuan. There was his salvor's uniform, of course, but also the way he carried himself: tentatively, confused, as if he were arguing life and death with his own ghost.

"Sorry," Anadare said to Valērija. "Been learning what's what while most of the salvors are off the ship. Turns out I had some business on Empress Deck, the one just below Jubilee," he whispered conspiratorially to her. Kuan, who was up ahead, did not react.

"What happened to your hand?" Valērija asked, passing him a napkin.

Wrapping it around his bleeding knuckles, he said, "Hurt it on some stubborn bolts." Nothing. She seemed lost in her own thoughts, so he gave up and asked, "How are you doing?"

"Everyone we know is getting murdered and we're delivering hot calzones and salvor hooch to the killers," Valērija said.

"Beats jumping ship in a hurricane." The attempt at gallows humor failed. He shrugged. "We must keep moving." Wind gusts blew their fury against the outer reaches of the ship as the deck rolled underfoot.

Kuan led Anadare and Valērija through various passageways as they dropped off food to those salvors who were still aboard. They found their way to the daycare. Anadare had tried repeatedly to see Taryn in recent days, but Isobel was monopolizing her time. She took her new protégé on tours of the fleet, instructing Taryn to perform simple medical checks. Anadare could occasionally spot them from the deck of the *Wyvern*.

"Meals on Wheels!" Valērija called out. Anadare snapped back to reality. He had no idea what that meant; it sounded like one of those obsolete phrases that turned up on comtutor.

Nurse Burk thanked them for the delivery. She and Taryn didn't want to venture out to the galley or dining areas. Between the storm and the fighting, the children were agitated and needed all the reassurance they could get. Taryn sat at a table with Maggie and two other TD patients, who looked around nervously.

"We brought you dinner," Anadare offered.

"Thanks. They might eat, but my stomach can't take it in this weather." Taryn accepted a tray of food, set it on the table, then pushed it away.

"I haven't seen you."

"I've been busy. Sorry. Isobel says nice things about your work."

"I don't want her compliments," Anadare said and instantly wished he could call back the rebuke.

"She's not that bad. You should give her a chance."

Her words froze his heart. Give her a chance? "Right now, she's attacking our families."

"As opposed to slowly starving them like my father did."

What? Anadare was confused at the change in her. When had this happened? What had Isobel been telling her? "It's not the same, Taryn. I can't believe—" He realized he'd raised his voice as more children drifted over to their table. Hoping to brighten the mood, he nodded in their direction. "It only took a war and a hurricane to get a rise out of them," Anadare said.

"They just need to get to know you. I feel as though I can help them. That's what I plan to do." She seemed to be telling him she was happy where she was, without him. How had getting angry at her father turned her against him? He wanted to tell her about their plans for getting off the *Wyvern*. His mouth moved, but no sound came out.

Valērija gently pulled him away from Taryn's table. They exchanged polite goodbyes with her and Burk and left.

Anadare and Valērija didn't speak much during the next several stops. Feeling the silence, he asked, "Why do people who've fallen off a cliff all have the same dream?"

"What dream?" Kuan spoke in a hesitant manner. Until this point, he had answered Anadare's questions, but said little more. The man was not well. It looked as though he hadn't slept in weeks. Anadare wasn't sure whether he cared about Kuan's well-being, but he let him join the conversation.

"To get back to the top of the cliff."

"They're stupid," Kuan guessed.

"Not stupid. Selfish," Anadare said. "Otherwise, even an idiot would make changes, change himself or give up something. No, they want—*we* want things to be the way we want them. Instead of making a sensible new plan, we go on doing whatever led to disaster in the first place. We go right back to the edge of the cliff. We cause ourselves to fall, and we'll do it all over again." He let his rhetoric rattle to a halt.

Valērija picked up the thread. Gesturing around, she said, "The salvors have all this stuff. This ship. Weapons. Hell, they have more than anyone else alive. They could help starving people instead of robbing them, but they like stealing. It makes them feel powerful. They're going to steal Gunn Island."

"Captain O'Malley tells us we have a right to such things," Kuan offered meekly and without conviction.

"Shark kūkā!" Anadare cried. "People have a right to what they earn." Looking accusingly at Kuan in his white uniform, he added, "You salvors already have plenty, but you keep taking more than you can use. That's selfishness. Futous are no better, with their caravans and their air conditioning."

"And wandering Latvians?" she asked.

"As far as my people are concerned, you're all refugees. We *original* islanders were doing great until you trashed your parts of the world and invaded ours."

"Nice," huffed Valērija. The conversation sputtered and died.

Ransom led his party up through the thick jungle behind the seawalk overlooking Losi Bay. A dozen islanders manned this cannon while as many more manned the other. The farther installation looked smart, even at a distance. People moved with purpose, firing their guns right up until runners arrived to announce that the Senate and Commissioner Hecht had surrendered to the salvors.

The nearer group was disorganized. They had no sentries, making it easy for the salvors to approach their position. Their leader, a skittish young man they called General Bentley, argued with his gunners. The citizen soldiers complained they couldn't see through the storm to aim. Bentley barked back that the enemy had no trouble aiming. The soldiers stood still, refusing Bentley's orders. He screamed bloody murder until a large, quiet man laid a leathery hand on his shoulder to calm him. The larger man appeared to be one of their fishermen, unbathed and rough, but with a presence that easily overpowered Bentley. It would make no difference in what was to come.

Ransom took a good look. These gunners were

fighting each other, handing victory to the salvors. Isobel would not miss their number. Ransom, meanwhile, wanted payback for the hits these gunnery crews had scored on the salvor fleet. His team broke from the jungle, whooping and yelling. The island defenders froze, gawping as the salvors' guns cut loose.

In the streets below, people were gaining control over the fires. Some looked up, searching for the source of a sudden cluster of gunshots. The sound came from the seawalk, where their friends and family members had gone to defend them from the invaders.

The elevator took Anadare, Valērija, and Kuan to Jubilee Deck with its sepulchral disco and long corridor of padlocked doors. A group of salvors drenched with rain streamed out of the nearby stairwell. One man carried a huge bird thing, its glass belly filled with snot-colored liquid. A gray-haired salvor woman grumbled, "This one never works. Piece of cac!"

"Dinner!" Anadare announced. The salvors split into twos and threes, each group heading for one of the cabins and unlocking the door. Anadare held out a tray and followed some crewmembers inside the nearest cabin to get a good look. As he'd deduced, it barely contained an enormous artillery piece secured to the deck with steel bolts the size of Anadare's fist. He had never seen anything this destructive in such a confined space. The cabin window had been removed, allowing the barrel to jut out over the suite's balcony. Heavy plastic sheeting barely kept the weather out; it fluttered and protested each storm gust. Stacked around the military-style piece were shells half as long as Anadare was tall. The flooring of the cabin sagged under the combined weight, separating the deck downward from the bulkheads.

"About time," a salvor with open sores around his mouth grumbled, grabbing a small jug and telling Anadare and Valērija to put the food anywhere. They noticed several empty jugs rolling around the pitching deck.

Valērija dared to ask, "So, when do we use these babies?" She said it as if she were excited at the prospect of a fireworks display.

"When the captain tells us to, little girl," said one of the men. "Hard to see what we're blowing up in this weather. Maybe Grace O'Malley has a plan. Now, go and get us some more hooch!"

The salvors hustled them out, slammed the door, and latched it from the inside. Valērija said, "Now what? Toss a match?"

"If I had one," Anadare answered. They rolled the cart down the corridor. "At most, we'd blow up some bottles of hooch along with ourselves. We just have to wait. Besides, Muriel doesn't want us killing anyone."

"My people have come to accept that dolphins are pretty smart. I'm sure she has her reasons for avoiding bloodshed."

Anadare rubbed his injured hand and hoped it was okay with Muriel if these salvors killed themselves.

They worked their way down the row of gun rooms. Anadare noticed there were different kinds of artillery; Isobel and her crew had taken souvenirs during their travels. He'd done what he could. He and Valērija could never hope to destroy all of these weapons. So, they served dinner to cutthroats and bided their time. The rest hinged on one curmudgeonly stowaway.

Isobel led Hecht to her dimly lit quarters, where she offered him conversation and something strong to drink. The liquor burned his stomach yet seemed to calm its churning. As he drained the bottle, Isobel's hands moved deftly in the darkness, removing his soaked clothes. She slowly toweled him dry. Unbuttoning her own wet garments, Isobel slipped into shadows that cheated his eyes of her callipygian charms. She returned minutes later wrapped in a man's tartan nightgown.

Hecht had always felt a certain sexual tension with Isobel, from their first furtive conversations over the shortwave. He never doubted her word when she described the power of her fleet and never doubted her intention to take Gunn Island. He only wondered whether he could insinuate himself into her emotions. As best he could tell, she did not have anyone aboard the *Wyvern*.

Odd. She was an attractive woman and a formidable presence. Maybe she felt discipline would suffer if she fraternized with the men under her command. So much the better for Hecht. The battle raging onshore was an unfortunate formality, a violent changing of the guard. Hecht's place was near the seat of power.

His clumsy hands groped at her as Isobel pushed him onto his back and mounted him. The sensations made him giddy. Hecht had never been with a woman who took full control. His wife showed up when she wanted something, then let him do what he wanted. An occasional affair spiced things up, but most of the women he chose were passive. Isobel was something new, exciting. Their lovemaking was vigorous, loud, and enthusiastic. The wild weather added a dangerous edge.

He tried to explain his feelings. She came back with one of her oddly timed quotations, this one from somebody named Groucho: "Marriage interferes with romance. Anytime you have a romance, your wife is bound to interfere."

Raising the sheet and climbing into bed, she pushed a fresh drink into his hands, in a glass this time. His head was already light, but he gulped. The extra booze helped take his mind off the incessant pitch and yaw of the ship. Hecht decided to make his real move.

"Isobel, I hope you'll excuse me for bringing it up, but I really need to know what's happening back on the island."

"I am in partial contact with my assault leaders. What

few radios we have don't work well in a hurricane. By now, my men should have anchored their ships and gone ashore. They'll have called for your people to disarm, probably had to shoot a few to convince them they're beaten. Then they'll have taken up residence in your—in our Senate Building. We'll also need the Exchange for now."

"That's what I wanted to talk to you about. Originally, we spoke of splitting the responsibilities."

"Kenny, Kenny, Kenny, Kenny, Kenny. Splitting? You mean sharing power, don't you?" In a nursery-school teacher's voice that gave him chills, she said, "My dear love, do I look like someone who shares?"

"I have been handling island administration most of my life. There's no need for you to take on the day-to-day nonsense of distributing food and supplies. I could—" She put a finger to his lips, then brushed her hands behind his neck. In one quick motion she removed the ruby-eyed gold lion necklace from his throat and fastened it around her own.

She got out of bed. Hecht watched the satin sheet worship the curve of her rack and rear on its way to the floor. Moving to switch on a lamp, she turned back to face Hecht. It was the first time he had seen her naked in full light. His eyes widened as the lust and alcohol haze evaporated. Seeing these womanly parts that had delighted him in the dark sent a shock to his system. They were discolored with a yellowish-green cast. There were odd bruises and blemishes all around Isobel's groin and a thick liquid leaking from small pustules on the insides of her thighs. He had touched and kissed her there. A new sickness welled up inside him, but this time it was not from the storm.

"Kenny, I hope you aren't disappointed to see me this way. Don't look so shocked. You'll get used to it. You'll have to. You are now every bit as infected as I am."

Chapter 12

By morning, things had changed. The storm had passed. Small groups of men and women in white moved people about the damaged docks, ordering them to load the salvors' ships with food, medical supplies, and fuel. This last item came from the small depot that serviced Gunn's fleet and the few skiffs that had working outboard motors. The islanders complained that the salvors were leaving them with nothing. The men in white only laughed.

Anadare's family and neighbors were busy prioritizing the hundreds of jobs that came in the wake of such a powerful storm, but they couldn't do what had to be done because the salvors were gathering up tools and young men to perform repairs on their fleet. Only one surgeon remained to tend the many injured (or gunshot) people in the hospital. The salvors took the rest of the doctors and most of the nurses off with them. To ensure cooperation, they also began rounding up hostages.

The islanders came aboard the *Wyvern* worn and grim-faced, having witnessed the fires and killings of the night before. Stepping off the launch under guard and climbing the steps to the gaping cargo hatch two decks above, many went slack-jawed at boarding the largest ship they'd ever seen.

Each small group passed an honor guard of salvors with wasp sticks before receiving a hearty captain's greeting: "Welcome aboard the *Wyvern*, an oasis of luxury and strength and your new home away from home." Isobel stood resplendent in her dress uniform, its gold braid gleaming in the storm-scrubbed daylight. She was clearly in her element. Turning to Taryn, she said, "It's vital to reassure them. They've been through a lot. They need to accept this as their new normal."

Taryn, wearing a fresh pink outfit Isobel had found for her, stood by the captain's side. "This is his doing," she said quietly, between greetings for the "guests." They included a doctor she'd interned with at Gunn's hospital and one of Anadare's neighbors. Each offered scraps of information about the decimation of the island. It was unreal. These were her people, and yet she stood with Isobel welcoming them aboard this ship, as if she'd always been there. That was not the strangest part, though. Her underpinnings had been stripped away. "You did this, Daddy," she said again.

Isobel put an arm around Taryn, who took her hand like a little girl. "Frailty, thy name is man," Isobel said. "People will disappoint you. Men, mostly, but people in general." After a moment, she added, "Try not to hate him; that just hurts you. He wants to see you."

"I don't think—"

"Trust me. This is how you take charge of your life, by learning to face the people who fail you." To lighten the mood, she broke into an exaggerated brogue: "We'll have breakfast first: brown bread buried in butter, black pudding, sausinger, and stewed tomatoes, plus an egg or two. I've a mouth on me this fine morning!"

The younger woman looked up at the tall redhead. She stood straight, strong, assured. She didn't have a man around to answer to. It was something to consider.

An hour later, they were below decks.

"As promised, father and daughter are together again," Isobel said blandly, ushering Hecht into the day-care center. None of the permanent residents turned to look at him. Neither did the newest staff member.

"Well, I'll leave you two alone," said Isobel.

Nurse Burk jumped in. "Maggie is more focused when you visit, Captain. She responds to your attention. Taryn's presence has been a godsend—"

Isobel's eyes skated past Burk to Taryn. "That's fantastic."

"—but what Maggie really needs is her—"

"I am so glad you're here with us, Taryn." The small

talk didn't last long. Citing ship's business, Isobel breezed out of the room. Burk sighed and went back to work.

Hecht moved to hug Taryn, but she stood as frozen as one of the children. They both felt the awkwardness. Hecht's eyes narrowed. "Your face!"

"What about it?"

"You're covered." She put a hand to her face. She'd barely noticed the effect of the sun on her skin, which now sported a constellation of freckles.

"Water water," she said dismissively.

He withdrew his hand. "I've come to take you home."

"I'll stay here where I'm needed."

Hecht saw it now: his daughter knew his role in everything. "Taryn, I did what I had to. They would have killed many more. I saved lives!"

"You knew what the captain was planning and you did nothing. And you sent Andy here to get rid of him. You threw in Val for good measure."

Hecht could summon no reply.

A guard took him back on deck. He spotted Anadare and Valērija, but walked briskly past them without stopping. A boat was waiting to return him to the island.

Isobel called Anadare and Valērija to the bridge late the next afternoon. Taryn was there, standing by the captain's side.

"Your people have been very generous, providing us with fuel. Of course, the island's entire supply barely nudged the needle off empty, but it will serve the immediate purpose."

"What purpose is that?" Valērija asked.

"We've hung offshore long enough. We're making way for Gunn Island. We'll anchor in Losi Bay before nightfall. Then, we'll have a lovely fireworks show!"

The two prisoners looked at each other, then at the captain and Taryn, who spoke: "We're going to finish what my father started. Gunn Island is about to be under new management."

"We?" Anadare asked.

Smiling at Taryn, Isobel answered, "Taryn is a salvor now."

Why didn't this surprise him? He wanted this news to hurt, but it was as if someone had been pounding on the same nerve over and over. He felt nothing.

Queen Isobel continued, "Your people will join us soon enough. First, we have to remove the last vestiges of the old order."

Isobel commanded her officers to start the main engines, something they had not done in many months. Long dependent on the solar tugs to move, the crew dropped the lines as the ship thrummed to life under its own power. "Set course for Losi Bay," Isobel ordered.

Defeat was not enough. Isobel required people to bow. Anadare struggled to think of something that would change her mind, but came up blank.

Valērija waited ten minutes before excusing herself. She said she needed to go to her cabin. "Girl stuff." Captain O'Malley nodded in assent.

Valērija casually stepped off the bridge, then broke into a run, ignoring the stares of the crewmen. She used the quickest way she knew to get below. Entering engineering, she climbed over the rail of a catwalk and scaled her way down to the lowest part of the hull. There wasn't much room to walk between all of the improvised fishery tanks. She looked left and right, squinting to try and catch sight of her ally.

Something clammy wrapped itself around her ankle, lewdly traveling up her thigh. "Stop that!"

"Stop what?" asked Norris.

"I don't have time to play. We have to do it now. You have to do it now. Right now!"

"So, you're saying you want me to do it now?"

"Norris!"

"Someone is certainly cranky today. I've already reversed the valves, I just have to adjust the flow."

"Hurry!"

"Now."

He oozed off. Valērija began climbing back up. She didn't want to be away from the bridge too long, but she had one more stop to make. On top of everything else, she really did have "girl stuff" to deal with back in her cabin.

All three islanders were on the bridge when the look-out sighted the gap in Gunn's outer reef. "We'll need to come to port fifteen degrees to make Losi Bay," she reported.

The helmsman called out the appropriate course correction, then added, "Captain, the ship is sluggish."

"What do you mean by sluggish?" Isobel demanded.

Before the helmsman could answer, red tally lights burst into life on long-dormant panels and a voice piped in. "Engineering here. We're taking on water fast. I don't know how, but the pumps are running backward, dumping the ocean into her belly. There's four feet of water in here and rising!"

Captain Isobel O'Malley put her hands on her hips and drew a deep breath. "Oh children, you've been naughty." She ordered her men to handcuff Anadare and Valērija to a pipe running down the side of one console. Taryn stood by, expressionless. Whatever happened, it would happen to all of them.

The next few hours were a blur of frenetic efforts to save the *Wyvern of the Waves*. The crew operated manual pumps to slow the rising water, but were unable to reverse the sabotage to the main bilge and ballast systems. The ship was sinking; it was only a matter of how fast. Her crew's best estimate put it within the next ninety minutes. Captain O'Malley knew damned well the engines would choke out and quit as soon as sea water reached the intakes.

"All ahead full!"

The giant roared in earnest, turning the sea behind her to boiling madness. Every gasket, bolt, and armature of the engines screamed at being prodded so rudely, but they held together and pushed the behemoth's great prow forward, slicing the ocean faster and faster. The *Wyvern* cleared the breakers at twenty knots.

From the forward windows, Isobel spotted familiar swimmers pacing them, playfully lancing the waves. "One big game, eh?" she said to the dolphins.

The helmsman called out the precise heading through the reefs. The first row outside the entrance to Losi Bay flew past. The helmsman barked the next numbers, the ones that would keep them from running over the submerged inner reef.

"Good. Set her bow thirty degrees to starboard of that point."

"Captain, we'll . . . oh. Yes, Captain!"

As the *Wyvern* came about, the full tonnage of the great ship skidded onto the tropical reef with enormous energy, jarring every loose object and person forward. Many, including some on the bridge, lost their footing. Metallic scraping noises overpowered all other sounds. The rocks and rapier coral below neatly slit the hull in three places. A second later, all noise stopped except for the straining propellers.

The captain cut the engines, and the *Wyvern* began to settle in place with a deep grinding sound like teeth chewing on steel. As a matter of luck, the *Wyvern* canted only a few degrees off true. As a matter of Captain

O'Malley's skill, half of the ship's improvised gun batteries now faced shore and the island's main settlements.

Helping one of her crewmates up from the deck, Isobel turned to Anadare and Valērija. "So you know: I was going to use my guns sparingly, just enough to teach your people who's in charge. Now, considering how you've bollixed things ... Mommy is going to spank you silly!"

While damage control worked to plug and seal the massive ruptures in the hull, Isobel radioed to her men on shore to clear everyone out of the Senate Building. She asked a crewman, "How many rounds of artillery do we have left?"

"Two hundred twenty," came the answer.

"Use them," commanded Captain O'Malley.

Anadare and Valērija tried to protest, but the captain ignored them. She was not seething, but had found a chilling level of focus and efficiency for the killing at hand.

The first rounds rattled every fiber of the *Wyvern*, which was, after all, not designed to be a warship. The gun platforms (formerly first-class suites) on Jubilee Deck blazed in anger, belching flame and acrid smoke.

Targets flared and vanished. These shells were magnitudes more powerful than the ones fired from the fleet vessels hours earlier. Homes vaporized three at a time. The gunners found one especially tempting target and hit it over and over, cracking it like an egg and reducing it to marble bits.

One of the guns near the middle of the array made

more noise than the rest. The crews ignored the fact that the deck under the weapons shimmied violently. The shaking increased with the second round.

On the third round, Anadare's sabotage paid off. The nuts he had loosened from underneath slipped free from the bolts restraining the guns to the deck. Gun number three took itself out of commission in spectacular fashion, tearing free of its mounts and rocketing backward. One salvor gunner with ugly sores around his mouth went with it. The gun flew straight through the former disco behind the room.

Observers in Piccadilly Circus below heard the explosion and looked up in time to see the gun blast into the open space. It was joined by dust and debris, a dead salvor, hundreds of flapping white shirts and shorts, and one madly spinning mummy. Detritus rained down on the courtyard, while the gun obliterated the bandstand and wedged several feet into the courtyard deck.

The blowout set off two loose shells and damaged a second gun room, taking it out of service as well. Three other salvors lost their lives.

Crewmembers scrambled to put out the resulting fires. The materials used in the *Wyvern's* superstructure were lightweight and shoddy, but fortunately they were also flame retardant.

Four guns remained active. In her anger, Captain O'Malley took potshots at the islanders' village and the Chinese shanties, and even lobbed a few blind shots over the mountaintops in the general direction of Daugava.

The barrage frightened dozens of shipboard animals literally to death, while chickens living two decks below the guns would never lay another egg.

On the shore, islanders had come out to call up to the bridge of the white wraith raining death upon them, begging mercy.

For long minutes, Anadare and Valērija begged Captain Isobel O'Malley to stop the attack. They pointed out that the islanders could raise no resistance; the slaughter made no sense. For long minutes, Taryn stood stoically in place.

Then, she turned to Isobel and spoke in a confident voice. "They've had enough."

As if discussing trivial matters over tea, the salvor leader answered, "Yes, dear." Only then did Captain Isobel O'Malley end her vengeance.

Chapter 13

It was a simple design, the kind of thing he'd ordinarily use to catch crab or lobster, though on a larger scale. This trap was not meant for shellfish. They were not fish at all, Sefa reminded himself. They could think and make choices. Their choices were supposed to prevent killing, or so they said. Funny, it hadn't worked out that way.

Rua and two other sailors had drowned because dolphins capsized their boats in a hurricane. Maybe the mammals had tried to save them, but dead was dead. While he and the other survivors pulled themselves onto the beach, the invaders seized Gunn Island. Sefa's best hope of repaying the dolphins for their treachery was to work with Queen Isobel. "The enemy of my enemy is my friend," she'd reminded him.

Sefa used a metal spar to latch shut the opening to the pen, which was bordered on three sides by a cove not far from the main pier. The spar was one of several bits he had salvaged from the smashed remains of *Hinatea*. An octopus might pick the pen's lock—in fact, he was sure one could—but the conical netting he'd artfully woven out of sturdy monofilament would prevent any escape.

There was one way into this pen, but no way out. His quarry would have a few dozen yards to swim around in. Queen Isobel had quietly put out a bounty for Muriel, but Sefa wasn't after any reward. He had his own reasons for working hard on this trap.

Kenneth Hecht found it easier to look at himself in the mirror while it was still fogged from the hot shower, or for that matter while his brain was shrouded in a hooch-induced fog. His clumsy fingers ran over the length of his manhood and around his groin, tracing the newest welts and blisters. He swigged down the last contents of the bottle and tossed it on the pile. It wasn't as though his wife or family were there to complain.

Two gunshots snapped him out of his torpor. He rushed to the window, nudity momentarily forgotten. Looking out onto the wide avenue, he saw his man, Fanchon, now in a crisp white salvor uniform, holstering a pistol and reaching down to pick up a bullet-riddled chicken. Children looked on with vacant eyes. All over the island, animals were vanishing as the salvors and some of Hecht's former collectors feasted. The revelry had already depleted Gunn's food reserves; shortages were now inevitable. He had drawn up plans for Isobel to review, but she had not responded.

Hecht dressed quickly, slathering on ointment to reduce the itching and choosing his loosest-fitting pants. The pustules were worse every day; no wonder Isobel no longer came by to see him. The caravan he'd ordered failed to appear outside his door. He'd have to walk. A full flask in his pocket kept him company.

By the time he reached the heavily damaged Senate Building, he had worked up a good rage. He burst through the chamber door and stepped past Ransom and over to Isobel.

"Your salvors are killing our chickens!"

Without looking him in the eye, Isobel said, "We were about to have lunch, Kenny. I see you've already drunk yours." She flinched at her own words. Taryn was in the room. "Sorry."

Taryn said, "It's not your fault he's a drunk."

"Taryn—" Hecht tried, but his daughter stared through him.

Ransom moved between Hecht and the others. "As I was saying, our teams agree with the local divers: the *Wyvern* is impaled on the reef. It may not be possible to float her free even if we can repair the damage."

"She deserves a better fate."

"We'd need to build a dry dock around her." He came around and rolled out some plans onto the long table where the Senate once sat. Light poured in from the shattered roof.

It occurred to Hecht that no one in the room was paying attention to him. "I have some good news!"

"Did I call for you, darling? No, I did not. Don't interrupt. There's a dear."

"I didn't think I needed an invitation to speak in the Senate."

"There is no more Senate," Ransom said, savoring the sound.

Isobel ruffled through some reports on *her* desk. "Well, what then?"

He considered asking Isobel to remove the guards she had watching the doctors. Instead, he said, "The doctors have had some success."

Ransom grunted. No one asked Hecht to elaborate.

Isobel rose and playfully stroked Ransom's ponytail, adjusting the silver clasp. She said, "Check on the production quotas again. See if you can teach Kenny's collectors to come back with something other than excuses. I want to see fuel production tripled. Put more people on it. If you can't find enough workers, expand the labor pool; go younger and older. Get me estimates on your dry dock plan. And get me something to eat other than fish. If I see so much as a scale, I'll eat the cook instead."

"That's something else, Isobel," Hecht interrupted, prompting Ransom to put one hand on the butt of his pistol. Isobel gave her man a reassuring look and sent him off.

Once Ransom had left, she spoke sharply. "You are not the almighty commissioner anymore, Kenny."

"I'm only saying you can't keep killing livestock every time your men get hungry. We're in danger of running through the breeding pairs. Once they're gone, that's it. If you put so many resources into fuel production and repairing that floating pleasure palace, we won't be able to meet our basic needs. We're desperately behind on repairing the damage you—the damage that happened during the hurricane and the recent unpleasantness."

"That's not job one."

"I've got families sleeping in lean-tos," he said. Taryn looked over at this. She knew those people.

Isobel beamed. "We could put housing up on the Exchange. Oopsie, I forgot. We could hold a lottery. Buy a ticket! Will it be a night on the beach with sea lice, or a nice warm bed in one of Morningside's finest homes? I do believe the Commissioner's Mansion survived the fires intact, am I right? And now one man is living there alone in . . . what?"

"Six large bedrooms and a dozen other rooms," Taryn answered her. "Plenty of space for the children. It's past time we moved them off the ship. Daddy could use the company."

"Now that is a good idea!" Isobel agreed. Hecht sputtered a protest. "Enough!" came the hissed rebuke. In recent weeks, Isobel had grown more mercurial; she displayed her temper often. She immediately switched tone and topic. "You said the doctors have a cure?"

"Not a cure. Treatment. Well, for some of the diseases. There are a number of diseases actually. They tell me they've been able to identify some of them."

Taryn showed her discomfort and announced she

would arrange the children's move from the *Wyvern's* daycare to their new home in Morningside. She left the room without saying goodbye to her father.

Isobel let loose. "I don't think there's a treatment for the bug that bit us, lover. I used to believe the lies my darling doctor told me. First he told me there was nothing wrong with our baby girl. A lie. My child never cried, never sang. In sixteen years, I have never once heard her voice! The good doctor could have warned me against trying. He plugged away and said nothing. My belly swelled three times before Maggie. Three times I wound up in sick bay with no baby to hold.

"I won't lie—I was grateful when my husband the doctor drank himself to death. Now your island quacks are pushing a new round of lies. I'll pass."

"It's a chance," Hecht pleaded. "At least, they may be able to help some of your people."

"We're close to the end now. I'm making the most of the time we have." Then she added something that made no sense to Hecht's wet brain. "*Wyvern* may sail again, but she may not. I want every delight this fetid little island can offer. I want a party so loud it opens the gates of heaven."

Hecht gasped. "I don't follow you," he dared. Isobel proceeded to explain her plan in every detail.

Through her mask, Valērija watched one then another and another of the wily animals pour themselves from a gaping wound in the ship's hull. Each carried bits of machinery.

"Fart-wit!" Only her respirator stopped her from yelling it into the sea. She tried to send a message: "The water's clear. Someone's going to see you dragging those things across the bay."

In reply, Norris and his comrades blushed camouflage to conceal their underwater theft. Their booty, cloaked by the octopodes' bodies, came from the *Wyvern's* main pumps. Norris said they were working on a "project for another time," but the inscrutable mollusk refused to elaborate.

Water, water. *Wyvern* would never float free again, so these sections of the ship would remain submerged. In the months since the grounding, Isobel's crew had let islanders handle the dangerous dives. Each day, Valērija concocted new misinformation. After surveying the wreck, she reported that the main hull in that section had cracked, not only in the pierced bit but in the surrounding plates, which was false. Then there was the idea of building a lock in the bay and draining it to create a dry dock. The plan was ridiculous, but it would allow them to dither about for years, so she encouraged it.

The salvors must have seen through her ploy. That's what bothered her. These were not stupid people; they'd made their livelihood out of salvaging wrecks and scrounging what they could. They must know the *Wyvern* was a lost ship. Yet Queen Isobel insisted she be saved, so the work continued. Why the pretense? Valērija couldn't stop wondering what Queen Isobel was playing at.

A male dolphin with a white star on his jaw, Bitsie, nudged her sharply. Valērija knew the signal; her wristband air gauge pointed to yellow. *How the hell do they do that?* Valērija rose to the surface at a safe, steady rate, finding a friendly face waiting. "Ahoy, netter! Give a girl a ride?"

"Climb in," answered Anadare. He helped Valērija onto his trawler and she rewarded him with a big kiss, drawing hoots and whistles from his crew. The couple was used to the catcalls.

"From up here, she doesn't look as bad." Valērija toweled off, looking over the now familiar lines of the ship.

"The portholes on the Esplanade have a bay view from two feet below the surface! Other than that, she's great."

The exchange was as comfortable as the handholding that went with it. Anadare felt a twinge of guilt at how much he enjoyed Valērija's company. He had visited Taryn only twice; they had barely spoken.

That night, Anadare and Valērija had dinner with his family. They were hosting four of Isobel's crewmen under their freshly patched roof. Technically, his family was still being held "hostage," but the term had lost its menace somehow. The salvors did chores and joked with the family.

Throughout the meager meal, Penina paid special attention to a security guard named Beauchamp, prompting glances between Anadare and his mother. Valērija giggled at Penina's audacity and they exchanged looks veiled in girlish code. Anadare's father held court, engaging the family's guests in fiery debates over fishing techniques and the proper way to serve in keffball.

After dinner, Anadare and Valērija made their way to the tent they now called home. Dozens of makeshift shelters comprised the island's newest and most crowded neighborhood. It was primitive; there was a single shower tent for more than two hundred people. Food was scarce. Rustic as it was, however, it was home. Funny how he could feel so rooted after only a few months, or lunas, as Muriel called them.

"This party is insane. You know that," Valērija said after their nightly lovemaking.

"What else would you expect from the queen?" Anadare had delivered his entire catch to the collectors, who now wore white shirts as honorary members of Isobel's crew. Using up all available food for this party was crazy, adding to the strain on the island's resources created by trying to fix the dead hulk in Losi Bay.

Valērija waited a moment before continuing. "Taryn says Isobel has been even more unstable than usual."

That hit him. "You've been talking to Taryn?"

"Yes. She asked about you, netter." That sounded like a lie to Anadare, but he didn't pursue it. "Point is, she's still on our side."

"You're sure? I think she likes Isobel a lot."

"If we're still breathing, I'm sure she's on our side."

"Got you." He agreed, Isobel had exacted no real price from them for scuttling the *Wyvern*.

"Taryn's confused, though. We owe it to her to try and understand. She'll be at the party tomorrow."

The event had been the talk of Gunn Island for weeks. Accompanied by armed salvors, the Latvians brought jams, sweet breads slathered with copious amounts of butter, and numerous chicken dishes. The Chinese provided hot pot, throwing anything available into the spicy boiling water. The people of Anadare's community outdid themselves with fish of all sorts, save octopus, thanks to his sister Penina's insistence. Even the weather cooperated, gracing the gathering with clement breezes.

Anadare decided to check on his boat before joining the festivities. He found several of the dolphins at the dock area, splashing about excitedly. After checking to see that no one was watching, he asked them, "What's going on?" Three smooth heads rose from the water and, in unison, made a bobbing motion for him to follow. They took off. Anadare rushed after them, heading up the pier, along the shore, and around a small bend.

There he spied several men and women in white hoisting a heavily laden canvas sling suspended between two long poles. Their burden was bleeding from one side of her face and crying in a voice that mimicked a human infant. She jerked and convulsed her long gray body—they had used their wasp sticks on her. Anadare doubted he could have survived such brutality. He could do nothing. The humans' leader was Ransom, who was heavily armed.

Anadare followed the group as they carried Muriel through the jungle in the direction of the party. He kept his distance, listening to Isobel's voice coming over loud-speakers mounted in the trees. She was in full regal mode, enchanting the crowd with talk of their "shared victory" and how they had earned a reward.

The salvors carrying Muriel made it to a curtained-off area behind the main stage. Anadare saw the four stretcher-bearers argue with four guards, insisting they get Muriel up the stairs. Reluctantly, the guards set down their guns and their poles tipped with wasp venom and took hold of the animal's makeshift sedan. Careful not to be seen, Anadare slipped closer to the backstage area.

Center stage, Queen Isobel was getting the crowd worked up. Anadare watched it all through a break in the curtains. The stage was set with a large table off to one side, holding hundreds of cups and one gaudy chalice. It was gold-plated with faux gems set all around the rim, plus the goofy face of Okey Dokey on one side. The sal-vors had set up a row of large casks, tapped and ready to pour.

Several people stood upstage. Taryn was next to Maggie. Isobel smiled and nodded to them. She motioned with a hand to her own head, acknowledging that Maggie wore new plaits in her russet hair, no doubt Taryn's work. It was a good look for what was to come.

Some of the islanders and salvors nodded or waved at

the girls on stage. Seeing them together making daily medical rounds had come to mean a moment of kindness or relief in these tense times. It became possible to set aside divisions, if only briefly. They were pretty girls, inside and out. That was enough.

From his hiding place, Anadare looked at the two young women as well. He wanted to call out to Taryn, but didn't dare. Scanning the huge crowd, he noted that many of the people in white had an arm around an islander, whether one of Anadare's community, a futou, Chinese, even a few Latvians. They'd been at sea a long time, but now these invaders were going native. Good. That might help matters. There was one more familiar face: Valērija, standing not far from the front of the stage.

Isobel wove her spell: "We've come through a lot together! Those who've served with me know there's nothing out there on the endless sea. Nothing for us. This is our place now! As much as I want it to be so, the fact is that the *Wyvern* will not sail again."

So, this was her admission, Anadare thought. All the threats and orders aimed at getting that hulk back into service were misdirection. She had wanted to waste their time while she prepared for today. Now what?

"I have decided," Queen Isobel said, "that we will make Gunn Island the final stop on our odyssey. The future for us ends here. And we will celebrate!"

As the applause boomed, Isobel motioned for the crewmen to bring Muriel, in her bloody sling, onto the stage. Her crew heaved the poles up and into four vertical braces. Muriel looked worse than ever. No one had bothered to pour water over her to keep her hydrated. Isobel almost felt pity for the creature—almost.

"This dolphin is confused. She says everything can be wonderful. She lies." Murmurs ran through the crowd as salvors and islanders took in the fact that Isobel acknowledged Muriel as a sentient being.

Isobel nodded to Ransom, who had taken his place on stage. He walked over to the table and took up an ornate carving knife. Loyal Ransom. The right man for this job.

In a flash, Anadare understood that Muriel was the main course. Without thinking, Anadare moved to the poisoned sticks and snatched one. He could have taken a gun, but he'd never actually fired one before. He was, however, proficient with a harpoon.

"No!" The word exploded from Anadare's lips, even as he let fly the wasp stick. All heads turned in his direction, including Ransom's. The salvor grinned ear to ear, raising his long blade while simultaneously dodging Anadare's throw. Ransom laughed at the failed attempt, then tumbled over as Taryn flung herself into the backs of his legs. Anadare did not miss his chance; grasping a second wasp stick, he threw it with all his strength. Guards grabbed Anadare around the arms and waist and shoved him roughly to the stage floor.

Ransom was staring at the lance hanging by its tip from his gut. He pulled it free, spreading a dull red stain onto his clean white uniform. He cried out, but within

seconds could make no coherent sound. The big man doubled over in agony. His silver clasp clanked to the stage,
allowing his hair to spill free. The crowd watched as the
toxins sent mad messages to Ransom's nervous system,
causing him to bite through his own tongue. Ruddy froth
seeped from his mouth as his eyes glared out from a body
he could no longer control.

Shock swept the audience. "Bring him here!" Isobel
commanded, stabbing a finger toward Anadare. The salvors backstage pulled him onto the dais. Others escorted
Taryn over, leaving Maggie in confused silence.

A dozen men and women in white rushed through the
crowd to help Isobel, but most didn't get far. A mix of
islanders and salvors tackled the captain's defenders,
beating them and taking their weapons. More of Isobel's
loyalists raised their guns, but found their fellow salvors
in their sights. The divided crowd looked at each other
and at Isobel, seeking direction. People murmured and
mulled about as a team removed Ransom, jerking and
twitching.

Finally, a salvor dressed in islander linens worked up
the courage and said, "Captain, we remain deeply grateful for your leadership. We ask only that you keep an open
mind. We've been at sea for so long."

One of the uniformed guards in front of the stage
added, "It's time to begin a new life . . . here. Please,
Captain."

Isobel turned off her microphone and set it aside.
Glancing at Taryn and then at the crowd, she summoned

a timbre of voice mastered through years of command. She struggled to find the right modulation, and in a moment recalled an all-too-brief time when she sang lullabies to her only daughter. The leader of the salvors, keeper of their mission and purpose, released this tonal mixture from her heart. "Oh, my dear ones, we face this moment together. I see that most of you would like to enjoy hearth and home. Believe me when I tell you I share your longings.

"In the end, I tell you it makes no difference. Until this moment, I have given you purpose, food and drink, and diversion. Now, know the truth: this is our last happy gathering." Patting the nearest wine cask, she said, "Let me lead you in one final toast together, and let us feast on the flesh of our enemy." A sweep of her arm indicated Muriel.

"We come to the end, my dears. We have sailed far and lived hard and well. It comes to dust. This," Isobel said, raising her hands to the trees and the distant waves, "will not last."

For a moment, Isobel thought of the people in her life, her grandfather, who taught her about the sea; her husband, who was once a lovely man until the drink and lies owned him; her daughter, who could have been so much more; and Taryn, who came into her life late and who would be better off avoiding the pain life held.

"No joy lasts. No island, no city, nor any community we have seen in all our travels has survived. The powers that made us have imposed a harsh judgment . . . and we will bow before it." Like a star closing a play, she lowered her head.

It seemed Isobel's sheer force of will had conquered all objections in the crowd. Then, a cluster of islanders began to scuffle with a group of armed salvors. One got off two quick shots into the air. Someone yelled a deeply personal obscenity and punched the shooter savagely until he dropped his weapon. That someone was a very pleased-with-herself Valērija. She swung about and saw the majority of the crowd was with her. Smiling broadly, Valērija turned to the stage and called to Anadare: "You're up, netter! Make it count!"

He looked to Taryn, who smiled. Not lost on Isobel, Taryn's gesture was not the smile of a girlfriend—just a friend. It was what he needed to see.

There was someone else weighing in. In Anadare's head, he felt her, weak and in pain. "Give us a future, Anadare-mans," she sang in *voce piangevole*.

Anadare shook himself free of the guards, who appeared unsure what to do next. "My friends, listen!" he shouted, his voice cracking with youth and passion. "We have been divided. Now, islanders and salvors are one community. The true enemy is the urge to give up." Anadare pointed at Isobel as if she were a mile away. "If you listen to this woman, she will take you into the darkness. She promised you would live the life you used to have. She promised to rebuild your fantastical ship, so you could sail on until you found some untouched place in the world. That will not happen! Even she admits that

. . . finally. She promised to rebuild Gunn Island into an oasis of food and celebration. That's a false dream as well." Muriel's feelings bloomed in his mind and Anadare felt joy pulsing from her heart to his. "The pain you feel is not from change, but from resisting change. You need not fear the future; embrace it.

"Look around! I'll tell you what I see. I see a new beginning, with families. Yes, I know some of you believe you can never become parents. Our doctors can treat your diseases, which have gone unchecked under Queen Isobel's watch. It's no miracle, no magic trick. It's a matter of hard work and the willingness to accept disappointment as well as joy. If you will consider yourselves members of our community, we can make a life and a home together. With the resources now at hand, Gunn Island can support us all. We can have the future that Queen Isobel cannot see and cannot give you. I promise you, we can have a life!"

So there was the choice: move forward together or embrace communal oblivion. Anadare honestly didn't know which way the crowd would go. Gunn natives would opt for the future, but Isobel's crew was fiercely loyal. If too many of them chose her way, they might convince the rest to drink the potent wine.

Isobel was unfazed. She hissed at Anadare, "I should have cooked you when I had the chance." This boy was not going to steal her crowd. She had one more card to play. In full voice: "You speak of a future because you are young." Isobel then turned to her daughter, checking for a direct response. Her lips parted to release a breath of regret. As Isobel turned back to the crowd, Maggie tilted her head a few degrees, raised her eyes, and looked directly at her mother. Isobel missed the moment, and instead began her final speech.

"We have seen many promises tied to the future. And we have seen *every one* of those promises mocked and ruined. Death is coming; we know this beyond doubt, but we will meet it on our terms. As the poet said, 'The readiness is all.'" She took the chalice and filled it with wine. "So, drink with me and meet death unafraid."

In a final thrust, Anadare said, "Fear cannot win while we keep moving and embrace the struggles of this life. If you would be free, then tell death to wait one more day!"

The speakers looked at each other. They had said all they had to say.

People stirred, but took no step toward the stage and the wine casks. Isobel held out one hand to Taryn, who stood still. Then, one person did move. Maggie, face streaming with tears, ran into Taryn's arms. All eyes were on the two women, now bonded as sisters. The islanders saw a meeting of their two peoples, while the salvors saw a girl they had known only as a mannequin suddenly come to life.

Every person there had seen enormous helpings of death served up with capricious delight. It had drained them. The odds of their long-term survival were terrible. Here was some small hope. It fed a spiritual need, no less than food feeds a starving body. If what Anadare had promised needed proof, Taryn and Maggie's public embrace provided it. Scattered applause grew into a crashing wave of excitement.

"Well," said Isobel, bringing the large goblet to her lips, "I guess I'm drinking alone."

Muriel sang *affannoso* and thrashed wildly in her sling as Isobel downed her wine to the dregs. Taryn and Maggie could only hold each other and sob.

Chapter 14

Valērija sipped a cool drink, watching at a distance as the baptism progressed. There was little ceremony, unlike the religious rites her grandparents had inflicted upon her until she grew old enough to resist. Instead, Taryn led a line of her children (some older than she was) thigh deep into the lagoon pen that had recently held Muriel prisoner. The mesh trap at the gate was gone, as was the young man who had built the prison. No one had seen Sefa in months, and Valērija suspected he had sailed off to take his chances on the open water. She felt guilty for all the mean things she had said to him.

Sefina and Fabia swam freely in and out of the partial enclosure. Norris and a juvenile octopod named Rongomaiwhenua joined in, offering a conduit for the less-sensitive acolytes of this ersatz Church of Recommitment.

As Nurse Burk and the TD patients watched from shore, Taryn took Maggie by the hand and looked her in the eye. These days, Maggie was able to meet her glance a little; it was a slow process, but Taryn was pleased with her sister's focus.

It was time for another session. Two dorsal fins moved

in a tight circle around Taryn and Maggie. Fabia couldn't help but peek up over the water and squeal in excitement. Meanwhile, erubescent limbs coiled up around each of the women's legs and tightened ever so slightly. The tableau froze for a few seconds and then washed away to reveal the smallest of changes: for the first time in her life, Maggie smiled.

"Hey! You've found your calling," said Valērija, coming over and helping the two women out of the lagoon.

"I won't lie—they may never be normal. The diseases damaged them, but interaction with the octopodes and dolphins somehow stimulates a deep level of their minds. They're more alert, more alive than ever."

"You might want to try that on your dad."

"If I can get him sober for five minutes."

"One day at a time." Valērija held Taryn's hand. "You seem happier than I've seen you in a long time. New guy?"

Taryn demurred, "Nope. I'm taking a break, focusing on the work."

Valērija switched subjects to the new tattoo on Taryn's thigh. "When did you get that? Do all of you have them?"

"Just Maggie and me. It's Norris' idea of art. That stupid octopod has the worst sense of style. He didn't even ask—and it hurt! Now, I have my very own octopod portrait! If you want one, I'm sure he'd—"

"No, I'm good. Already have my blue finger," she said, wagging the digit in front of her. They laughed. "Complete change of subject: come to dinner tonight?"

"Oh, I really . . ."

"Anadare gets back in the late afternoon. We'll see you at seven."

She wanted to get things ready for the dinner, but first she had a drive to make. The last of the freed detainees were loaded on to a caravan. They were headed to various destinations around the island. Valērija was there to see two of them back home.

Māris sat up front with her. She pressed him about his plans, but he said nothing. "My parents will help you find a place," she told him.

"No! I can't face your mother." His eyes welled up with tears and his face turned tense. He looked like a child terrified of monsters. She realized Māris saw himself as the monster, still alive while her uncles were dead.

"You could take one of the salvors' boats and fish."

"I don't fit there anymore, Taryn. I don't fit anywhere. You can't understand."

"I think I do. Look, the Justice and Reconciliation Council made its ruling. What's left of Ransom will live on Hell's Reach, along with his inner circle. The other salvors have a new chance. That includes you and Kuan." She looked over at the silent man next to them.

The caravan pulled into Chinatown. Pickers were busy making their rounds on bicycle, finding useful scraps from the refuse piles that rose between the homes. Māris and Valērija climbed out of the carriage. A number of salvors followed them, including Kuan, who stood shifting his weight from one foot to the other.

A short way off, two women stood. One of them held a baby. The other, an elderly woman, was crying. Kuan lowered his eyes to the sand.

"The Lord don't like cowards," said Fanchon, stepping out of the caravan. "This homecoming maybe won't be so sweet."

Valērija leaned in, threatening him, "One more word and I'll personally put your ass on the next boat to Hell's Reach."

"Water, water." Fanchon blew out a chuckle of sorts and started to walk away. "People didn't like me when I worked for the commissioner," he said to no one in particular. "People didn't like me when I worked for the captain. Maybe the Chinese will appreciate a man who carries his loyalty wherever he goes."

He stopped in his tracks and looked back. Kuan had not budged.

Fanchon shook his head. *Merde!* He quick-stepped back, took Kuan by the arm, and manhandled him over to the two women. He spoke without introduction or preamble. "Madame Zhang, your boy is home. He's done some bad things, but no one's gonna talk about that no more. Have a happy life." The family said nothing. Fanchon sauntered off, leering at the pretty women around him. "Time to put some cream in my coffee."

It took some moments for Kuan to speak, and then he said only one word: "Mama." Tears pooled in the rimples of the woman's face as she wrapped frail arms around her son. Kuan's sister joined in the embrace, shifting Duo Duo from one arm to the other.

Valērija realized she was staring . . . and misting up. She turned to Māris. "Your turn, *mans draugs.*"

What the meal lacked in calories, it made up for in camaraderie. It would be months before they saw chicken or pork again. That hope only existed because some families had risked their lives by hiding breeding stock before the animals became part of Isobel's spectral buffet. Sitting in the tent in the intimate light of a few lumens strips, Anadare, Valērija, and Taryn let the conversation flow. They talked about how families were supplementing their paltry fish diet by eating snakes or bugs; aficionados added island chilies.

The friends traded stories of how each spent their days. Taryn said, "The dolphins and I are teaching the children how to swim."

Valērija said, "I hope the children don't try to ride a dolphin the way a certain netter does."

"Ha! If I were any better, I'd *be* a dolphin." When they finished laughing at him, Anadare told them he and his crew planned to open trade with the salvors on Hell's Reach. The tiny bullet produced rare medicinal plants.

The islanders had stripped the weapons from the salvors' fleet and begun using the craft to improve their scant fishing catch. Next, they had to work out a plan to share the material wealth coming off of the *Wyvern*. Between plumbing, electronics, housing supplies, and the surviving pigs and chickens, the ship was a veritable horn of plenty. There was, at present, no distribution system in place; the Exchange was a jumble of marble chunks. Anadare vowed that whatever system they established, it would not play to people's worst instincts of greed and desperation.

Valērija took that as a cue to make her announcement. "The newly elected Senate has decided to use a couple of the salvor ships to resume exploration. They've renamed one of them the *Gints*. We're making it ready for a trip far to the west, to Japan or even the South China coast. We've never gone that route before."

"We?" Anadare asked tentatively.

"I meant to tell you first, Anadare, but it's just as well you're both here. I'm going on that expedition," Valērija said.

Taryn and Anadare exchanged a look. "Well . . . maybe I could go, too," he ventured.

"No, netter. You need to stay here. You're our best fishing captain. Plus, you have a future in the Senate." He had become an ancillary member.

"Th'fuh? I don't want to do that . . . alone," he said. This led to an awkward pause. All three knew Anadare and Taryn had made their individual choices. As for Valērija . . .

"I'm not ready to grow roots. I need to be part of something bigger. Anadare, when you talked about families, people listened. I swear, half the women I know are knocked up, so . . . good work! That means more mouths to feed. We need a world, not just a tiny island." Then: "Don't worry. You won't be alone for long. I see those little netter girls following you around the docks."

This made Taryn crinkle her nose in a genuine show of good humor. "Of course, you've already dated the two prettiest women on the island."

"It's all downhill for me now," Anadare said, holding his bracelet so the gold lioness played near to his new silver dolphin earring. Along with Dakuwaqa, these made him a living array of animal wisdom and strength. The young women exchanged compliments on the jewelry and sternly warned him to never remove them.

"The main thing," Valērija continued, "is that you have to stay here where Muriel can tap into you for her array."

"You've seen Muriel?" he asked excitedly.

"From a distance." Her voice dropped. "She doesn't look well."

"Can't the rest of her pod help?" Taryn wanted to know.

"She's become a loner," Valērija said. "We've tried to get her back to the pen to feed her, but she won't come."

Anadare asked, "What do you mean she wants to tap into me?" ("Big pattern. You." Oh.)

"I've pieced together what I can from our old conversations and from what little the other dolphins can tell me. They don't understand much either." Valērija took a sip. "Muriel is ready to try her array. Anadare, you're a big part of that now, especially since Muriel lost Isobel and some other special contacts in the war. That's why she tried so hard to keep us from killing each other. She needs enough powerful minds linked together to maximize the array's range and focus. She's weak, thanks to the salvors' poison. Her plan isn't perfect, but she feels she'll never get a better chance."

Taryn asked the obvious question. "So, what is this array of hers? What does it do?"

"It's a way to send a message. If she's lucky, she'll send her whole consciousness," Valērija said.

"Where?" the others asked together.

"Not where. *When*."

Taryn was incredulous. "You're saying our buddies are not just psychic cetaceans, but time travelers as well? Yuh. I can see that."

"I know it sounds like pig kūkā," Valērija said. "Maybe it is pig kūkā, but Muriel believes it. She's the only one who can do it, if she's strong enough. Without enough people, her network won't give her control over where or when she'll show up in the past. Regardless, it's a one-way trip. She hopes to communicate with someone *before* the Fall, but close to those events so humans can grasp the danger."

"Isobel believed we're already finished as a race." Taryn looked at her hands.

"I know you liked the captain, but I'd rather trust Muriel's vision," Anadare said.

"Even if Muriel can go back," Taryn said, "I don't see how a dolphin is going to convince arrogant humans who are dead set on doing something stupid."

Anadare said, "Only two things can happen: one, the person she talks to ignores her; two, the person starts preaching about talking to dolphins and gets locked up."

Taryn added, "Maybe she could found a cult of nature lovers."

Valērija responded, "People would screw it up like all the other religions, make it about themselves. Details fuzzy? Polish 'til you see your own reflection."

"People love magic and flattery," Taryn agreed.

Valērija shrugged. "I believe Muriel's planning to make her attempt soon."

"Will we even know if she succeeds in changing the past?" Anadare wondered.

"I can't answer that," Valērija offered, "but I think those of us she's touched will know when she makes her attempt."

Taryn raised her glass, prompting the others to do the same. "Well then, to the past, the present, and the future, whatever it may bring!" The three friends drank their toast together.

The next spring, Valērija set off in search of green lands to the west and Taryn committed herself to her medical studies. Anadare threw himself into his work in the Senate. They had to build a proper school for all of the children, they needed to build up the fishing fleet, and he had to gather support for a constitutional review to narrow the gap between islanders and futous. Anadare pressed himself hard. He barely made it back to his tent to rest. The effort took its toll. One night, utterly spent, he fell into a deep sleep and had a vivid dream.

Anadare stood on a beach, watching the orange sun quaver and plunge through a line of clouds on the horizon, striking the Earth with an emerald flash like a beat from the green heart of all life. Among the distant waves, he could see a grinning gray face looking back at him with fiercely intelligent eyes. "Hello, my friend." As he watched, her features subtly altered, becoming indistinct, causing him to blink involuntarily. Then, she slipped under the waves.

The air felt more temperate than on his island, while the breeze gently reassured him it held no thought of storms. The cries of seabirds punctuated the susurration of the waves. One more sound broke in the distance along the bend: a ragged rush of noise from two lines of lights, white in one direction, red going the other way. Up the shoreline, he became aware of a beacon tower, its twin beams reaching for opposite infinities on a slow circuit of the world. Then, as if they had just appeared, he registered an unbroken row of tall buildings, hotels, painted in muted pinks, greens, and blues. The lower rooms' lights were off. A few guests were out on their balconies, speaking softly and drinking fiesta-colored liquor. He saw one young couple, barely dressed in bathing attire, point to a spot near where he stood. He followed the line they indicated to see something as foreign to his life experience as the rest of this vision: a huge green loggerhead turtle.

She was brushing back wet sand to cover a clutch of eggs. She was exhausted, having just laid her life's prize and safely buried it away from greedy seabirds. The turtle's lids languorously swept the sand from her eyes. He wanted to help her with her chore, but it was not his place. By now, the sun had passed the horizon, leaving the new mother to finish her work in the eventide and return to the ocean.

It was a moment apart from all others. This hour did not belong to Anadare; somehow he was allowed to stand inside a living echo surrounded by waning shadows. He wanted to shout to the ghosts around him, though that was against the rules. He ached to tell them, to warn them: you still have a chance to push back against the endless empty night. He wanted so very much for these strangers to cherish the fragile gift they had, so they might keep it just a little longer.

III

A Clear Call That May
Not Be Denied

Chapter 15

Joy as delicious as fish. "Yom," sang her life. Terror drifted away as the Great returned her to the world of time and sensation. Salty water flowed over her skin, sunlight stippling its surface. A group of dolphins reached out in song. All of life could be discovered anew in this moment. It was perfect. Almost.

Something troubled her, a missing thought. It had been there in her mind before . . . before . . . Now, she felt a needling absence. There were slivers of comprehension, as if someone had taken a lovely view of a thriving coral reef and shattered it into bits. The image was not a coral, or anything she had actually seen. That was the problem. Somehow, she had emerged from the Great with an idea, based on images and knowledge that lacked scale or reference.

The plan. The plan? Must. Here now, she thought.

"Hi. Who's here? I like your song about fish." The second voice sang "yom," adding her own distinct melody. She glanced around and discovered that she was in a brightly lit tank several body lengths in diameter. Along part of the perimeter, a window looked outward to a darkened area. A sliding partition hinted at an adjoining enclosure, but that part of the pool was shut off for now. She could see no other dolphins; she was alone. No, not quite. On the bottom of the tank sat a large, clear vessel containing a mottled brown mass from which one eye tracked her every movement: an octopod. The voice did not originate from the octopod; the mollusk was characteristically standoffish. In fact, the voice did not arrive via any of her senses, but rather was there within her.

"Myeruhl." She tried again: "Merr-aye-ll."

"Merle." A giggle that emitted from her, but not her giggle. "Welcome. I'm Gabby. Merle, why are you in my head?"

"They're Atlantic *Tursiops truncatus.* These four are from the same purchase"—the young tech stopped himself as the smartly dressed woman from the head office cleared her throat—"acquisition last month from . . . the dealers. The director says we'll keep one female and one male here at Mystic and sell—*share* the others with Ocean Park once we work out the details."

"I see we've segregated the one you called 'creepy,'" Dr. April Findley observed, moving past the technician (his badge said Stoeffler or Stiffle or something) to the edge of the holding pool. Three dolphins swam in a circle on one side of the partition, while one swam alone.

"The pinkish one with the eyes, yes," interjected Kitty Kaplan, a stout redhead with lacey hair ribbons. Findley performed an up-and-down visual review of the girl's loose sweatshirt and overstuffed mini-skirt-and-fishnet combo, making a mental note to issue a dress code for interns. "She and the octopus there are buddies. We've tried to remove it, but octopuses are great escape artists, you know, and it keeps showing up in her tank. So, now we leave them together."

Findley ignored the dark lump on the bottom of the pool. She focused on the dolphin whose head bobbed on the surface. Its eyes met hers. Findley took a step to one side. The dolphin's gaze moved with her. Dolphins loved to make eye contact for a second or two; she'd never seen one focus like this. Findley pulled a thin gold case and a lighter from her jacket pocket and lit up. As she did, the dolphin dipped its rostrum below the waterline, then rose a few inches and squirted a stream of pool water at the burning cigarette. Findley dodged the salvo, then reconsidered and held the cigarette at arm's length. A perfectly aimed gush of salty water put it out. "Bad for my health, eh?"

Hughes, a mop-haired teen, joining the trio by the pool, pushing a cart laden with pails of cod and mackerel. "Who's hungry?" he called playfully to the dolphins.

Findley's pocket beeper sounded; the brass wanted an update. To Hughes, she said, "Keep a close watch on these animals," and to the interns: "You two, do whatever it is you do." Casting her half-finished smoke into a pail of fish, Findley headed off. Her bosses were always looking for unusual opportunities. This was her chance to bring them something valuable.

"More fish!" Gabby called out excitedly as two young mans pushed a food cart toward the pool. The partition was open and the other dolphins circled close to the mans, steering well clear of Gabby. They did not usually play such cruel games. Ever since Merle had shown up, the others avoided Gabby as if she had ick.

"Need to tell the mans."

"Tell them what, Merle?"

"Not Merle! Tell. Warn." She tried to call to each of the mans, but she felt weak, as if she were losing herself. She let Gabby do most of the communicating with the rest of the dolphins. That was not going well, either. They should know already. Why didn't they know? It should be in—they should know. In—dolphins should know. Transmemory. The Great. Why didn't it work? Why didn't the dolphins know?

Muriel squeezed their stomach and clenched their jaw tightly, as if using the muscles would help focus their shared brain. Nothing happened.

"There you go again, Merle. What are you trying to do?" Gabby asked.

"Not sure," Muriel responded. "I touched the Great, but there is no change in transmemory."

"I have a great memory. I know all the best places to find fish."

"Failure. Must reach out to the dolphins and the mans. The TransPacific is in danger!"

"You mean the Pacific Ocean?"

"Yes. Danger."

Gabby tittered, "How can a whole ocean be in danger? That's silly. Besides, that's a long way from here."

"We have to get there. If I explain to the others, they could begin now. They could—"

"Whoa! You want to take a trip around the world? My aching peduncle!" Gabby sensed the rising panic in her new melon-mate. She added, "I have family down south who might be able to help you. What is this big message you have to tell?"

"I can't say it," Muriel said. "I know it, but it's locked inside, in a place I can't quite reach."

"Oh, let me try!" Gabby began rummaging around in their shared inner bits. She saw herself now as a cute little Gabby, poking and probing around in a much larger Gabby-shaped ocean. Perceiving her circumstances this way, Gabby could discern Muriel as a vague, separate shape, one that chased her about this continuum of thought in a vain attempt to rein her in. Silly. Delighting at the new possibilities, Gabby flung her mental self through imaginary currents and corals. Ah, there was a shiny shell that begged for attention. With little effort, real Gabby directed tiny Gabby to the desired object. Got it!

Like a balloon popping, the three young mans around

the pool collapsed. The one who was taking notes dropped his clipboard and crumpled to the deck. The light-haired one nearly fell into the pool. The redheaded female mans fell into the cart, pulling several buckets of fish on top of herself.

Chapter 16

"See the sawfish! Isn't he scary?" Lisa asked her handsome young beau as they viewed the captive ocean life.

Transfixed by both the fish and the girl, Quinn responded, "The sawfish is scary. You don't want to swim with the sawfish." JD watched his little brother communicate, in his own limited way, with JD's pretty blonde girlfriend. Quinn had a tendency to flirt with his hazel eyes, the way an infant does without knowing he was doing it. That endearing look shifted without warning as Quinn clutched his fists and grimaced as if in pain or laughing silently. Then, just as suddenly, a smile reappeared on his face. It was what he did when he was excited. The doctors called it "stimming."

"The sawfish looks like a hedge trimmer," JD joked, trying to regain Lisa's attention. "I could plug him into an electric eel and cut Mom's shrubs." He struck a roguish pose Lisa usually liked, flashing his blue eyes and shaking out his dark spaghetti-in-a-blender hair. Quinn and Lisa did not laugh or even respond; they were on to other fish.

They strolled, JD trailing, past the windows of the enormous tank, which threw a rich blue cast over the crowd. Inches away, a toothy barracuda slipped over the strange migratory eyes of a flounder, while sharks and rays patrolled in their ceaseless hunt.

They circled the main tank twice before JD suggested they hit the snack bar. A waiter came over with a tray of frozen sugary treats.

"Jimmies, please! Jimmies! Jimmies!" cried Quinn.

"Chocolate-covered ants," Lisa teased.

"Ants! You don't want to eat ants. Jimmies!"

JD thought about the two lonely dollars in his wallet. He thanked Lisa again for treating them all to ice cream. She had also paid for the tickets.

JD was grateful he didn't have to disappoint his little brother. Otherwise, they'd have heard Quinn chatter about jimmies the entire forty miles from Mystic, Connecticut, back home to East Greenwich, Rhode Island.

Last summer, JD had made the mistake of complaining in front of Quinn when their mother refused to let them see *Poltergeist*. She insisted the film was too scary for Quinn. JD really wanted to see the film, and nearly yelled "Jesus Christ!" at her refusal. Instead, he caught himself, and said "Jeepers Crow!" That's all it took. Quinn said nothing but "Jeepers Crow!" for a solid week. "Jeepers Crow!" at the market. "Jeepers Crow!" on the bus. "Jeepers Crow!" at church. Finally, they figured out it had to do with the decision to not see the film. Their mom relented. It turned out they enjoyed the movie, but jeez!

Quinn went to work on his bowl of ice cream with jimmies on top. JD and Lisa shared a thick chocolate cabinet, two straws standing straight up in the semifrozen sugar cloud. JD had to lean across the table to share the drink with his girlfriend; Quinn had wedged himself in next to her in the booth.

"I was thinking, after we get back, you and I could take a drive out to Beavertail. Some guys from my poly-sci class are gonna build a bonfire tonight."

"Can't make it tonight. Sorry," Lisa said even before he'd finished.

He tried: "I know how to get into the lighthouse."

"You said that last time," Lisa said. "We were outside on the cold beach until three a.m. I came home with sand everywhere." She raised her perfect golden eyebrows. "Everywhere."

"Is that bad?" JD tried to take her hand, but she pulled it away.

Quinn began grimacing again. The doctor said stimming was normal. JD thought it made Quinn look mental. The time he tried to get Quinn to stop making that face, Quinn broke into a burst of squealing, like noises Shemp from the Three Stooges would make. Then he cried. There was no winning. This time, the hand-waving and stressed facial expression lasted so long, JD was sure everyone in the snack bar was looking at them.

"We go to see the dolphin!" Quinn finally cried out. Loudly.

"Shhhh. We saw the fish. We saw the big tank. They

closed the dolphin exhibit to let them rest or something," JD said.

"We go see the dolphin!" This time, Quinn screamed it, and several customers looked over with concern.

"Okay, buddy. We'll go," Lisa promised, rubbing Quinn's shoulders. "JD, you have to take him."

"Fine. Where?"

"The pools are roped off, but the lower viewing area is over there," she said pointing to a set of doors across the lobby.

"You're not coming?"

"I have a phone call to make. I'll meet you back at the car."

He wanted to protest, but his little brother was already out of the booth and yanking him by the arm toward the doors. A sign read, "No Guests beyond This Point," but the doors were not locked. Checking to see no one was watching, JD led them inside.

They walked down a dimly lit corridor with a wet floor that smelled like low tide. It led to an open area with two sizeable tanks, separated by a partition. Sunlight filtered down from the surface of the water. Climbing up a cat-walk along the front of the tanks, JD and Quinn could see one pool held three dolphins, who circled the narrow perimeter of their domain. The other tank held only one dolphin, who slowed and came toward them.

"Okay, Quinn, look at these dolphins," JD said, directing his brother toward the crowded tank.

"No! See the dolphin!" Quinn knelt by the side of the

tank containing the solitary animal. JD decided he'd give Quinn two minutes to stare at the dumb fish, then haul his brother, probably kicking and screaming, out of the restricted area.

Quinn looked intensely at the dolphin. It looked back, bobbing its head (well, its forward half), as if the creature and his brother were speaking to each other. A grimace appeared on Quinn's face, then he began mouthing something. After a moment, JD asked jokingly, "What are you two talking about?"

"Not-Merle. We go to the beach. Save mans."

An electric bug crawled through JD's stomach. Quinn typically repeated one or two phrases, occasionally turning something into a question. He rarely came up with anything new. These words had come from . . . somewhere.

"We go to the beach. Take Not-Merle. Save mans," Quinn said again, never breaking eye contact with the dolphin.

As JD bent down to take his brother's hand, noise filled the chamber: agitated voices and the sound of boots running across the wet floor and up the metal steps. Two uniformed men hurried onto the catwalk, one yelling into a radio, the second yelling directly at them.

"We go to the beach. Save mans. Not-Merle save mans," Quinn repeated. The guards looked at each other.

Strong hands led JD and Quinn out a side exit of the Mystic Aquarium, into the dazzling sunlight. The guards demanded their names and address. JD was trying to apologize, saying (lying) that he didn't realize they weren't allowed in that room and that his brother just wanted to see the dolphins.

A woman in a dark suit joined them. With acrid cigarette breath, she said, "It's okay, sir." Sir? She pressed a bundle of passes into JD's hands, then added, "We hope you'll come back once the quarantine is over," she continued. "You understand, we have to do what's best for the animals as well as our guests. Please drive safely." The woman led the guards away.

JD stood dumbly for a moment before it struck him: they were not in trouble.

JD drove his mom's mildew-colored Ford LTD station wagon north on I-95. Lisa sat in the back with Quinn, leaving JD to act as chauffeur. She barely spoke. Quinn smiled and giggled, but said nothing.

Watching them in the rearview, JD finally asked, "What are you laughing at?" Quinn did not reply, but continued to giggle. "Quit it." Quinn put his hands over his mouth and giggled harder. "Quit it!"

"It's okay," Lisa said, rubbing Quinn's shoulder. "Something's funny."

"Nothing's funny. He just does that. He looks . . ." JD trailed off. He wasn't going to use the r-word.

Lisa glared at JD then looked out the window. What? He hadn't said anything mean. God, she was confusing!

For miles they listened to the Eurythmics, Men Without Hats, Prince, and Dexys Midnight Runners on the radio. JD dropped off Lisa at her green ranch-style home off Middle

Road. She gave Quinn a quick kiss then walked off in her Daisy Dukes. JD tried to make eye contact, but he saw only the sweep of all that lovely blonde hair flowing down her back.

"Lisa is fun," said Quinn, five minutes later on the trip home.

JD drove, but said nothing.

The octopod kept one sideways-canted eye on its roommate while surreptitiously snatching morsels of food, living and otherwise, from its immediate area.

"How are you doing?" Gabby asked the soundless cephalopod, but got no answer. Then, to Muriel: "And he's supposed to help?"

"His kind possess an innate ability. I'll work with him on his technique. We'll need his help dealing with the mans."

"Why do mans matter?" Gabby tittered, not really interested in the answer. She went back to singing country western music.

"They just do," Muriel obliged.

"Well, we won't be getting any more mans visitors, thanks to you. You tried to contact the fish givers. They fell down."

"That was your fault. I was trying to contact them, but you were running around out of control—"

"It's *my* head!"

"—and I accidentally pinged them too hard. You can't do that with mans. I managed to give the young female mans a suggestion, but that's all. The little male mans, the one who came to visit, is different. He can hear me, I'm sure of it."

"Are you still trying him?" she asked, simultaneously starting a musical refrain involving loneliness, a cowmans place known as a honky-tonk, and beer.

"He's too far. Very foggy. I might be able to send some images." She huffed, "Your singing is not helping. You sound like a dying porpoise."

"Critic."

Hospital rooms were all the same. Kitty hated the pistachio walls. It was the same color as the hospital room they had stuck her in for a month (three days really, but it seemed like a month) when she broke her leg as a kid. The smell of the room was the same, too. The nonstop noises of bells and commotion on the other side of the door was the same.

One thing was different: this time she knew her roommate, Hughes from the aquarium. He was unconscious. That worried her.

Another nurse came in. That made five or six. Someone said the aquarium was footing the bill, so that was okay, but still, how many nurses did she need?

"The scans are fine," said nurse six in a bright, sunny voice. "Your appetite is good. No more headache?"

"No." Fortunately, Kitty woke this morning with a clear head. She didn't mention the vivid dream. If she told the doctors, they'd never let her leave.

"You should be able to go home this afternoon. Your father is coming to pick you up."

"Great!" Kitty hated to pull her dad away from work, but it was always nice to see him. Then, looking over to the next bed, she asked, "What about him?"

"We sedated him. He was a little more shaken up than you, but he should be out of here by tomorrow." The nurse busied herself with both sets of charts.

The door to the room opened. Three people stepped in, Findley and two other corporate types. "Hi. How are you doing?"

"I'm busting outta this joint this afternoon."

Findley moved closer. "Good, good. We're still trying to learn exactly what happened. We've put the dolphin in isolation."

"It wasn't her fault. I'm sure she didn't mean to hurt us."

"We think you're right. We just want to know what happened. We think you and that dolphin have some kind of special connection. It's tried to contact others as well."

This was news to Kitty. "Are they all right?" she asked.

"They're fine. Fine. In fact, we're trying to do a follow-up on two of them, an autistic boy and his brother. It turns out the brother is a classmate of yours at URI. We thought you might be able to help us with them, let us know what they're up to . . ." She added with a smile, "For extra credit on your internship."

Their mom was a pink blur in her RN scrubs. JD hated to see her working third shift at the elderly group home; she tended old drunks whose families didn't want them.

"What if I got a job?" he pleaded with her.

"We've been through this a thousand times." Looking around, she sighed, "Dammit all! James Donovan Brennan, where did you leave my keys this time?"

"Top of the fridge."

"I looked there." Carol Brennan reached up and found them farther back than she had expected. "Jeez." She checked through her purse and noticed her flip-top box of Saratoga 120s was crumpled, as though it had been pawed by an ape—an ape who didn't like her smoking. No time for that argument now, just a quick wince and sigh. To the culprit: "Look, I wish your dad's job brought in enough, but they're charging him for his housing now. Plus, everything in California costs double. I don't even know why he . . . Point is, money's tight. Quinn's school costs a bundle."

"It's not helping." JD regretted it the second it came out.

"It is, a little. I know, you could sell your car. You always drive mine anyway. You never put any gas in my tank."

"I put in two gallons. From now on, I'll drive my Chevelle. I just have to put in the new brake pads. Tomorrow!"

"Let Quinn help. He enjoys it. And paint that rust bucket while you're at it."

"It's not rust; it's primer." He almost said, *I'll paint it in metallic flakes suspended in a candy apple–red enamel like a carnival rocket ride. It'll be awesome!*

His mother's voice jammed the joystick forward, bringing his daydream rocket in for a hard landing. "That car is the color of an old bandage." She hurried to the door, narrowly missing JD's friend who breezed in and past her.

"Hello, Mrs. Brennan," Dom said, turning on an ingratiating smile that went with the sharp leather coat and twenty-dollar hairstyle.

"No!" she told them.

"No?" JD and Dom asked together.

"The beer in your trunk, Dom," she said.

"You and my nonna Theresa have that same second sight. It's scary," Dom said.

Mrs. Brennan shot Dom a look, but spoke to her own son. "You're watching your brother, JD, not sitting around getting stink-faced."

"It's just beer! For the love of—I can't go out," JD tried.

"And you can't drink. Quinn needs you." She motioned to his brother; JD hadn't even noticed Quinn come into the room, he was so quiet. "He's been having nightmares. So, no sneaking off to Newport."

"What? I don't—"

"If you don't want to get caught drinking at Newport Jai Alai, maybe you shouldn't keep the souvenir chula glass in your room." A chula was both a wicked shot that was impossible to catch as well as the name of a wicked strong drink.

"You went in my room?!"

"The repairman had to fix the wall." She glanced at the scabs on the knuckles of JD's left hand, prompting him to swing it behind his back. Yet another argument she didn't have time for. "I'll call later to make sure you're okay. Gotta go!" An air kiss later, she was in the station wagon and driving off.

Dom planted himself on the couch, picked up the remote, and found MTV on the set. It was the video about a long-haired Brit who wouldn't pay for a ferry ride to hell. Lots of fog and cheesy lighting.

"Thanks a lot," JD said.

Quinn grabbed JD's arm hard and hugged his brother. JD had to shift to keep from losing his balance. "Dolphins like mackerel. Porpoises are stupid," Quinn said.

Chapter 17

Quinn told himself he was having a dream, though it seemed an odd thing to be aware of. Still, it was a fun dream. He was back at Mystic Aquarium. This time, JD and Lisa were not there. Lisa was so pretty, it made Quinn feel funny-good inside, but anyway, she was not there. Quinn was alone in the viewing room, staring at the one dolphin in its own pool. Except, that one dolphin was really two dolphins in one. He knew that because it was arguing with itself in two voices. Both sounded female and musical, but each had a different tone. One was urgent, frustrated, and a little confused; the other giggled at everything.

The first voice said, "My name is not Merle. You're thinking of Merle Haggard."

"Stop picking through my memory, unless you want to share, too. Yes, I heard fishing-mans play Merle Haggard on the radio. I've never seen a radio. How odd. You put that word in me. Neat trick. Anyway, I like fishing music. And sad songs about hope." Gabby began to sing, her voice taking on a dark, smoky timbre. In her unique manner, she used her clicks and perfect high tones to convey the loneliness of a life on the road, mixing in dimly lit roadhouses, late hours, and beer. "Sad, but good."

"Fine. Merle is good. I'm not Merle. I'm Morrell . . . Myrtle . . . something, but not Merle!"

The bickering petered out. They began to address Quinn directly. "I'm Gabby. Merle popped in my head without asking," part of the dolphin's thoughts said. He tagged one of the speakers as Gabby. Flighty, happy.

"Not-Merle!" the other said. Oh so serious.

"Now she wants to get in your head. She's kind of rude," Gabby told Quinn. It was then that Quinn realized two things: they were speaking directly to him, and it was easy to speak with these two. When he spoke with JD or his mom, he could barely make the words do what he wanted. Other thoughts and noises jumped in the way and he pulled back inside himself.

"Why did you pick me?" Quinn asked.

Muriel took full control of the talking dolphin. "I have to show you." There was no transition; Quinn was abruptly inside the tank with the two-in-one dolphin. Oddly, he was not afraid of drowning. The water felt fine and he could breathe normally somehow. "I have given you my part of the story. I need you to come back here and take me . . . take all of us . . . to the beach." The dolphin indicated an octopod in a jar on the floor of the pool. The boy thought "octopod" was a strange way to say "octopus."

"How do I do that?" he asked.

"Find a way. I will tell you more later. I am having

trouble remembering all the details. Trust me. I need you. I need to help you."

"I don't understand. You need to help me? Why do I need help?" Quinn asked, enjoying how smoothly his words came out in this dream.

"I want to tell you more, but I can't focus," said Muriel.

"Try," he urged them.

"Not-Merle has a lot in her memory. Sometimes she shares, sometimes not." This was Gabby chiming in, in her corny country-music voice. She sounded like the big-bosomed lady who sang about working nine to five. "Not-Merle doesn't like it, but I can help her share. Like this!"

Not-Merle cried, "No!" It was too late. Quinn felt fire in his head; he screamed in his dream and screamed in his bed back in his bedroom. He woke up screaming.

Someone was blasting Duran Duran, the rhythms of its Roland TR-808 drum machine thrumming through the young pelvises of dozens of party guests. Lisa loved "Hungry Like the Wolf." Lisa wasn't there. Lisa wouldn't answer her phone. JD wished painful death on both Durans.

"When did you call these people?" JD demanded.

"You peed," Dom answered, taking a swig of beer.

"I don't know half of them. Ma doesn't let me have parties."

"You are not having this party, I am. And this is a moving

musical festival that happens to be in your house right now. See?" Dom was pleased with his own cleverness.

"I'm gonna ask my mom to kill you in front of my eyes before she kills me. Take these people back to your dorm."

"Can't. It's still wet."

"Crap! Really?" JD said, dodging a couple that was dancing and swapping spit at the same time. "I told you it was stupid to put a hot tub in your living room."

"It was working fine. Sally and I were sharing a dip, then my roommate walked in, took off his clothes, and climbed in. He has the smallest wiener in the State of Rhode Island and Providence Plantations. Sally laughed her ass off. Anyway, that's when the drain pipe split off and it flooded the room. The RA is pissed."

"I don't care. Just get these people—"

"Are you JD?" someone interrupted. It was a chunky redheaded girl trying to pull off the Madonna look.

"Yes," JD answered.

"You'd better come see your brother," the girl urged.

JD and the girl rushed into Quinn's bedroom with Dom close behind. JD found Quinn sitting up in a knot of sheets, his knees pulled tightly to his chest. He had stopped screaming, but was still visibly upset.

"What's wrong, Buddy?" JD asked.

"The beach is on the ocean," Quinn said, his eyes fixed on something a mile away. JD was used to Quinn's non sequiturs. This time, though, there was something about the way his brother said it. "The beach is on the ocean. Not-Merle has to go to the beach."

JD and the redheaded girl exchanged a look. "Who's Not-Merle?" she asked.

"He's mentioned him before, but I don't know," JD told the redhead. Who was the redhead?

"Huh?" Dom struggled to follow what was going on. Outside the bedroom, someone switched the music to an old AC/DC album, whining that JD didn't have it on compact disc.

"He was screaming in his sleep, then talking. He kept saying 'transmemory, transmemory goes one way, transmemory goes forward only.' I have no idea what that means, but it's very unusual," the girl said. As if to answer a question JD and Dom wanted to ask, she added, "I'm pre-psych."

"You're psychic?" Dom asked.

"No, genius. I'm pre-psych," she repeated. "I'm studying psychology at URI. I'm also pre-law. Daddy doesn't care, as long as I get a degree before I get a baby." She noticed JD's open-mouthed expression. "I'm Leah Kaplan. People call me Kitty. Your brother—"

"Quinn."

"That's no nightmare Quinn's having." The way she said it seemed both earnest and far too maternal for someone dressed for a disco. "You need to listen to him. There's something he needs you to do."

"You see, if we do . . . *this* . . . the little dots get brighter." Gabby was enjoying this.

"I don't want to make the little dots get brighter," Muriel told her. She had finally remembered her name, but had yet to get Gabby to acknowledge it. Muriel did not like being poked and prodded, and had no interest in playing games.

"But it's fun, Merle. Give it a try."

"*Muriel!* It's what the mans want us to do, and I don't like these mans. I wish they'd take these metal wires out of our head and release us from this stupid harness."

Three of the mans, including the female mans who was always there, were working at the box of bright lights and dancing pointers. They wore big metal helmets, presumably to keep Muriel/Gabby from making contact. They clearly didn't understand that the helmets were not what was blocking the dolphins; these mans' puny brains simply did not receive them as well as some others did.

"I don't trust the female mans. She reminds me of seaweed that's shriveled in the sun, and I don't like the way she looks at us," Muriel said.

"They give us lots of fish. Look, she's bringing us a new toy."

The female mans took a burning twig from her mouth and threw it to the floor without looking. She walked over to a pair of doors, which slid open and led into a tiny room. (Muriel: "It's called an elevator." Gabby: "How do you know?" Muriel: "You'll see.") The female mans walked in, and the doors closed behind her. A moment later, she stood above them, her image rippling through the pool's surface. She was carrying a telescoping silver pole, with a long pointy part attached to one end, much longer than the pins already sticking into them. A curly cord trailed off the new thingie.

The female mans was speaking mans talk. Muriel could grasp it and passed the gist along to Gabby: "I hope that rig is on tight. This is gonna hurt."

The Chevelle noisily rolled down Route 138, along Upper College Road, and onto the understated campus of the University of Rhode Island, JD's safety school. Students called URI "You Are High." It was only twenty minutes from home; that and the familiar faces made JD feel as if he'd never left high school. Bright-eyed seekers on the cusp of life wandered in and out of stonework halls rendered on a budget. Future nurses, dentists, and accountants crossed the grassy quad past a rusted cannon from some forgotten war.

"It goes off every time a virgin graduates," Kitty joked.

Quinn grew restless in the back seat. "Not-Merle needs to go to the beach," he repeated.

"He's back on that again. Earlier, he was talking like a normal person," JD said. "It practically scared my mom to death. It also convinced her to let us try to do this thing."

"I don't know how, but I believe this dolphin has been in touch with your brother," Kitty said. "I . . . heard she did the same to other people at Mystic Aquarium. One guy got bad headaches, had to go to the hospital. And . . . there's a girl, who keeps having flashes of images and thoughts, like Quinn's, but not as clear."

"Where'd you hear that? When did this stuff happen?"

"That's not important," Kitty answered. "What matters is the dolphin has to be free. We have to free her."

They made their way through halls shrieking of rock music and smelling of pot, arriving at Dom's room. Young men laughed and talked about the Sox, the Pats, the Celts, and girls. JD tried the door to the dorm, but found it only partway open, barely enough to squeeze through. The wreckage of Dom's do-it-yourself indoor hot tub took up all of the floor space. He'd stacked the beds into rickety-looking bunks to clear space. Since the accident, the room looked like a broken lavatory.

"Fine. Haul out all these hoses and clamps and the brushes, too. We've still got to disconnect the pump and filter, and then we're good to go."

"Cool!" said Dom, who was on his third beer.

"You're a crapload of help," JD said. Dom flipped him the bird and gulped another swallow.

In one awkward step, Kitty stepped through the doorway and over the side of the ruined hot tub. The setup left her nowhere else to stand. She was grateful she was not wearing her best shoes, because there was still an inch of water at the bottom.

"So, this is a good start," she said, gesturing around at the sad contraption. "It might work to haul a dolphin, assuming you have something to haul her in? I don't think you can jam her in the trunk of that bitchin' cool muscle car." She let her sarcasm drip like the dirty water she stood in.

"Got it covered. My cousin Tony has a Winnebago. It belongs to his parents, actually. They moved to West Palm Beach and—"

"How much?" JD asked bluntly. Dom mentioned a likely price and JD sighed.

"I . . . could get that," Kitty offered. The others looked at her like she had grown antlers. "What? I'll sell a bond. My dad's kinda rich."

"Must be nice," Dom said. "There may be a way to work out a deal to borrow the Winnebago for free."

"What—" JD began, then thought better of it. Instead, he went on to the next question. "What about the water? How do we get the right mix of salt and water?"

Kitty spouted the information, delivering it as if she were answering a final exam. "I know where they keep sacks of premixed stuff at the aquarium. No one guards salt."

"Did you learn that in pre-psych or pre-law?" Dom asked.

"Marine biology. Pre, I mean," she said.

"You're a jack-of-all-trades. I suppose you have a plan to get this dolphin out of the aquarium."

"Well, they shut down for maintenance on Mondays.

Next week, they're taking Tuesday off as well, making it a long weekend. At night, staffing will be at a minimum, and I can get us in."

JD and Dom looked at each other, then back at Kitty. Then JD looked at Kitty again. It was more than curiosity, or else it was a different kind of curiosity. Kitty noticed him checking her out, but didn't acknowledge it. She decided it was okay. He was cute enough.

"Okay, I'm a docent, at Mystic Aquarium," she said. "You'll need this, too," she added, pulling a clear plastic flask from her pocket. "It's a hydrometer, to check the salinity."

"You're that other girl. Not-Merle messed with your head, too, right?"

"Yeah." She rose up on her tippy-toes and unleashed a proud smile. "That's me."

JD let the information sink in. "So, we've got an insider. We might pull this off yet!"

Chapter 18

The brakes issued a metal-on-metal call for attention, drowning out the noise from the Chevelle's throaty 454 engine. The 8-track *kerchunked* from song to song, randomly spitting out cartridges it didn't like (especially *Toto IV*) as the trio wound through the early-morning woods of Westerly. Eventually, they came to the cluttered property belonging to Dom's cousin, Tony. Weeds grew up through the frames of auto carcasses parked around the yard.

Tony Giordano came out of his office, a prefab shack on cinder blocks, carrying several beers that dripped condensation. He was a big man with huge arms and the beginnings of a belly; a silver crucifix hung below two dark, sunken eyes that identified him as a stoner. "Dom!"

Dom introduced JD and Quinn as they made quick work of the drinks. Quinn stood looking around at the cars, smiling.

"You're sure it's all right for us to take the Winnebago?" JD asked.

"My folks haven't used it in two years. I told them I'd sell it for them. First, I want to fix it up, get rid of the granny fixtures, and put in track lighting and a good sound system. And I have some other plans." Dom and JD looked at each other.

Tony led them around the side of his shack, where he'd parked the Winnebago. It was about a decade or so old, with the big "Flying W" on the side in shades of mocha and vanilla. In fact, the whole color scheme looked to JD like one of the candies Grampa kept in his sweater pocket to give to the kids, the kind JD couldn't wait to spit out.

"I call her *The Foxy Lady*."

"Like the strip club in Providence?" JD asked.

"It's a great place. Five-dollar pitchers. So, the deal is this: we get her in shape for your trip, then later you give me a couple of weekends helping on other work." JD and Dom knew what Tony meant by "other work," and it had nothing to do with remodeling. JD filed it in the back of his head. Maybe.

They climbed up the stairwell into the RV. Tony wasn't kidding about the old-fart décor. Somebody loved sunflowers; they were all over the place, on curtains, upholstery, even the overhead. Dark wood paneling and orange deep-pile carpeting turned the vehicle into a time machine set for 1972.

"Groovy," Dom said.

Noticing that Quinn was getting fidgety, Tony took him to the driver's seat, a swivel captain's chair, and let him play with the CB radio. "Breaker, breaker!" Quinn beamed. He was in hog heaven.

Tony called over to JD, "I heard your brakes a mile

before you got here. Before we do anything else, we should fix those. I have some replacements parts."

Quinn put down the CB handset. "Needs shoes and rotors."

Tony laughed out loud. "I think I've got a new assistant. C'mon, buddy!" Together they rummaged through Tony's shelves and found the parts they needed. Tony pointed out what had to be done and Quinn addressed each new task with a giddy precision. It took them two hours, but when they were done the Chevelle stopped on a dime without the grinding protestations.

Next, they turned their attention to the job at hand: converting *The Foxy Lady* into an aquambulance. Tony called the shots, including choosing the music: The Doors, of course. While Jim Morrison crooned on about a lonely woman in the city of angels, the trio ripped out everything rear of the stairwell. That meant taking crowbars and claw hammers to the tiny kitchen unit as well as the couch that doubled as a bed. They left in place a two-seater meal nook and the rear lavatory. The latter connected to a sizeable water tank; they'd need that. Next, Tony installed a garage door runner in the overhead, while the others added S-hooks to seat belts cannibalized from cars in the yard. These would fit into the runners. They made extras in various sizes. Their cargo couldn't just sit on the floor; they needed to suspend her in shallow water in order to distribute and displace some of her weight and allow her to breathe comfortably.

"We need to keep her wet," JD told the others.

Looking at Dom, he said, "We can jury-rig the pump from your failed sex experiment in the dorm, but we need a pool liner. Ideas?"

"What? You think because I'm Italian, I steal?"

Tony looked up from his work. "You need a pool liner? I know a guy."

"Jimmy, you can't just take off for the whole weekend with Quinn in some broken-down RV." His mom's eyes bulged as she spoke. "Dammit all, I wish your father were here." At the thought of Danny, the word *coward* leapt into her thoughts and she wondered for a second whether she'd said it aloud. "I can't keep track of all your running around. I'm not a magician. What is this all about, anyway? What road trip?"

JD drew a blank. The cover story he'd cooked up sounded lousy. For a moment, his mouth hung open.

"We have to save her, Mom. We have to." It was Quinn. He was smiling, but not his usual painted-on doll's smile. This was softer, intelligent. "She needs to go to the beach. We have to help her."

"Honey." Carol Brennan leaned down and took her son's face in her hands. In his life, she had never heard him put so many words together. She looked over at JD, but did not ask how this was possible. She was not going to question a miracle.

"There's one other thing, Mom," JD said. "We kind of need a little help."

As CEO of Futura Mundi, LLC, Greg Majenski had his critics, but no one could say he failed to surround himself with talented people. He'd plucked MBAs and PhDs from various university faculties across New England, while plundering other corporate boards for the best cutthroat players. Findley tried to keep up with the conversation around the conference table, but it was like trying to decipher arcane code. One board member who had more titles than Findley could hold in her head was talking about redesigning the equipment to better measure the dolphin's brainwaves.

"We need more than an EEG," the board member said. "Call it a CEEG, cetacean electroencephalogram." This drew a few good-natured chuckles from around the Spartan boardroom.

Another said, "Call it anything you like, but we have to fine-tune our efforts to learn whether this animal is an anomaly or one of many."

"She was part of a pod," Findley jumped in. "We harvested only her, but there were others. We can get them." There it was. Speaking out without first stroking the egos of the people at this table was risky, but Findley resented being summoned here only to answer a few questions. She wanted to take charge of this party, not serve drinks.

"Dr. Findley, are you suggesting this dolphin's pod-mates may also be double-brained?" asked Majenski, whose saturnine features and baritone voice commanded attention.

"Double-*lined*, Greg. Again, we're exploring new territory. We'll come up with a better term for it. Jargon aside, what the conventional EEG registers is not two brains, but rather two lines of discrete activity going on inside one brain. And, of course, there have been all the incidents."

Majenski spoke. "At least five people who have been touched by this 'double-lined' dolphin have shown profound reactions. Yes, this is something our friends want us to investigate further." He waited a moment while Findley stood wondering whether it was her turn. A nod; it was.

"I propose we launch a new expedition to locate our dolphin's pod, and harvest as many as possible. I have already made certain preparations.

"As for the people who've been touched, several lost consciousness. One suffered minor trauma. Some of them report odd . . ." Here it came. The board members knew everything up to this point. What they hadn't heard yet was: "Dreams."

The board members all began talking at once. The CEO looked Findley in the eye, paused, then cleared his throat and raised one finger slightly. The cross talk petered out.

Findley continued, "After-incident interviews with one intern named Hughes and one of the security detail members named Morelli suggest the dreams they have been having include snippets of"—Another pause. Go for it, Findley!—"of messages. Something about a mission. There's also a name: Muriel. Plus, a request for more fish. That's normal enough, except that both of our people agree the request involved a second voice, distinct from Muriel's." Now, the board broke into fervent questions. "In short, the dolphin speaks."

Findley kept her eyes on Greg Majenski, who seemed to look at her with . . . respect? Attraction? As the other board members fought to be heard over one another, Findley sat down, confident the hook was in good and deep.

Chapter 19

He was tall, slightly heavy, but not bad. He had all his hair! He set down two coffees and joined her at the table. The back of her chair bumped a filing cabinet in the aquarium's cramped security office.

"Thank you so much for finding my keys. I don't know what I would have done without your help." Carol Brennan jiggled the keys the officer had found exactly where she'd planted them minutes earlier. So much lying—first to get out of work, now this. "I'm sure you have a lot to do," she said, smiling coquettishly. *Good Lord! When was the last time I did that? Next I'll be complimenting his uniform and asking if I can touch his gun.*

"No, the last of the guests will be gone by now. We're locked down tight until Wednesday morning. Actually, I could offer you a look around, behind the scenes. Miss . . ."

"Brennan. Call me Carol. Smoke?" She offered the pack, before noticing the condition of the cigarettes. "They're a little crushed. Kids." *No! Don't bring up children.*

"Thanks, Carol." He took one and produced a lighter for both of them. "I have a son in the army. How many kids do you have?"

As she took a drag, she answered, "Two boys. Fourteen and nineteen."

"Then you know." They both nodded; yes, boys were tough. Keeping the momentum going, he added: "It's Johnny."

"Officer Johnny," she laughed. *Damn, it's working! Danny is not going to like this. Then again, what difference did that make anymore? He's obviously got his escape planned; it's only a matter of admitting it.* "I would love to see the seals." *Ow. Whiplash! Get ahold of yourself, woman! Okay, Officer Johnny seems to expect a little something . . . which could be interesting. Anyway, he's the only human being on site tonight. Good. Let's go see the seals—far away from the dolphin tanks.*

"What about the cameras?" JD asked in a hoarse whisper.

"I turned off the recorder," Kitty answered. "There's only one guard tonight. As long as your mom takes care of him, we'll be in and out with no one seeing us."

"What do you mean 'takes care of'?" Dom snickered. JD slugged his arm.

Carol and Officer Johnny walked over to a glass wall

that offered a bottom-to-top view of the seals, who were nudging human toys with their noses.

"So, seals have ears." She blinked. "No. Sea lions. I meant sea lions." Carol could hear her own nervousness.

"Sea lions are the ones that have ears." Officer Johnny took her hand. "You didn't come here to look at the animals." He was smiling.

"Um."

"I was a cop for a lot of years before I started my private security firm. The sucky part about owning your own business is having to work so your employees can take the long weekend off." They laughed. "All of my training taught me to notice details." Looking down: "Like a woman with two young sons who comes to the aquarium alone . . . and the white mark where a wedding ring used to be. Plus, you're a little nervous."

"A little?"

"You're new at this." He was smiling intently now, enjoying her like a cat enjoys a mouse.

For the first time, it really struck her what she was doing. She had come here to commit a crime and Officer Johnny knew it. She wanted to get up and run out of the office, but her legs wouldn't work. She was not frightened, just resigned.

"Are you going to arrest me?" Then, bravely attempting humor, she asked, "Are you going to strip-search me? I've never—" Her voice became a stammer, so she jammed the cigarette back into her mouth.

"Never stolen a dolphin before? Me neither."

"What?! I'm not—how—what?" He was definitely toying with her. Rat bastard. Handsome rat bastard.

"It's okay. Muriel's been in touch," he said, tapping his temple with one finger. "I figure your friends need another fifteen minutes to fool me."

"If your bosses find out, they'll fire you," Carol said.

"From what little I can make out of the nonsense that dolphin put in my head . . . it's pretty important for her to get out of here. I can always find someplace else to guard."

Someone was coming into the room beyond the glass. Muriel/Gabby tensed up. The last few rounds of tests had left them drained. The probing sessions included strong jolts of lightning that shot through their inner parts. They felt medium-rare. Gabby now agreed with her skullmate: some mans could be mean.

"Maybe if we bite them," Gabby suggested.

"Do that, and they'll take a blade and peek inside our head to see what make us tick."

"We tick like any dolphin. What's the mystery?"

"Wait!" Muriel said as the visitors got closer. "It's not the bad female mans. It's Quinn!"

Over the next several minutes, the two inhabitants of the shared dolphin body tolerated attention that was a mix of unpleasant and outright painful. Quinn and a

larger mans came up in the elevator to the side of the pool.
They jumped in, carrying heavy straps with them.
Moving awkwardly in the water, they positioned these
under Muriel/Gabby and cinched them tightly. They took
advantage of a crane and windlass—presumably the same
one that originally dropped them in here. The mans used
it to pull Muriel/Gabby up, up, up. One moment, their
shared body hung buoyantly in the water, as normal; the
next it seemed made of boulders as they swayed in the
open air. They dared not move too much for fear their
peduncle might snap.

They were dripping wet, but so far the job had gone
smoothly. Then came the part where they had to move
the dolphin from the hoist to the dolly. JD's back protested as he briefly took the weight of the hoist rings attached to one strap. An odd sensation of a wet something
caught on his back diverted his attention. He tried to
shake it off without dropping his load, but the gooey plastic bag or whatever it was only shifted around. JD
grunted. He couldn't deal with that now. He hooked his
ring on to the dolly's frame. Surprisingly, Quinn, Dom,
and Kitty each managed a similar maneuver. They got the
last two rings on the frame, ratcheted up tension to keep
her belly from dragging on the ground, and thus had a
dolphin they could wheel around.

"How the hell much does this thing weigh?" JD asked.

"She's a little girl. She's only five hundred pounds." Of course Kitty had the answer. She continued in whispers as they made their way down in the elevator and out of the aquarium. "Hey Dom, did you know that a dolphin does not have a nose? The bottlenose knows no nose!"

Happily taking the bait, Dom offered: "Really? How does she smell?"

All three at once: "Smell? She stinks!"

"I'll never get used to being hauled around like this," Gabby squealed.

"I've had worse."

"Huh?"

"Wait," Muriel said to Gabby. "I know why I feel so different. I'm not a bottlenose."

"You are now, girlfriend."

There was one consolation. Muriel/Gabby was able to focus now on Quinn.

"Merle/Gabby, I can hear you and . . . see myself." Quinn was looking back at himself through their eyes.

"My name is not Merle, and it's certainly not Not-Merle. It's Muriel!" Muriel's thoughts declared emphatically.

"It is?" Quinn and Gabby responded in unison. Then, Quinn added, "Now, we are three." He giggled like a dolphin, relishing the absurdity of it all.

"Four," corrected Muriel, indicating the bundled octopod clinging for dear life to her and Gabby's dorsal fin. "I have no idea how you got into this sling, but welcome aboard!"

Removing all the cabinet fixtures from around the stairwell made all the difference. Dom, JD, and Quinn maneuvered to transfer the dolphin from the dolly's frame to the reinforced runner mounted into the Winnebago's ceiling. They moved Muriel/Gabby gingerly, keeping her weight distributed. Kitty and Carol used the time to mix the sacks of salt water into the makeshift reservoir. The pool held eighteen inches of water. A spray hose, hooked to the Winnebago's shower, provided their passenger with a briny mist. It wasn't pretty, but it worked.

As they adjusted the final belts around Muriel/Gabby for maximum comfort and safety, Carol looked the dolphin in the eye. "I don't know whether you can understand me, but you're taking both my sons on this adventure of yours. Keep them safe."

The mammal's large, expressive eye offered her an unexpected assurance, emboldening her to add, "And please, if you can, help JD."

The Foxy Lady lumbered along Route 27, away from Mystic Seaport and the aquarium and toward I-95, carrying a doubled dolphin and four humans. JD drove while Dom rode shotgun. Quinn sat by the pool, stroking Muriel/Gabby, with Kitty looking on.

"Eeewww!" Quinn called out. He pulled his hand from the dolphin's side and found it covered in a filmy residue. "She's melting." JD noticed that his brother's speech seemed almost normal when he was with the dolphin.

"It's okay," Kitty said. "She's sloughing off skin. She'll do that a lot. It's normal, but we'll need to keep an eye on the filter."

"We'll be there in less than two hours. We can beat the morning traffic," JD said.

Quinn touched Muriel/Gabby's melon and spoke softly. "We'll be to the beach soon, girl. Be to the beach." Quinn pictured Beavertail. It was a long stretch of land, dotted with beaches and rocky jetties. A circular road led around the old lighthouse to some rocks, and then to the waves and freedom.

The animal became agitated, then began opening its rostrum and emitting audible clicking and whistling noises. "She's upset about something," Kitty called forward.

"Wrong beach! Wrong way! Wrong beach!" Quinn, still in physical contact with the dolphin, raised his voice to a shrill squeal.

"Good God, Quinn! Is that you talking or the stupid dolphin?" JD demanded.

"She's in contact with him," Kitty offered. "I don't know how."

"Yeah, whatever. What does she mean, 'wrong beach'?" Dom wanted to know. He was fumbling with a Triple-A road map, trying to spot other beaches. There were plenty along the Connecticut coast, but none as familiar as the ones in Jamestown, especially the squared-off black-and-gray lighthouse at Beavertail.

Quinn looked around, trying to form words. After a struggle, he said, "Home. Gabby's home."

"Where, honey?" Kitty asked Quinn.

He looked over to his brother, who was already frowning, then whispered into Kitty's ear.

"Uh . . ." Kitty made a face.

"What? Which beach does this beast want?" JD demanded.

"Head south!" Kitty replied. She squeezed Quinn's hand. "She wants to go home, right?" Quinn nodded.

Dom piped in, "She can swim anywhere she wants to."

"No. She'd be swimming with the whole New England fishing fleet. We need to take her south . . . a bit."

"How far?" JD asked.

Kitty and Quinn shared a nod. Finally, she said: "Savannah, Georgia."

Chapter 20

J D drove southward through the dawn and into the early morning. They stopped to pick up new maps. Kitty used her father's card to pay for the gas. It took forever to fill the enormous tank; *Foxy Lady* was a guzzler.

Cars whizzed past on the road. JD noticed one dark-blue Buick sporting an elaborate antenna. It had prongs and silver spirals that looked like a UFO had crash-landed on its roof. The sedan slowed almost to a stop in front of the station, sped up, and then came back again from the opposite direction. He waited, but it did not return. The gas nozzle jerked and died, indicating the tank was finally full. The price on the pump made him cuss out loud. The others returned from the little store and they headed on.

The hours rolled on. Quinn hugged the dolphin, both arms wrapped behind its face. He could feel Muriel/Gabby's thoughts. The fuzziness lifted when they touched; communication went from clipped phrases to full sentences. Right now, they were side by side. He could see, through her eyes, the inside of the joined dolphins' makeshift pool and the octopod trying to make itself tiny. He tried to form questions, but Muriel/Gabby seemed more interested in him than her/their own predicament.

"You will grow," Muriel said in her head voice.

"When?" he asked, without moving his lips. He could do it!

"Sooner, if you let me help." With that, the dolphin began singing a low, soft song. It felt very good. Quinn could not be sure whether it was intentional, but this was also the moment she chose to let down her guard. It took his brain a few moments to sort out what was happening between them. She had something to say, but did not want to say it.

"Tell me," Quinn urged her.

"It's about the mission."

"Yes?"

"We have to stop something. Something bad," Muriel said, and she showed him the world she came from.

Carol felt foolish, sitting in Jimmy's car in her own driveway. Hoping to catch a nap, she slid the driver's seat back, exposing a hole that looked straight down to the pavement below. The grubby leather seats stank of furtive teenagers; she remembered that time, not too long ago. Try as she might, she could not keep her eyes closed.

It was obvious she was not going to sleep until Jimmy called on the CB. She practiced working its controls.

Originally the CB had been Danny's. He loved to show it off to her. The family had gone to the Hill Top Drive-In to see *Smokey and the Bandit.* Jimmy and Quinn watched the movie from a blanket on top of the station wagon's sturdy roof. She could hear them laughing and playing all through the film. (The commotion made it hard for Mommy to enjoy her private thoughts about Burt.) It was a good memory. The boys had never stopped playing with the CB after that. They'd pretend to have a two-way radio conversation, although Quinn only repeated a few phrases, like "Pig Pen, this here's the Rubber Duck." That wasn't from the movie, it was from . . . Anyway, the CB had eventually found its way into Jimmy's hormone-mobile. Now, it was her only link with her two sons, who were off on a wild adventure.

"Breaker. This is Foxy Lady. Come on back, Big Mama!" Her eyes shot open. When had she dozed off? Jesus, it was midmorning. Why weren't the boys home?

Carol picked up the handset. "Hello. Where the hell are you?"

"We're in . . . New York. The smelly, boring part." It was Dom's voice.

Now she allowed her anger and frustration out: "Dom, what the f—*hell* are you doing in New York? Get back here!"

There was a pause. Jimmy's voice came on. "Ma, we're going to make a side trip, to Savannah." He paused, no doubt waiting for an explosion, but she held it in. "We'll be back in a few days. I'll call by phone later. Ten-four?"

"I'll ten-four you! With a two-by-four! Jimmy, if anything happens to Quinn, I will hold you personally responsible."

"I know. I know. We'll be careful. I swear, Ma."

There was nothing to say. They were doing this. At least they were doing it together. That weird dolphin was getting a free ride. She wanted to say more, but what came out felt good for the moment. "Fine. I'm going to use your Chevelle to do my errands. In fact, I need to run to Almac's and get some cigarettes and maxi pads."

"MA!"

The next call was to Tony, who sounded stoned. He told them the Savannah run was no problem. He wanted them to make a quick stop in Atlanta on the way back to pick up a package. They needed to connect with a trucker who would set them up. Tony gave them a CB frequency and told them to ask for Pratt.

By noon, they were deep in the bowels of New Jersey. Marshlands and spewing smokestacks flew by. Kitty came forward to sit with JD, who refused to surrender the wheel.

She set the frequency as directed. "Breaker. Hi."

Quinn called forward from poolside to correct her. "Breaker, breaker!"

Kitty smiled. "That's right." She began again. "Breaker, breaker."

"Darlin', you gonna talk or play?" It was a man's twangy voice.

"Hi. We're looking for Pratt."

"This is Mudflaps. I don't know Pratt, but I bet I know somebody who does. You hold on to your sweet fanny a minute and I'll check." A burst of static and a high-pitched squeal sounded from the speaker.

A different voice came on the CB. Kitty hadn't known they could network like this. She wondered how many truckers they could reach. She said, "I'm a star!"

JD rolled his eyes and swigged a soda. There was another short burst of static, like the machine was clearing its throat. "Hey, sugar breeches. This is Sam from Nam. One more switch will get you to Pratt. He's somewhere on a Miami run, I think. Hang on."

"Pratt here. You read, ten-four?" The voice was hard to pin down. It came in clearly enough, but it was either a little too high for a man or a little too low for a woman.

"Hi, Pratt. Is that a first or last name?" she asked, hoping to satisfy her curiosity.

"It's just Pratt. One name, like Cher. I have her posted over my bunk in the back of my cab." So, it was a man! Then again . . . "What's your name, darlin'? I can tell you're a greenhorn."

"I'm Kitty. We're in a Winnebago in New Jersey."

"Acknowledged, Camper Kitty. What in the world does Saturday Night want to bring you into this for?"

Saturday Night? It took her a second to connect Tony to Tony Manero of *Saturday Night Fever*. He obviously thought he was as hot as John Travolta. Stoners!

"We're on a kind of a mission to Savannah. We're carrying—" She looked at JD and Dom to make sure it was okay to say it on the air. JD raised his hands palms up, then motioned one hand to the CB, meaning, *Why not?* "We're carrying a telepathic dolphin who needs to get back to her people."

A full two seconds of silence, then: "That's better than what I'm hauling. Savannah, eh? I could meet you there."

They agreed and exchanged details.

Octopod. That was a new one, another of the mans words. He wasn't sure he liked the title; it felt so limiting. He was used to using full-bodied concepts to frame his world. They had color, texture, and most of all, taste. Using mans words was a flavorless affair, like reaching a carcass after the sharks had been at it for a while.

He tried to understand Muriel's intentions, but her plan was so . . . what was the mans word? Grandiose. She wanted him to pass these new thoughts and skills to octopodes the world over. She said there was some great danger coming. Mans again. All in all, he wished he'd stayed in his tank back at the aquarium and never gone to check out the funny new dolphin music. Muriel's songs were beguiling, but confusing. At least she was generous with the food the mans dropped in their tiny pool. He pulled another helping of mackerel to his beak, savoring the fish as his radula reduced it to bits. Understanding could wait.

At first, Kitty thought Quinn was asleep. He was still pressed against the dolphin; they were practically attached. At the edge of her vision, she spotted a furtive gray limb withdrawing to someplace hidden from view. She was wondering what had drawn their extra passenger out from hiding, when she noticed something else.

"Honey, what's wrong? Why are you crying?"

"She says it's bad. It's very bad." Quinn was shaking.

"What is? What's bad, sport?" Kitty moved closer and rubbed his shoulders.

Dom took notice. He swiveled his chair backward to face them. "What's the problem?" Kitty answered with a shrug.

"The cities are sunken or burned. The people, so many people, are . . . gone. Muriel/Gabby says it's coming. She says she has to get to the beach to warn the others."

"The other what? The other dolphins?" Dom asked.

"And people, if she can." Quinn snuffled up tears and snot and composed himself. "She can't do anything from a tank. She has to get to the ocean." He was adamant.

"It's okay, we're going as fast as we can," JD called

back from the driver's seat. "What do you mean about the burned cities? What's going to happen? A war?"

Quinn looked around at the faces of his brother and friends. "The Fall is coming."

No one spoke.

"Your girlfriend . . . tells the future?" Dom asked.

The dolphin *skeejed* and *skeeled* in an oddly musical display, bobbing about in the pool.

Kitty sighed. "No, guys. She is *from* the future."

JD cursed. A couple of minutes later, he pulled the RV into a rest area. "You want to back up and give me that again?" he demanded.

"This part is what Muriel shared in *my* dreams," said Kitty. "There's a bad thing coming. I can't tell whether it's tomorrow or a hundred years from now. I'm not sure she knows when, but it is coming."

"So, she's a time-traveling psychic dolphin on a mission to save the planet." Sarcasm dripped from JD's voice.

"Cool!" said Dom. "Since we know about it, we can prevent it. It's like a sci-fi movie. We'll tell people. Scientists can build whatever technology we need to stop this Fall thing."

Quinn looked up, his face lacking any trace of the familiar humor that usually animated his features. He said, "Mans tried. It did not work." No one missed the fact that Quinn referred to them as "mans" or that he spoke in the past tense.

Later, when Quinn was preoccupied with Muriel/Gabby, Dom whispered to the others, "That was Muriel talking. The dolphin told Quinn, 'It *did not* work.' Muriel's seen the future."

"And it sucks," added Kitty.

Chapter 21

Back on the road, the day dragged on as they passed out of New Jersey and on to Maryland and then Delaware. JD figured they could make it to Savannah by the next afternoon, but they would have to stop somewhere for the night. He noticed the car they had spotted at the first gas station, a Buick, hanging back behind them like all the bad guys on TV drove. Its windows were darkly tinted, offering no view of the driver or passengers. JD tried slowing down to allow them to pass, but they veered off an exit and out of sight. Hours later, the car was back.

"Someone's following us." Dom checked out the rear window. "Same bad-guy car." Kitty said nothing.

JD pressed his luck for a few hours after dark until he worried his fatigue could get them into a wreck. Dom suggested the nearest 8-Ball SuperStore. The big ones had hookups for RVs, so they could replenish their water and dump their sewage.

Kitty spotted the giant beacon in the shape of a glowing eight ball (more purple than black) calling acolytes to worship at the all-night altar of consumption. Attention 8-Ball shoppers, there's a big bargain break on: pink flamingos and garden gnomes, coolers for the beach that wind up next to his Barcalounger, a *Donkey Kong Jr.* game cartridge with a never-used math program included, 100 percent–polyester Hawaiian shirts, deodorant to take some of the stink out of the 100 percent–polyester Hawaiian shirts, lava lamps and black-light posters, sixty-five million copies of Michael Jackson's *Thriller*, cases and cases of Miller Lite and Tab, cool Members Only jackets, cooler Swatch watches, and totally cool Ray-Ban sunglasses.

They ate burgers that spilled glops of ketchup onto Styrofoam trays, bought from a fast-food joint next to the 8-Ball. It was a satisfying meal after a day of chips, sodas, and Slim Jims. "Yom," said Quinn, jamming fries into his mouth while stroking the dolphin.

Dom pulled out a bottle of Boone's Farm Strawberry Wine. "If we still had the stove, I'd whip up some bruschetta," he said and passed the bottle to JD and Kitty.

"Coke is it! Coke is it!" Quinn mimicked the jingle, the notes sustained then staccato, and drained his soda. He considered offering some to Muriel/Gabby, but gave her some fish instead. (As Pratt had promised, there was a fish market in the same plaza.) Quinn wanted to talk to the dolphin some more. She said she was distracted. Something was hurting her.

"Pain," Quinn told JD. He could feel her presence feeding into the current that carried words from his brain to his mouth. "Please help her, JD."

His brother climbed around the others and moved

back to the dolphin's hind section. The water was clear; they had just cleaned the pool again. "I don't see anything," JD said, then thought to look under their passenger's heavy tail. Muriel/Gabby was good enough to lift it, exposing the underside. "Bastards!"

"What is it?" Dom asked.

"There's a cut. It's inflamed a little. It's not bad, but that's not the problem."

Kitty looked closely. "It's an incision scar."

"They planted something in her fluke, a tracking device."

Dom went over and took a closer look. "Someone stitched it closed."

Kitty sat back and heaved a sigh. "Oh Lord, I didn't expect that!" She added, "If we try to remove the tracker, we'll make a bloody mess. It does explain your mysterious car, JD, the one with the funny antenna," she finished, her voice becoming thready.

JD wore a statue's face. Now she talked about the car. Not a word earlier.

Quinn stroked the dolphin's side and fed her more fish, which she eagerly gulped down. "We have to do something," he said.

"I'll make up an ice pack. That should help," Kitty said. "I have antibiotics, but I'm no vet. I wish I'd taken more courses."

"Whoever's tracking us has to be with the aquarium," JD said, looking directly at Kitty.

"I hate aquarium cops," Dom said through gritted teeth.

Kitty said, "They haven't stopped us yet. I wonder why not. The best thing is to keep going."

Kitty made a quick trip to the convenience store and returned with enough supplies to strap an ice pack on Muriel/Gabby's fluke. She also gave her a shot for the pain and to take down the inflammation. The dolphin appeared to relax.

It was late. The four humans made do sleeping in the captain's chairs and on the floor of the Winnebago. Dom and Kitty volunteered to take turns checking on Muriel/Gabby. JD faced away from the smelly tank. He slept in the driver's seat, with Quinn to his right.

His brother was getting tall. JD wondered how much longer people like Kitty and Lisa would see Quinn as a cute boy. Once he got full grown, his hand-waving and twisty faces wouldn't seem so cute. JD didn't let himself continue that line of thought. His mind wandered and sank into dreams.

Christmas. No doubt it's Christmas. The room is hung in excitement and youthful greed. The tree is huge, owning the living room and packed underneath with boxes and mysterious shapes sheathed in color and expectation. One package is my GI Joe with Kung Fu Grip; I had him all through junior high. Another is my magic kit, wand, and cups that make the ball disappear, but no magician's hat. I need to get a silky black top hat to be a magician. Sloshing. The tree is so tall. No, JD is small. Not JD. I'm Jimmy. I'm looking up at the red-and-gold angel. She got lost years ago. No, my angel is here. My favorite lights are all here, the Chinese lanterns and the little snowballs that blink red, blue, green, yellow. Barney is here, yapping, tearing through the shiny wrapping paper. Barney got hit. Barney's woofing for more paper. His woof sounds like splashing in the bathtub. Dad is here. He's happy. Dad is grabbing Mom's bottom, and she squeals like a little girl. They think I can't see. They kiss. Quinn looks upset, holding his arms out to Daddy and Mommy. "Jealous!" Mom laughs and they both give Quinn a kiss. Water. I want a kiss. They say I'm too old for that. Quinn's my baby brother. He's funny, but not the ha-ha kind. He's supposed to play games with me and do what I tell him to do. No dice. Sounds like piddle in the toilet. Don't hit the seat, young man! Then, red-and-green lights all winking out at once, Christmas is gone. The walls are gray and all my toys are gone. Dad's gone. Where'd he go? What work? Why can't he be here? No. Not fair. I heard them. The walls were yelling, "I can't look at that boy." "He's our son!" The yelling sounds like gurgling water. Quinn won't talk. Not for years and years. Mommy says he's artistic. Then, Quinn talks, but says things funny. He's no fun. I want another dog. The sound of water.

Gurgling. The water from their makeshift aquarium refused to be silent, intruding on his dream. JD rubbed his eyes and discovered that his left hand was wet. In fact, the cuff of his sleeve was soaked. How had he gotten on the floor? Stupid dolphin. Stupid dream.

He needed air that didn't smell like a cannery. JD was glad for the garbage strewn around the RV; it gave him an excuse to leave. As quietly as he could, JD grabbed up their trash then stepped over Muriel/Gabby's pool and down the stairwell. His boot heels tapped a staccato tempo on the asphalt.

JD dropped the burger wrappers and empty bottles onto a full trash can in front of the entrance to the 8-Ball. The garbage cascaded over the top and onto the sidewalk, where the wind lazily rolled it out to the parking lot.

There was no sign of the blue Buick, but there was a black limousine, also with darkened windows and bearing the exact same UFO antenna he'd seen on the Buick. Great.

It was their move, whoever they were.

JD found a phone outside the store entrance next to the coin-eating kiddie rides. He made a mental calculation of the time difference and figured it wasn't too late there.

Quinn told Muriel he was tired of hooking and unhooking hoses; he wanted to use a restroom with real toilets. Dom was still dozing, Kitty was nowhere to be found. Quinn left the RV and made his way to the brightly lit store. Inside, he found the men's room and did what he needed to do.

Finishing up, he walked to the toy section of the store. He didn't have much money, so he just looked at the brightly colored packages. The toys here looked like the toys in the stores at home: a Darth Vader action figure, those ugly baby dolls that girls loved, and a *Dukes of Hazzard* set with Bo and Luke and *The General Lee*. He really wanted the orange car with the funny flag on it. Maybe he could convince his mom to get it for him.

Bored, Quinn headed to the front of the store. He looked down one aisle and noticed Kitty, her back to him, talking to some lady in a suit like what men wore except for ladies. A sign for "8-Ball Specials Half Off Sale" blocked the woman's face. He couldn't hear the words, but their tone made it sound as though the two women were arguing. Mom said not to butt into other people's conversations, so he kept walking.

Outside, Quinn found JD talking on a pay phone. Quinn got excited as he heard their father's voice on the other end of the line. He reached for the receiver with both hands and uttered a guttural moan; unfortunately, the dolphin's effect on his speech had worn off.

JD held up a finger to his anxious brother and focused on his phone call.

Danny Brennan's distant voice said: "Hey, kiddo! How's it going? How's Quinn and your mom? What are you up to?"

JD picked the last part of the question, and lied. "Uh, nothing much."

"Okay. Well, I'm glad you called. I'm a little busy right

now, though." JD could hear movement in the room where his father was. A television was playing some cop show. There were people. Some of the voices were women. JD's stomach felt funny and his boots were suddenly four sizes too large.

"I wanted to ask you when you thought you might be coming home." He phrased it so passively. JD could hear the pleading in his own voice. He felt the strength draining out of his knees and a dull ache growing in his gut.

"I'm not really sure, Jimmy."

"It's JD now, Dad. I go by JD." He almost yelled it. He sucked in a quick breath and tamped down the anger as best he could.

"Okay."

"So . . ."

"I have to finish this job. There might be more work, too." As their father spoke, JD's face turned strange; Quinn figured he was in pain or holding in a fart. "You're the man of the house. You have to look after your mom. I'm counting on you."

"Why can't you just come home?"

"Jimmy, I told you—"

"I just want it to be the way it was."

"Jimmy, I have to go." There was a click and then silence, and finally a dial tone.

JD held the phone like he'd forgotten it was in his hand. Quinn saw the tears on his brother's face. Quinn didn't know what to say, so he gave his brother a hard hug.

After a moment, JD led Quinn back to *The Foxy Lady*. He told Quinn to get inside and get some sleep.

JD was furious, but couldn't figure out how to focus his feelings. Anger was a clumsy weapon. Dad was letting them down, him, Quinn, Ma, but didn't his father have a right to do what he felt was best for himself? He was earning money. But . . . who was that with him? Why did he have to have someone else? Mom was still pretty, wasn't she?

JD heard the *clack-crunch* of heels and pavement as Kitty approached him.

"You couldn't sleep either?" Kitty asked, with deliberate casualness.

"I keep thinking, I don't even know why we're doing this. They'll just catch another dolphin. Even if we get Muriel/Gabby back to the ocean, odds are she'll wind up in two hundred cans of tuna."

"We gotta try."

"I'm not her hero. Not hers or anybody's."

Kitty put her hand on his arm. "You could be. If you wouldn't push people away so much."

"What's that supposed to mean?" JD asked.

"Nothing. Just . . . maybe a hero doesn't have to swoop in wearing a red cape and save the day. Maybe all a hero has to do is care and try his best. That can change a lot of minds, you know."

"I don't want to save dolphins or change minds. All I want is . . ."

"Want what?"

"I want . . ." He looked her in the eye, and in one quick motion he pulled her to him and kissed her hard on the lips.

Kitty pounded her fists against JD's chest and pushed herself back from him. "What?!"

JD pulled her close again and gripped her by the hair with one hand, while his other explored her chest. Kitty began to struggle as JD thrust his tongue past her lips. He was strong enough to hold her in place. She tried to escape his hands, but had no luck. Seams ripped, hair ribbons fell out, press-on nails tore off. She began to scream, but the sound got muffled in the unwanted kiss. Plus, she was afraid of what might happen if Dom and Quinn found them like this. Kitty used the old standby, jamming her knee into JD's crotch. He easily dodged it and ground his mouth even harder onto hers, causing their teeth to click jarringly. Kitty twisted and beat her fists on his arms, then bit down sharply on his lip until they both tasted blood.

JD let out a yelp. "Jesus! What's wrong with you?!"

"What's wrong with *you*?" she demanded, somehow keeping her voice to a harsh whisper. The tone in her voice stung him worse than if she had slapped him. "Your brother and my boy—your best friend are like ten feet away."

"I'm sorry." His mix of anger and machismo melted into the face of a toddler who'd lost his mommy. She almost felt sorry for him. Almost.

Walking back to the door of the RV, she turned and

said, "You need to get your head together, JD." With that, she was gone.

JD sat down on the pavement and dug his fingers into his disheveled hair. His thoughts played like music jangling on the radio while someone kept switching channels. This was a stupid situation. Everyone else was calling the shots, and he was doing . . . what? *What am I going to get out of this?* he wondered. He desperately wanted to sleep, hoping against hope that the morning sun would bleach away the ugly stains inside his head.

He had one more thing to do first. He stood up and began to walk from one light pool to the next. He fixed his eye on the car, parked many rows away. A rear window was open a crack and wisps of smoke rose out. From behind the tinted glass, he saw a dancing red dot, flaring each time someone drew a poisonous breath.

Customers seemed unconcerned that the tile flooring and walls in the restaurant's dining area continued unbroken into the restrooms. They lined up for a breakfast of greasy hash browns, dry biscuits, and spurious sausage. When the travelers returned to the RV, Quinn offered leftovers to Muriel/Gabby, but the dolphin held her rostrum tightly shut.

On the road, traffic slowed to a crawl. They'd made the mistake of hitting the Capital Beltway during morning rush. At a pit stop, Dom slipped into the driver's seat before JD could say anything. Dom fumbled a bit with the odd dashboard configuration; the automatic shift was mounted to the left of the wheel, requiring him to shift downward to get from park to drive. He adapted his skills to the demands of *The Foxy Lady*, grinning from ear to ear.

"Is she asleep?" Dom asked, using his head to motion to the rear.

JD looked back. Quinn was stroking Muriel/Gabby. Kitty was curled up on the sunflowers of the narrow bench/couch. "Kitty? Yeah, she's still napping."

"Guess I wore her out!" His smile was immense.

JD took a moment, then gave him a long glance sideways. "What's that supposed to mean?"

"You know."

"What? With my brother sleeping inches away?"

"No, we didn't *do it*. We made out a little and slept, you know. Third base."

"Wow. I'm impressed," JD said.

"Me too," Dom shot back. They didn't say anything more.

Findley's back was killing her, as was the smell that wafted up from her travel-weary jacket. "At least this car's got working air conditioning," she commented into the limo's phone. The sliding panel on the tinted partition was closed. She didn't want the liveried kid on the other side to be listening in.

"The board is antsy about sending what you asked," said the voice on the other end of the phone. She felt annoyed at having to deal with a vice president, some jumped-up assistant.

"Tell them I've got confirmation now. They're headed to Savannah. Reroute the *Talon*. The ship just left port, so it should be a quick turnaround."

There was a click on the line loud enough to make her wince. A new voice came on. "April, this is Greg. In fact, the change of course costs a small fortune in fuel and other expenses. I hope you know what you're doing."

"I do, Greg." *Figures he'd be listening in.* "Our inside . . . girl . . . expects them to be there by late this afternoon."

"April, do you trust her?"

Findley remembered the little intern's uppity attitude at the 8-Ball the night before. The girl had doubts, but Findley had to believe she'd follow through. "Absolutely, Greg." Findley did not mention the side deal she'd made with the Brennan boy. Keeping details like that from Majenski constituted another risk. Instead, she said goodbye with just the right touch of warmth and hung up.

Making sure her acne-faced driver was eyes front, she reached for a little square bottle in the mini-bar.

To herself: "This had better work."

Chapter 22

The radio filled the hours. They said nothing as the industrial duns of Delaware and Maryland slid into the rolling greens of Virginia.

They had a bit of excitement when a balding tollbooth operator in a bright orange vest commented on the smell coming from their RV. The vehicle's height prevented him from getting a clear view of their passenger.

"You got a marlin back there? You better get more ice on him," the operator joked. "I have one on my wall. Caught him in Cabo San Lucas. The guy threw him to me for thirty bucks." He winked to ensure JD knew this was the funny bit. He'd bought a stuffed fish. Hilarious. "Anyway, you need some ice pronto. There's a store about two miles on."

Back at the wheel, JD faked a laugh, said, "Yeah, we'll do that," and hit the gas. The incident prompted them to reinspect the filtering system, which was on the verge of quitting.

As signs began advertising their approach to the Carolinas, Kitty took a moment to freshen up in the ersatz bathroom. She couldn't enjoy full privacy; hoses ran from the faucet out the door so Quinn could give the dolphin a regular spritz. She did what she could.

JD noticed signs were beginning a mileage countdown to the Carolinas. Without really thinking, he said, "You could do better."

Dom was daydreaming, looking at the passing cars and trying to guess which ones belonged to millionaires. The comment penetrated his fog and he turned to his friend. "Better than what?"

"Kitty." JD's words poured out, sour as curdled milk. "She's nice. I like her. But, you know—"

"No, I don't know. Why are you being such a dick?" He saw the cutesy face JD used sometimes and got angrier. "Is this how you act with girls? No wonder Lisa dumped your ass." With that, he swiveled his seat around, got up, and moved to the couch.

The Winnebago turned off the interstate. On the other side of the windshield, it was as if some stage manager had redressed an enormous set. Spanish moss dangled in gothic fashion from the centuries-old live oaks. The streets led one to another with no particular theme, except for a notable absence of fast-food joints and retail chain stores. In their place stood quaint restaurants and clothing stores housed in early-nineteenth-century brick warehouses that had once serviced tri-masted sailing vessels. The RV lumbered down a steep hill and onto a cobblestone lane. Here, crowds strolled the waterfront at a tempo that belied urgency, spying through small-paned display windows at the singular treasures inside. Savannah.

Dom worked the map. "East River Street becomes West River Street—makes sense—then we need to get on Seventeen. We should be able to find a reasonably private spot at the edge of the Savannah River. It'll be dark in a few hours. We probably should wait. I saw some great restaurants."

"We need to keep going," Kitty called from the small rear window she was peering out of.

"Go where? We're here: Savannah," Dom said.

Quinn was rubbing Muriel/Gabby's skin gently, running the hose over the long slope of her body. The pressure was low, reducing the water's flow to a trickle.

"We should discuss our next step," JD said slowly without making eye contact with Dom or Kitty.

They chose a parking area next to a giant anchor surrounded by picture-snapping tourists. Nearby, an anachronistic paddle wheeler lay tied to the wharf, its stacks smoking idly. A local TV news crew was stopping people to interview them on their way up the ramp.

The three of them stepped out of the RV, leaving Quinn with their passenger. "Guys, what?" Dom asked, as he tried to stretch the kinks out of his back. "I've been smelling sardine farts for two days. Tell me we're almost done."

"We need to take her somewhere else." Kitty's voice betrayed nervousness.

JD had had enough. "Something you want to tell us?" he asked.

Dom looked from one to the other. "You both look like you're hiding something."

"Ladies first," JD said, folding his arms.

"Fine." Kitty opened her mouth to say something to Dom, then exhaled sharply. "No apologies," she said. "We have to keep going because Dr. Findley is somewhere around here."

"Who?" Dom wanted to know.

It was JD who answered. "The lady from the aquarium who talked to Quinn and me after Muriel made contact. The lady who put the tracker on Muriel/Gabby. She wants Muriel/Gabby back, but not before the dolphin leads them to more dolphins like her." Kitty knitted her brow at that last detail.

"Whuh?" Dom wanted to know how JD knew all this, but Kitty's expression distracted him. "Wait. You're working with . . . with Findley?"

"I agreed to keep an eye on you guys while you moved Muriel/Gabby," Kitty explained. "We didn't know where the dolphin wanted to go until we were already on the road. I didn't think about it. I was thinking about myself, and what this could lead to for me.

"Hey, JD, don't look at me like I'm some kind of monster. Maybe you can explain how you figured out that Findley is after more dolphins?"

On cue, Findley rounded the side of the RV, accompanied by a young man. (He wore a black hat and shirt that buttoned at the collar. He looked like Kato from *The Green Hornet*, but not as cool.) "You've both been very helpful. Now, we have to get our friend into the water. It's simple, we all want the same thing." She lit a cigarette. JD and Dom both fidgeted in disgust at the stench.

"Your girlfriend's a spy, Dom," JD said in a steely monotone.

"And you're a turncoat, JD." Dom stood rigidly.

"You're both overreacting," Findley said. "Let's wait until dark. We can have a meal that doesn't come in a wrapper. First, though, I'd like to see our little lady."

They invited Findley inside *The Foxy Lady*. There was no point in trying to keep her out. Her driver, who didn't talk much, stayed with the limo. Findley admired their makeshift life-support system, but noted it was failing.

"Get her into the ocean," Quinn said. He looked up at Findley. "You're a bad mans."

The line stretched out the door, including two men wearing WSAV-TV ID badges: a black man in a navy-blue blazer and sport slacks, and a white guy dressed like a slob. Finally, the waitress wedged Findley's party into a booth, with a warm "Welcome, sweetie." Dom and Kitty laughed at their first exposure to a Southern drawl. The decor mixed crumbling factory bricks with Day-Glo-painted ducts and fixtures. They picked at the meal of seafood and pasta, keeping one eye out the window at the RV parked across the street. Quinn hated leaving Muriel/Gabby and their tank buddy alone. He grimaced and stimmed throughout dinner.

Dom took a break from eating long enough to ask, "Why the cloak-and-dagger crap? Why didn't you just ask us or ask her?"

"The dolphin is tough," Findley said.

"We don't serve dolphin, ma'am. That's swordfish!" a passing waiter said.

Findley shook off the comment and continued, "She doesn't like to cooperate with us. She can communicate with Kitty and some other people only up to a point. Your brother is unique, as far as we can tell. I needed the dolphin—Muriel/Gabby, as you call her—to feel safe, so she'd take us to her pod."

"I didn't get this detail until we stopped at the 8-Ball," Kitty insisted. "I figured they were going to release her and track her." Then to Quinn: "I swear, buddy! I wouldn't hurt her."

Quinn smiled at Kitty. He now recognized Findley from the 8-Ball, and understood now why she and Kitty had argued. The pleasantness faded from his face as he addressed Findley. "You want to hurt her. You're a bad mans."

"Please stop saying that. I'm not a bad man. Not at all. We want her and her family to teach us about them," she said.

"And how do you learn? With a scalpel?" Kitty

vehemently stated her case, knowing full well that Findley would deny it. "There's something you need to know about Muriel/Gabby."

JD, who'd been hanging back in the conversation, jumped in. "It doesn't matter. We have a deal. I made sure we got her here. I expect you to keep your end of it."

"Of course," Findley said. Kitty dagger-eyed JD, who looked back defiantly.

"You don't get it, do you?" Kitty shot out, not caring who was listening at the other tables. "Dr. Findley, there is no pod. We don't know why Muriel wanted to come to Savannah. She's not from around here."

Dom blurted it out: "She's a psychic time-traveling dolphin on a mission to save the Earth! Cool as hell, right?"

"What in the world are you talking about?" Findley demanded.

"He's right, Doctor. We'll prove it," JD said. His face betrayed frustration.

As they left the restaurant, Kitty bought some insurance. Waiting until Findley was focused on the boys, she went over to the TV news crew. The man in the blazer introduced himself as Benton Bradley and his cameraman, Joe. Kitty caught the sly leer and decided to use it.

"I can't help but notice you two handsome men are with the TV news, right?" she said, vamping Benton Bradley for all she was worth. "I've got something to show you. It's the story of the century, right out there in the parking lot." She motioned to the RV.

Playing along with Kitty's game, they agreed to take

her up on the offer, right after they finished eating. "Good enough," Kitty said.

Back in the RV, JD and Quinn exchanged whispers. "Are you sure?" he asked his younger brother.

Findley stepped over to the tank. Muriel/Gabby squealed a bit. Findley crouched down closer to the dolphin and said, "Don't worry. I'm a friend."

"Not a friend!" Quinn cried and swung one of the octopod's suckered limbs onto Findley's face, where it slapped into place with a wet *thwuck*! Two more limbs clung to the dolphin's melon. Before Findley could peel herself free, Quinn yelled, "Go!"

"The reception is lousy," Gabby said. "She's not as open to us as Quinn. I don't see how this creature is helping."

"He's not as advanced as the ones I'm used to," Muriel answered. "He barely listens; he's more about eye-linking and chemical communication. Turning an octopus into an octopod requires incremental precision. Still, he has the basic ability to transmit images and some language."

"I still say you're speaking dolphin to an ape." Gabby made a farting noise with their blowhole.

"Never mind. Let's just show the mans what we need her to see."

Findley did not cry out. She could not. She felt as if she had fallen into a tank of thimble jellyfish, but instead of actual pain, she felt a curious immobility.

Images assaulted her consciousness with a mass-free force of sensation and intuition. The wave hit her like a truck hauling emotions. By itself, each image shone like some ancient glyph found in the depths of a cavern. An indefinable influence stitched the colors and feelings into a cohesive design. This patchwork revealed itself to be experiences drawn from many witnesses over many lifetimes. These watchers told a tale:

Harbor pilings stood surrounded by sunken boats of all sizes, their hulls scorched. What should have been a lively ballet of fish was a fetid swell and sway of ghastly clumps.

New image: Impossibly bright suns broke through the waves. Too many. Too close. The water boiled. Calm returned, but illness grew inside. A creeping fatigue. Darkness won.

Another change: A view from the water toward the shore. Mans in rags. (Mans?) They fought with their hands. They ate . . . something. No. No. Next image.

A sense of time. More than a whole lifetime. More than several.

Close to now, Muriel's now. There were limits in the trackless currents where no boundaries should rise. Vast sectors of the ocean were poisoned. Ruptured barrels lay wedged amongst the thermal stacks where hydrocarbon molecules formed to call forth new life, laced with death from the onset. To trespass was to die.

Muriel wondered whether this was the end. Would we all wind up in the Great? Was the Great still the Great if there was no one left in the world to dream of it?

A final vision: A small cluster of life in the open water, then an island. She could change things. Muriel could teach the living to eat the poisons, a little at a time. It would take many, many lifetimes, more than they had left. Time was nearing an end. It was better to start earlier. She could go back with a warning. Muriel had to take the chance.

For a moment, her world was dark and without form. As light and mass returned, Findley heard a strangely melodic voice: "All things end in failure. Failure is the chance to begin again."

"I tried to tell you. She's a weird dolphin," Kitty said.

His hands waggling in stim fashion, Quinn added, "She's the only one! Only one weird dolphin!"

Digesting all she'd seen and felt, Findley fell backward into a puddle on the floor.

She sat for a moment, then said, "My ass is wet."

Of all the random static that frizzles and fries within mans' brains, *names* were the most pointless. He couldn't understand why the dolphins liked them so much. Hermes. He neither wanted the moniker nor appreciated it being thrust upon him. Muriel. Gabby. April. Worthless noise now rattling through his brain. He'd been intrigued by the two-in-one dolphin; now he wished he'd fought that fascination. A plan, they had said. A plan that meant his elegant, simple, organic language got pushed back into the depths of his consciousness in favor of the mans' jumble of glottals, plosives, and sibilants. And why? To whom was he supposed to pass these mans words? The others of his kind weren't weighed down by words. At least not yet. He supposed communing during a meal or procreation would pass this affliction on to others. What a joke! Let the mans ruin their land. What did that mean to him or any octopod? *Octopod?* What kind of a word was that?

Mutely curmudgeoning his future, Hermes hung for a moment by two of his limbs, now suckered to April's arm. Silly, rigid thing, useless for propulsion and barely dexterous enough to convey food to the female mans' mouth. She walked him over to the barnacle-encrusted retaining wall and extended her arm above the gentle swell.

These were not the waters of home, but they would take him to his new domain in the ocean. Fine. Hermes released his grip and fell with a barely registered plop into the Savannah River.

"Well, that was interesting, I guess," Joe said, clicking off his camera. "Got the lead at eleven right there. This is the story that's gonna land you in the anchor chair, bro!"

Ignoring his cameraman, Benton Bradley turned to the woman in the business suit. "Now, if we could get a word on why you did that, Miss . . . ?" Getting no response, Benton Bradley snapped his fingers. "Hello?"

Findley stood glassy-eyed and said nothing. Kitty walked up to the news crew and began, "That's just the beginning. Dr. Findley is about to release a very special dolphin."

She was about to continue when a taxi rolled up within two feet of the group. Out stepped a distinguished-looking man in a three-piece suit and aviator glasses.

"Excuse us for a moment," the man told the news crew in a confident voice that extinguished any argument. He pulled aside both Kitty and Findley. "Enough. No one said anything about bringing in the press."

Halfway back from her dream state, Findley managed, "Oh, Greg. Good, you're just in time."

"Where is our property?" he demanded.

"She's fine. She's in *The Foxy Lady*. The Winnebago," Kitty offered. He narrowed his eyes.

"It's all right, Greg. Kitty knows," Findley said. "In fact, they all do."

"April! What have you done? I trusted your judgment. Have I made a mistake?"

"Things are under control," Findley parried. "We're finalizing the release of Muriel/Gabby."

"Who named it?" Majenski's eyes darkened. "Look,

the *Talon* and the support ships are standing by in the harbor. They have a lock on its transponder signal. It's getting late. Find an open spot along the shore and get the thing in the water. We'll take care of the rest."

"How many dolphins were you hoping to catch?" Kitty asked.

"That's not something an intern needs to worry about," he shot back.

Findley found her composure, then amped it up to swagger. "Okay, let's do this. Greg, you take the limo. We'll ride in the RV with the kids and our dolphin."

Dom and JD walked over to where they were talking. Benton Bradley and his cameraman stood by, making a questioning motion as if to say, *Are we talking or what?*

Dom asked to ride in the limo, saying it was something to brag about to Tony. The others climbed aboard the RV and took off, with the news crew following.

Chapter 23

Aboard *The Foxy Lady*, Kitty said to Findley, "Your boss has to notice we're blowing by a bunch of likely spots along the shore." Kitty perched herself between the two forward seats, which now held Findley and JD. Quinn was in the back with Muriel/Gabby.

"I'm going to one up ahead. I asked and the waitress said that beach is closed at night. No people," JD said. "We're gonna dump this fish."

"You can't!" Kitty protested.

"Why not?" Findley asked.

"How long before your people realize she's not hooking up with other dolphins?" Kitty asked.

"Muriel wants to hook up," Quinn piped in, giggling at the term "hook up." "She wants to tell them about the future."

"Those are normal dolphins! Vintage 1983 dolphins!" Kitty shouted.

"A dolphin is a dolphin," JD said, and Findley agreed.

"No, they're not." Kitty pulled Findley's swivel chair so they faced each other straight on. "You start cutting into them, you'll discover our dolphins don't have any magical bits inside. They can't communicate with humans as well as Muriel/Gabby can. The dolphins developed—*will* develop a gift, but it hasn't happened yet. What's your excuse going to be?"

"I'll think of something later," Findley said, fidgeting in her purse for her cigarettes.

"Think now!" Kitty was screaming. "You can't kill innocent, intelligent creatures. You're a doctor, right?"

"I am a fully qualified marine biologist," Dr. Findley said with practiced gravitas. It all came clear: what Kitty was saying as well as the meaning of the images the dolphin had jammed into her head. "I don't want to hurt any of the animals, but if your friend back there isn't more cooperative, I'll have to do something. We have to understand them if we're going to avoid the future she showed me." Findley did her best to explain the myriad insights Muriel/Gabby had imparted.

"That's exactly why you have to let us release her as far away from your ships as possible. She has to find other dolphins and warn them."

Findley thought for a moment. "I understand that, but it's pointless. The ships will find her eventually."

"That's a chance we have to take," Quinn said.

JD looked back in the mirror to see his younger brother's face. Instead of Quinn's usual comical mask, he saw a worried young man. A sandy road rolled up on the left; the sign read "Beach Closed at Sundown." It hung from a chain that was hooked (not locked) on to a post. JD took his foot off the accelerator.

"This beach is fine. If we keep going to Tybee Island, what are the odds I'll get my money?" JD asked in a quiet voice.

"I'll figure that out, too!" Findley insisted. JD snorted in disbelief.

Kitty tersely added, "Daddy will pay you, okay? Keep going."

"Don't quit now, JD. She needs us," Quinn said in a good, clear voice that sliced deeply into him.

JD hit the gas and let the turnoff slide away from the dusty beam of his headlights. "Fine," he said with resignation. "What about Greg? Your boyfriend's not going to allow you to dump her into the ocean where she can escape."

"Let me take care of that," said Kitty, reaching between them and grabbing the CB mic.

"There's plenty of beaches along these exits. Where are we headed?" Majenski demanded. Findley's acne-faced driver said he was following the others. As the sun faltered on the horizon, the news van pulled ahead of them. Majenski began to worry. He went to fix himself a drink from the mini-bar, only to discover it had been pilfered; a considerable number of tiny bottles clinked in the trash pouch. "April," he sighed under his breath.

"So," said Dom. "You two, huh?" He sat with his hands

folded on his lap, smiling at the man in the expensive three-piece suit.

Majenski ignored the boy's forwardness. Instead, he picked up the car's phone and began to dial the office. Suddenly, he and the boy were thrown off their balance. The limo lurched as it narrowly avoided a hit from ten tons of steel.

"What the hell!"

Within seconds, two more big rigs had boxed them in. Majenski banged on the partition, urging their driver to do something. He tried. Slowing down, honking, cursing out the window; none of it did any good. They were in the rocking chair, as the truckers say, and these eighteen-wheelers were not going to let them out.

This nerve-racking state of affairs continued for an hour, until they crossed the bridge eastward to Tybee Island. All at once, the trucks hit their screeching brakes, stopping and blocking the limo's path. Majenski picked up the car phone and hit one button. Their driver picked up a receiver and spoke quietly with Majenski. Dom marveled at how the businessman could speak, not two feet from him, without his hearing it.

The driver hung up the phone, then reached over to the glove box and pulled out a Smith & Wesson 586. The young man awkwardly held the massive black pistol to the glass for Dom and Majenski to see.

"*Porca miseria!* No one said anything about shooting," Dom said.

The driver then displayed the gun for the benefit of

the truckers. Looking down from their cabs, one feigned terror, one stared, and the third held up a sawed-off shotgun. The chauffeur rolled down his window and called up to the armed trucker, "Don't worry, no bullets. I'm just driving until I get my real estate license."

Majenski rubbed his temples with thumb and finger. They were going to sit here. "April," he muttered for a second time.

Night held court. Looking out, one could see a ribbon of glossy black ocean carrying the moon's comet trail. Tybee Island's shoreline held a few scattered cottages and one or two shabby hotels, but not much more. Streetlights were few and far between. JD guided *The Foxy Lady* into a parking spot near Tybee's fishing pier. One slot over, the WSAV-TV truck rolled to a stop and the two journalists began unpacking their gear from the back.

JD called over to them, "All right, guys. This is what we came here for." Both teams stepped out. Their weight combined with their eager burden caused the pier's weathered beams to creak beneath them. JD urged his friends and Findley, "Let's get her in the water."

"Wait. You aren't going to throw her off the pier?" Kitty was aghast.

Quinn smiled. "They want us to. They say it's fun." It

clicked in Kitty's mind that sometimes Quinn was speaking for Muriel and sometimes for both dolphins inhabiting that one body. Apparently, they were both ready to take the plunge.

"So . . . final touches." Kitty climbed halfway up the RV's stairwell, plucked the CB mic, and said, "That's fine. You can let him through now."

"Oh God, let this work. You don't have a drink, do you?" Findley asked.

One hand on Muriel/Gabby's melon, Quinn's eyes focused on the radio. "Done with CB?" he asked in the clipped structure that suggested the question came from their passenger.

"I guess so. Why?" Kitty asked.

"An idea." Quinn looked at the twinned dolphin, then back to the others. "Her idea."

The news crew was set up at one end of the pier with field lights blazing. JD, Quinn, and Kitty did their best to steady Muriel/Gabby in her sling as the dolly trundled over the uneven planks. Sea turtles flew between the pilings below.

The limo tore over the parking lot's blend of gravel and seashells, stopping in a cloud of dust with one wheel on the edge of the pier. Majenski launched his tall frame out of the back seat and ran across the boards, screaming for April.

"April, help me to understand what you're doing here." Majenski spoke without raising his voice, which only made her feel worse.

Rushing to meet him, Findley implored, "Greg, trust me."

"No. I'm afraid I don't."

Kitty joined them. In a schoolgirl's conspiratorial whisper, she said, "Fine, don't trust her, but you might want to think twice before you try to stop her. Our friends from WSAV-TV would love to lead a dull weekend broadcast with the news that a major company is trafficking in hot dolphins."

"What?" Majenski demanded.

"You get them from a shady company that poaches the animals illegally. Then, you put them in your aquarium and sell tickets. Not good for public relations." Kitty got the words out with confidence, and just a touch of self-satisfaction.

Majenski's face went as blank as a resident of Pompeii. At that moment, one of the trucks that had hazarded and then released his limo pulled into the now bustling parking area.

"Excuse me, I have something to do," Kitty said and walked over to the big rig. The cab door swung open and out stepped an epicene figure in black denim and a Culture Club T-shirt. "Pratt, I presume."

"After all this excitement, I had to get a good look for myself," Pratt said in the now familiar gentle voice and offered her a firm handshake.

Kitty fumbled for small talk, but found herself oddly speechless.

"Oh," said Pratt, reaching back into the cab and producing a bundle wrapped in brown paper and twine. "This is for Tony." In his hand was a single mistake followed by years of trouble for somebody.

"Got it." Kitty discreetly tucked the bundle into her purse before JD saw it.

At the end of the pier, Findley and Quinn did the honors of ratcheting the straps holding Muriel/Gabby's hind section, raising her flukes higher than her head.

JD released some of the forward hooks to help her slide out. He was careful to make sure the makeshift collar Quinn had attached was in place and the CB it held was switched on. A small red tally light gleamed through the heavy plastic sheeting they'd added to protect the improvised transmitter. Quinn's handiwork impressed him. It might only last a few minutes, hours maybe, but it was brilliant.

"My brother is brilliant," JD said aloud and patted Muriel/Gabby on the melon.

"Yes, he is," Muriel told JD with a clarity that knocked him off balance and nearly sent him plunging backward into the water.

With that, the dolphin slid out of her sling and executed a flawless dive into the water. JD looked over at the TV news photographer, who gave him a thumbs-up. They got the shot. JD then looked over at Quinn, saying, "Well, buddy, are you ready to go tell Mom a fish story?"

Majenski was in front of the camera in a heartbeat, explaining that this was all Futura Mundi's doing. He claimed his company had nursed a sick dolphin back to health at great expense so they could reintroduce her—he said "her"—into the wild. Benton Bradley made his face serious and nodded at the businessman's every word. JD doubted the journalists believed any of it, but it made for good TV.

"Is your truck's receiver set to the right frequency?" Quinn asked. Joe the photographer assured the funny/serious boy that a tape was running, with the audio set to pick up the CB signal. They were not disappointed.

The group on the pier stood for a moment. They heard noises coming from a few yards offshore, a high-pitched chattering and a splash. Muriel/Gabby began doing flips in the water. The news crew turned its lights toward the sounds, piercing the darkness. Right on cue, the laughing dolphin shot like a missile above the water, flipped, and fell prone into the rolling waves, spewing brine in all directions.

"I'll drive, you shoot!" Gabby said, diving them straight down. The package strapped behind their melon tugged, but did not slow them. With a perfectly gauged twist, Gabby reversed and pointed their rostrum straight up at the undulating surface and a moment later shot through it like a flying fish or a stupid porpoise.

On each flip, Muriel/Gabby curled nose to tail, shrimp fashion. Able at last to get a line-of-sight lock on the thing stuck in their fluke, Muriel blasted it with an effector pulse, knocking it out of commission. No one would be tracking them from this point on.

Gabby kept them close enough to the shore for the others to see them in the quicksilver moonlight. Muriel found herself amazed at the power this dolphin commanded. Muriel's old spinner dolphin frame had been sleek and fast, but Gabby's bottlenose physique possessed both strength and an excess of pure spirit.

"Now, sing! Do that fancy stuff you like," Gabby ordered her body buddy, who complied in full *voce giojoso*.

Human ears could not discern the melody, but the complex tones and whirs inscribed upon its listeners an unmistakable testament to bliss.

Kitty made sure Pratt had his CB equipment set not only to pick up Muriel's song, but to broadcast it to Pratt's network of truckers. They in turn sent it out to ham radio enthusiasts. In all, hundreds of people listened to the live broadcast, while the WSAV-TV crew recorded it for *The Nightbeat at Eleven News*.

A drug-related double murder and a fire at an empty warehouse stole the lead position that night. The dolphin-release story got pushed to the second news block.

Even so, thousands of people in Savannah saw Muriel/Gabby's release. For a few, the idea of people helping an animal made an impression that informed their decisions for years.

"May I borrow your phone?" Kitty asked Majenski. Not waiting for a reply, she got on the line. "Daddy! You remember you told me to work hard in college so I could bring you million-dollar ideas?" Being sure to mix in plenty of father flattery, she machine-gunned the idea to him: a video for MTV starring a singing dolphin complete with song and pictures, courtesy of WSAV-TV. (The photog nodded at this.) "It shouldn't cost more than a few thousand, and it's bound to make . . . well, as much as music videos make!" There was laughter on the other end.

Away from the others, Majenski turned to April. "You have no idea how much you've cost me. This release is FUBAR." He delivered the military curse as calmly as if he'd read it from a phone book.

"Greg, I can turn this into a public-relations bonanza. You'll be known as the man who loves dolphins. I'll get you on *Johnny Carson*. The cover of *Time*." She was spreading it a bit thick, but so be it.

"Fine. Do that," he said, getting into the limo. "You can coordinate everything from the Muncie office." And he drove off.

His abruptness caught her off guard. The Muncie office was the size of a Fotomat and consisted of two old men and a Xerox. She doubted Greg ever visited. It hurt, but somehow not as badly as she had feared. She took out her cigarettes, then put them back in her purse. She thought, *I've done it. Not according to plan, of course, but I took charge and made things work.*

Dr. April Findley had no regrets.

Chapter 24

When a dolphin leaps and dives, she punctures the surface of the world and makes a ring of water. This ring spreads outward until it mixes its peaks and vales with the ocean waves. The change is infinitesimal. The change is real.

In addition to the TV audience, many people heard the broadcast over the ersatz CB network. Pratt's minions loved the idea of a dolphin who could sing. They passed the story and a recording on to anyone who'd listen, making it part of late-night conversations that flitted about the interstates for years. Truckers told their kids, and took family vacations in Savannah. They took dolphin cruises, where they told the stories again to doubting tourists.

JD dropped out of URI and drifted for a while. He made mistakes and paid the price, but he finally found his center. From time to time, people would ask him to speak about the singing dolphin. It's funny what a small slice of fame can bring. Eventually, JD strung one opportunity to the next and earned enough to open a used car lot: Brennan Brothers. His best mechanic charmed their customers with an endearing giggle.

Kitty pestered her father and his friends and associates about helping dolphins. Her father invested in a start-up company, of which Kitty became the head, that made special nets for trawlers, to extrude dolphins. The project reduced the number of deaths of not only dolphins but sea turtles and octopuses. It helped.

Dom and Kitty dated for months and even toyed with the idea of marriage. In the end, they committed to a life-long friendship.

As hoped, Muriel/Gabby was able to remove the CB collar. Gabby made a flirtatious show of asking a bulky male bottlenose named Aaron to aid them. She brushed up against him, pretending to try to use the motion to help work the collar free. The motion was largely pointless. Gabby had a different point.

"What are you doing with this guy?" Muriel asked. "We need to make plans. I have to talk to more mans and dolphins too and get them to understand—"

"There'll be time for all that. Life comes first."

Aaron, a dolphin of few words, asked, "Wanna mate?"

"It's the only way to get you a melon of your own, Muriel. Not that you haven't been a great partner, but I prefer to fly solo."

"You mean?"

"I'm getting pregnant, so get ready to use some of that fancy psychic stuff to move into your new body."

Muriel found birth more disorienting than time travel. It took her many years to focus her thoughts enough to try and organize a group of followers behind a single philosophy. They saw her less as a dolphin than as a mystical figure. Try as she might, she could not impress upon them the need to begin the hard work of seeking out and ameliorating toxins created by the mans. Her mental abilities were greatly reduced in her new body, perhaps because it was outwardly male. Her mission made no sense in the here and now. The others promised to remember and to communicate with mans whenever possible as the coming troubles unfolded.

Muriel came to understand she was not going to solve the biggest problems. She would get few if any of the answers she sought. So, in the end, she lived a life.

The old man's back protested; rowing didn't agree with it. He couldn't tell by looking at the sky whether it was summer or winter. It made little difference anymore; the seasons had quit their jobs and moved on, as had his youth—only winter lived in his bones now. He put up the skiff's oars and looked back across the bay. The sun was setting behind the darkened city. That skyline was not the way he remembered it. Staccato gunfire sounded, along with indistinct cries, the sounds of a beast eating itself. The old man fumbled with his meager meal. He wanted to share it with his old friend, but he knew she was not there. How long did dolphins live, forty years?

She was long gone, like the others. He was the last of their band of friends.

"She is between her lives," came a voice. It played through his head and his spirit, like the strains of an aria achingly sad yet lovely. "She will be back to play the part she has already played."

"That makes no sense."

"Perhaps."

"And what about the part we played all those years ago? What good did it do? Things now are so . . . wrong. Everyone is so selfish, so angry."

"Those are the same thing. You should rest. The world is unfolding as it should."

"There's so much pain," he said.

"Sometimes pain must happen, though there may be less of it because of those who listened to one dolphin's song. They did what they could. You did what you could. Be at peace."

"I want the world I knew when I was a boy. I want blue skies and seasons and . . . apples." He grimaced and clenched his fists; that happened less often now.

"The Great watches," said the voice. There were movements under the water. Trim gray shapes flitted about the tiny skiff.

"What happens now?" the man asked.

"We'll see," said the voice.

Coda

A Sweet Dream When the Long Trick's Over

Chapter 25

"Approaching the target, Admiral," Captain Bartolomeu reported to Lord High Admiral of the Seas Qing Yuan as the senior officer jetted into the control room.

The captain called up images from the sail cameras as well as some CGULS wheeling overhead. Limbs busily adjusting the focus, Bartolomeu observed the target in detail on the big control-room screen. The admiral suckered himself to the bulkhead, his eye turning ninety degrees as he observed the screen. It was the island they had been hunting. They refused to name the awful mass that loomed large before them.

Centuries of dumping had filled Earth's waters with dross. Currents, storms, and wave actions reduced these insults to tiny bits that spread as enormous clouds. This island was one mass that had not broken up. Rising tides invaded the mans' dumping grounds, washing out thousands of hectares of semi-solid waste at a time. Various refuse heaps drifted into the open ocean, occasionally merging as the sun fused them into giant accretions of cast-off plastic amusements.

Since the Fall, the island had grown and accumulated dust and sand enough to support a few hearty wind-borne seeds. Eventually, drop foliage composted into fertile pockets big enough to support shallow-rooted palm trees and myriad midget flora. Aquatic life darted in and around the ragged skirts of sun-bleached plastic, while clouds of seabirds fed on the water skaters that thrived there. Despite the natural camouflage, the floating mass appeared anything but natural. The general shape was lumpy, but lacking the peaks or a caldera found on so many fixed islands.

Looking at the blob now on the screen, Bartolomeu pictured some minor god using the ocean for his toilet. Its colors, though greatly faded, included lurid greens and provocative magentas no self-respecting flower or fish would claim. As they got closer, details provided the final proof that this was the work of mans. The island was one colossal, irresponsible, indigestible, irrational con-glomeration of want and waste: soda can rings, deflated bouncy balls, collapsible chaise lounges for ten thousand lazy monarchs, miles of automobile tires discarded like old shoes, old shoes, nets for fishing or badminton, jew-elry now reshaped by age and sun into fantastically hide-ous art, millions of metric tons of microbeads once used in toothpaste, and more, and more, and more. The island wasn't going away. Disposable diapers would be with them for another three or four centuries, while monofila-ment fishing line could last centuries longer than that. Adding to the problem, decomposing plastics were giving off chemicals suspected in causing everything from cancer to asthma. (Their scientists were working on safer polymers. Nothing was perfect.) They had to deal with it soon, before this mess did more harm.

"Quite a sight, eh, Admiral?" Captain Bartolomeu prompted.

Admiral Qing Yuan encouraged the informal shortening of his title while they were underway. He eschewed using coloration to signify rank, choosing instead to erect devil-fish horns above his eye slits as an affectation of command. The crew had been in close quarters aboard the *Yiming* for weeks. A casual atmosphere pervaded their daily routine, allowing them to fuse their talents smoothly into one collective effort.

Some of the crew grumbled that things were not collective enough. Captain Bartolomeu adjusted the boat's trim, triggered a repeating sonar ping off the approaching plastic island, updated coordinates in the torpedo targeting system, and played a game on the chart table with a junior officer. Bartolomeu's blue tip moved an amber stone in place to create a row of five: Pente.

Admiral Qing Yuan pulled himself along the walls and deck of the bridge, checking in with the octopod at each station, while casually gulping down herring released into the confined space to help them maintain their stamina.

"Your captain has neglected to protect two of his ruby-red stones. You can surround and take them," Admiral Qing Yuan pointed out to the junior officer playing Bartolomeu.

"No kibitzing, Admiral." A captain's authority must never be questioned on his own bridge, not even by his admiral.

Bartolomeu blushed his pride, prompted by the frames, plates, and hatches that encased him and his crew. The octopodes had discovered dozens of sunken vessels over the years, but few in as good of a condition as this boat. Whoever sailed her last had gently nestled her into a sandy seabed, as if planning to one day return for her. The octopodes had no trouble getting past the locks; the mans had always been naive about their security. During the refurbishing, the interior of the boat held stale air. The octopodes did not enjoy working in the dry spaces, so they learned to carry water bladders to moisten their skins without dousing the sub's exposed circuitry.

It was an octopod named Norris who appreciated how valuable a submarine could be for exploring the Earth's oceans. Norris and his fellow octopodes "borrowed" pumping equipment from a recently disabled surface ship and used it to pressurize the boat's ballast tanks. Once they lifted it off the bottom, they still faced several hurdles. Electronics were ruined by years of submersion; however, the mans who built this boat had left maintenance manuals featuring simplistic pictures, so that a mans child (or a particularly dim octopod) could comprehend. In lockers, they found replacements for damaged computer cards. They studied up on the concept of "least-repairable units" and decided when to pull an entire assembly and replace it, using the abundant spare backplanes left about the boat in protective envelopes.

Norris said the fuel that remained in the boat's tanks was "sour," but it retained enough potency to get them back to Losi Bay. That was where the real work had taken place over many years, adapting the boat and its electronics to a liquid environment and turning the so-called submarine into a true marine vessel.

Reconditioning certain weapons was simple, but time-consuming. They had only a few working torpedoes, barely enough to split the bulk of the miles-wide plastic island into manageable chunks. They'd need more of these torpedoes to seed the seas with servile bacteria. Teams were combing the TransPacific for more salvable torpedoes. Here, the salvors and their children lent invaluable skills.

It took Captain Bartolomeu no time to sucker his way over the keyboard, which was designed for a mere ten digits. He called up Umed's swarthy image on the monitor. The extra hair around the mouth and jaw looked so . . . well, mans-ish. Umed had led the effort to recondition *Yiming's* onboard controls to resist the deleterious effects of salt-water immersion, prophylactically encasing consoles, conduits, and jacks in a special gel. The effort had earned Umed the right to serve as *Yiming's* sole crewmans. The honor consigned him to the few chambers that remained dry. The air inside accommodated his need to breathe as well as the boat's need for buoyancy, "a win-win," Admiral Qing Yuan liked to say.

"Greetings, fellow travelers." The final member of the boat's senior staff swam in from the forward torpedo room. Sister Myune affected an Orphic presence, as was typical of all members of the Circle of Muriel. In Captain Bartolomeu's opinion, the sisters were an odd pod. They tagged along on the reclamation missions, offering stray bits of encouragement, which were mostly nonsense. The crew treated her politely, but avoided engagement. Even the admiral offered her little more than small talk.

"We're in luck," the captain said. "The island's course has taken it nearly to the center of one of the largest of the poison patches in this region. Commissioner Mataeula will be pleased; we'll be able to conduct both phases of our mission at the same time."

"The torpedoes will do their job, Captain," Umed added, unnecessarily, over the link. It required discipline to maintain eye-to-eye-slit contact via the link in order to understand each other; there were plenty of miscues. "How are the conducrobes working?"

"Well?" Captain Bartolomeu looked around at his bridge crew. Most were concentrating on various readouts, neither looking directly at him nor making physical contact.

"Read you loud and clear, Captain!" came one response after another.

"It would appear, Mister Umed, your psychic stew is working well." The conducrobes, Umed's latest project, were undergoing testing during this voyage. So far, they only worked in a limited space, serving as supplementary lines of communication between the various sentient species now serving in the fleet. In the case of the octopodes, the tiny creatures allowed communication without the need for touch or line-of-sight linkage. The microbes possessed no intelligence of their own and were not truly "psychic," but they did convey most of one's conscious thoughts to others in the immediate vicinity. As a side benefit, they tasted good.

Twenty minutes passed slowly. The crew checked all lines of communication aboard and beyond the boat. Everything showed green and ready.

"Would you care to do the honors, Admiral?"

"Thank you. Ensign, fire one and two!"

Twin cavitation streams burst forward from the boat, like silk tracers from some industrious spider. Directed to within a sucker's width, each torpedo found its target and exploded in a piercing thrum that resonated through the bones of those crewmembers who possessed them.

The warheads were packed with high explosives, shaped to both exploit known fissures in the island and fill them with a super-hot chemical that propagated fire equally well in the air or underwater.

After the concussive wave, the giant faux landmass remained unaltered. So large was it that, at first, the effect of the waves of destructive energy was not readily visible. Birds startled then returned to the same spot, palm fronds rustled, but to the naked eye slit, the target was implacable.

Slowly, fractures drew lines in acrid curls of smoke and flaming petrochemicals. It was as if a powerful artisan had drawn a red-and-orange letter Y across the face of the isle, causing it to neatly cleave into three parts. Two sections of the broken plain heaved horizontally, like tectonic plates in collision, subducting their lesser sibling. Owing to buoyancy and resiliency not found in stone, the final section bounced back, ultimately forcing all three calves to part ways for good. The ocean showed its face under the new channels as the last of the fires died down. Screens and periscopes transmitted the welcome sight to the eyes of dolphins, octopodes, and mans alike.

The admiral made it official: "Well done, friends! Well done!"

With a blush of approval from the captain, Umed supervised the launch of the final two torpedoes. These bulkier models came equipped with sonar and a guidance system that allowed them to circumnavigate two of the newly calved masses. They delivered a thin necklace of water-soluble ampules containing concentrated swarms of bacteria, manipulated by mans and dolphin to consume poisons. If all went well, these bacteria would thrive in the shelter of the remaining two isles, devouring the local toxins as well as those encountered roaming freely in the currents. This was only the latest battle in a very long war for the survival of the planet.

Umed and a spinner dolphin named Philo were in charge of the third island, the one they had come to claim. Umed climbed into the escape hatch. Too flooded to actually surface, the *Yiming* sailed at periscope depth most of the time. Making an exit at this depth was perfectly safe. Still, he had to fight his own instinctive fear of drowning in order to open the valves, intentionally flooding the claustrophobic space. The turbulent water pressed in on him, mashing his filter mask against his face. The process took seconds, but felt much longer. Umed opened the outer hatch and swam into the enormous ocean.

He located an anchor line and followed it slowly to the surface. There he found the raft he'd provisioned with food and supplies to last a few months. *Lunas*, he reminded himself while speaking to his partner; dolphins were stubborn about their vernacular. Philo was waiting for him, having taken a much simpler exit through a modified torpedo tube. Umed had not taken a radio, so Philo was his liaison to the sub, as well as to their volunteer workforce.

"Our new home," Umed said. He had no problem speaking normally with his partner, despite the absence of conducrobes. It was also possible the creatures had managed to survive his digestive system. Umed and Philo had worked closely for many months now. He postulated that long-term proximity strengthened their link. Or else Philo may have done something. Dolphins didn't ask permission.

"Thank you for your help," Umed said, holding tightly to Philo's pectoral fins as the inverted dolphin used his powerful flukes to tow him along.

"We try," Philo answered, dismissing the approbation.

"Yes, you do, though after all my people have done, I'll never understand why yours are so accommodating."

"Dolphins are as dolphins are."

He enjoyed their discussions. They'd found a certain intimacy and trust, like brothers or perhaps kindred spirits. "There are times I wish men were more like dolphins. We get caught up in our own selfishness."

Philo erupted into a droll snorting. "You're only mans." With that, he dunked his passenger.

Umed spit out ocean and shook the wetness from his curly hair. "Indeed," he said.

The two made their way to a jagged inlet. Umed tied off the raft and stepped ashore. The land crackled and compressed beneath his feet, as if it were made of eggshells, but it supported his weight. Umed got to work, moving his supplies inland to a relatively flat area and setting up his new home near a water hole, which he nicknamed Bagh-é-Tarikhi.

Philo was off, heading to a rendezvous with the final members of this mission. Those members originally wanted nothing to do with the poisonous island. It had taken long negotiations to convince them that the danger could be turned into an opportunity. The pod had agreed.

Umed was fishing when they arrived. His breath caught in his throat. He had never seen whales. Centuries ago, the last men to see bulls at full girth had pierced the animals' lungs, cut them to bits, and rendered them into oil. The creatures that rose before Umed now were not merely giants among the waves, they were giants among the giants.

More than twenty of the black bulls—called back from their rogue wanderings to mate and help protect the calves—split from their pod and found positions along one shoreline.

Philo explained the plan to push the plastic berg toward Gunn Island, where crews were ready to break it into bits and haul it to the synth district for reclamation into new materials and fuel. Priority one was to build sprawling greenhouses for the islanders' crops, now that things were becoming so unsettled.

No one talked about charting the course; no one needed to. The bulls were masters of their world. They knew where everything was.

Their enormous heads butted the isle's false shore with irresistible brute force. The living engines sang encouragement to each other, in sweet high notes and endless lows, as they pounded round grooves deep into the pliant waste. In perfect rhythm, the array of great tails tore up from the surface of the ocean then slammed back down in a gush of salty spume. Avians danced in the updrafts above the long wake, eyeing the confused fish below. It took time, but the artificial island began to move in the desired direction.

Umed checked his readings to confirm their new direction, not that he had any doubts. He seemed to remember some factoid about these whales having the biggest brains on Earth. They could travel without stopping to consult a star map. Moreover, the behemoths were indefatigable in their task; at any given time, each rested half of its great brain while letting the other half control its broad flukes.

Umed thanked Philo and asked him to pass along his thanks to the pod.

Their trip would take many weeks. Philo spent his free hours blowing bubble rings for his own amusement, and to confuse fish long enough to catch them. Umed used the time to run tests on the composition of the various plastics, relaying the data to the crew of the *Yiming* below. The routine was not as mentally challenging as he would have liked, but it required him to bend his back to dig into the island's many warped and tangled strata and the exertion left him with a welcome fatigue at the end of each tetra-tide.

On the third night, Umed slipped into an odd dream. He found himself face to face with Philo. They had to be in the water, but the feeling was different than the usual sensations of swimming, more like flying. He felt more in control, more at ease. Another dolphin swam nearby. Though he did not recognize the visitor, her song struck him as familiar. The wispy melody she provided, replete with haunting cetaceous gleaks and clucks, rolled through his mind and down into his body, taking up residence within his chest and limbs. Umed tried asking Philo what was happening. His companion offered no explanation, but reassured him all was as it should be. In the morning, the dream's details faded, leaving only a feeling of well-being like a half-recalled childhood holiday.

Umed ran the logistics in his head. Providing the islanders with a new source of recyclables was a good thing, but only a temporary reprieve. *What's gone is gone for good,* he thought. *There is no magical fix. The world is on a new path, and it will take eons for the future to find its true form. Whether humans fit into that plan . . . well, odds are . . .*

There was no knowing. Umed called up to a murder of raptors overhead, "Water, water. Let tomorrow come, says the man standing on a floating mountain of trash!" Indifferent to his laughter, the scavengers pulled their wings in close to their bodies, making themselves into dive bombers. They knifed under the water, then popped up again with a gullet full of lively morsels exposed by the blasts.

Dining in the *Yiming's* mess hall that night, someone used a comtutor to locate an ancient recording, then played it over the sub's internal speakers. Familiar sweet strains of clicks and knocks floated through the water as if she were there with them in the sub. Muriel's song spanned generations, buried deep in one of the mans' archives, called "The You Tube." The file did not include any background; all they knew was it was the voice of

Muriel, the dolphin who had lived twice. (Some say she had lived three times.)

"Amazing thing, comtutors. They tap into archives from our mans brothers. In some ways, the little devices mimic the Great," observed Captain Bartolomeu.

"So, the Great is watching and recording us?" asked a skittish midshipfin. "So . . . who will watch that recording when we're gone?"

Captain Bartolomeu pondered that for a moment. "That is a very good question. I imagine the Great is more like a song in many parts, composed over the eons. The ultimate score is more beautiful than anything our minds can conceive. In the end, maybe no one listens; maybe no one can." His brindled mantle darkened as the thought played through him. "Still, I'm glad it's there. Gives me a good feeling inside." With that, the captain returned to his dinner.

The Circle of Muriel had a different take on the long-ago song from their prophetic sister. Theirs was a nascent faith, giggling at its own nakedness. The circle held but one tenet, contained with the rhythms of twin prayers, one part for each of Muriel's doubled life. From the far reaches of the boat, the sisters' voices joined the melody on the speaker, reciting their Homily of the Fall:

> *Shun the selfish who insist*
> *that Earth abides all wounds,*
> *that contrition amends poor choices,*
> *that yearning summons the dawn.*

Embrace hope with clear vision:
see small acts stay grave mistakes;
see opportunity reward sacrifice;
see, ever and always, the waters flow.

Ignoring the cetaceous catechism, Admiral Qing Yuan turned his attention to a gossamer net, hungrily admiring its lively contents. These biodegradable dinner nets allowed the crew to travel farther, stockpiling rather than stopping where they could to go out and catch food live. They worked well, though they reminded them of the seriousness of their situation. Good seasons, bad seasons; so much depended upon whether the poison patches dotting the TransPacific intersected with the fish nurseries they maintained. The octopodes worked to isolate and secure areas from the danger of drifting contaminants, both for themselves and the other species. They were diligent and smart about their work. Even so, there were no guarantees.

Admiral Qing Yuan said, "Sometimes I wonder whether we're really making progress. How long will it take until the seas run clear again?"

"A few centuries," sniggered Sister Myune, entering the wardroom. Dolphins always laughed at the serious bits. "It could have taken much, much longer. Sister Muriel be praised."

"Cryptic, as usual," grumbled Captain Bartolomeu, rolling his eye slits upward in as near a mans-like gesture as he could manage.

"Will we last that long?" the admiral asked, pointedly.

"Umed says it's problematic." Captain Bartolomeu paused to think. "He says creatures in the water have a better chance. He's not certain his own kind can survive on land, because mans take too long to adapt and evolve."

Circling the mess, Sister Myune responded in a lilting contrapuntal composition with enough twills and fwicks to weave a *giocoso* ditty: "Working on it."

Stupid dolphin, Captain Bartolomeu thought.

The conducrobes dutifully delivered the unintended message, prompting Sister Myune to giggle even louder.

Acknowledgments

I wish to thank the dolphins who spoke to Muriel Lindsay, author of *The Dolphin Letters: Vital Information from Sea to Land*. I tried speaking with dolphins, but they chose to remain inscrutably silent, so I wrote what I could imagine.

I thank authors Ray Bradbury, who taught me the beauty of words, Douglas Adams, who taught me to laugh at words, and George Orwell, who warned us all about the power of words to do either good or evil. I hope I've learned well.

About the Author

Chris Riker is a writer, father, and journalist. He grew up in Rhode Island and now makes his home in Georgia with his wife, Ping. He has always loved books, from science-fiction and fantasy, to historical novels and biographies. Building on a background in broadcast news, including a stint at CNN, he is now focused on telling stories with strong characters and moral resonance. His premiere effort blends a love for our beautiful Earth and her myriad life-forms with a sense of wonder at our shared purpose and fate.

To get the latest ecological news
and information, follow
Come the Eventide and Chris Riker
on social media:

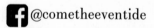 @cometheeventide

 @chris_w._riker